"Damn you, Gabriel, put me down!"

"Once I do, you foolish chit, and you see what I've in mind, you'll be begging me to pick you up again." He tossed her on her back onto the bunk.

Mariah landed with an indignant yelp, skirts and hair flying. She yanked her skirts back down over her bare knees as she scuttled back against the bulkhead, her eyes glowing with rage. "*Begging* you, indeed! I wouldn't waste my wind begging you to do anything decent or gentlemanly!"

"Then you won't be disappointed, will you?" Breathing hard, he unbuckled his sword belt and let it drop clattering to the deck. "You with all your orders, wagging your finger at me like some kind of preacher in petticoats! You'd unman me before my own crew!"

She watched as he tore off his waistcoat, buttons spinning across the deck. No doubt his breeches would be next ... !

Dear Reader,

Harlequin Historicals welcomes you to another sizzling month of romance. With summer in full swing, we've got four titles perfect for the beach, pool—or anywhere!

From popular author Miranda Jarrett comes another swashbuckling tale set on the high seas—*Mariah's Prize,* her next book in the thrilling SPARHAWK series. In this story, a desperate Mariah West convinces Gabriel Sparhawk to captain her sloop, never guessing at his ulterior motives.

Scottish chieftain Dillon Campbell abducted Lady Leonora Wilton as an act of revenge against the English. But one look into Leonora's eyes and it became an act of love, in *The Highlander* by favorite author Ruth Langan.

In Julie Tetel's stirring medieval tale, *Simon's Lady,* the marriage between Simon de Beresford and Lady Gwyneth had been arranged to quell a Saxon uprising, yet this Saxon bride wants more from her husband than peace.

And finally, if you liked Merline Lovelace's first book of the DESTINY'S WOMEN series, *Alena,* you'll love her second book, *Sweet Song of Love.* When knight Richard FitzHugh was called to battle, he left behind a meek bride given to him by the king. So who was the curvaceous beauty who now greeted him as *husband?*

Next month, our big book selection is *To Share a Dream,* a reissue by author Willo Davis Roberts. Don't miss this moving saga about three sisters who dare to build a new beginning in the American colonies.

Sincerely,

Tracy Farrell
Senior Editor

Please address questions and book requests to:
Harlequin Reader Service
U.S.: 3010 Walden Ave., P.O. Box 1325, Buffalo, NY 14269
Canadian: P.O. Box 609, Fort Erie, Ont. L2A 5X3

MIRANDA JARRETT

MARIAH'S PRIZE

Harlequin Books

TORONTO • NEW YORK • LONDON
AMSTERDAM • PARIS • SYDNEY • HAMBURG
STOCKHOLM • ATHENS • TOKYO • MILAN
MADRID • WARSAW • BUDAPEST • AUCKLAND

ISBN 0-373-28827-1

MARIAH'S PRIZE

Copyright © 1994 by Susan Holloway Scott.

MIRANDA JARRETT

is an award-winning designer and art director whose writing combines her love of history and reading. Her travels always include visits to old houses and historical restorations.

Miranda and her husband, a musician, live near Philadelphia with their two small children and two large cats. She is still trying to figure out how to juggle writing, working and refereeing disputes among preschoolers in the sandbox.

For Jake, as always, with much love

Chapter One

Crescent Hill, Aquidneck Island
The Colony of Rhode Island and
   Providence Plantations
June 1744

"I'll lay you five guineas that the Spaniards have captured Newport!"

Gabriel Sparhawk didn't answer. He stood at the open window with his hands clasped behind his back, watching the bright glow from the flames in the distance against the soft gray dusk and the smoke drifting out across the bay.

Men seldom ignored Anjelike. Impatiently she slid her hand beneath Gabriel's shirt, her fingers spreading across the broad muscles of his back as she pressed her body to his. "If the Spanish *are* here, then I couldn't possibly sail tomorrow," she murmured. "But I'd be safe enough here with you to protect me, wouldn't I, my pretty, brave Captain Sparhawk?''

"No Spaniard's ever shown his long nose this far north, Anjelike, and they won't come now, not even for the chance to ravish you." Deftly Gabriel eased himself away from her and walked to the sideboard to refill his goblet. Even with every window thrown open to catch the breeze from the water, the room was hot, and his gold-haired mistress did little to cool the evening air. In New York, when he'd been a guest of her husband, he'd been too intent on bedding Anjelike to notice how much scent she wore, but after a week of her company in his own home, he was weary of her and of attar of roses, and thankful he'd soon be rid of them both. "The Spaniards are done, and so is their war."

"Don't scorn the Spaniards, Gabriel," said Anjelike, pouting as she twisted her fingers in the double strand of pearls around her throat. With studied carelessness she let her dressing gown slip lower over her bare shoulders. "You've made your fortune from their war."

Gabriel only shrugged. From the Holland cambric of his shirt to the wide, polished floorboards beneath his feet, every inch of Crescent Hill and everything in it had come from his success in this war. In three years, twenty-six Spanish merchant ships had struck their colors to him, more than to any other English privateer in the Caribbean.

He'd been exorbitantly lucky and he knew it, and if there was any justice in the world he should have been equally content. He was nearly thirty-three, and God knows he shouldn't expect much more from life. But the peace he'd sought when he'd left the sea two years ago still eluded him, and nothing—not his grand new house, not the procession of lovely, willing women like Anjelike—nothing eased the restless emptiness that still ate at his soul.

"I'm not scoffing at the Spaniards, sweetheart, only at the notion that they're here burning Newport," he said lightly, as the brandy splashed into the heavy blown glass. "More likely it's just the pipe of some drunken journeyman, set fire to his master's warehouse. I'll see you off tomorrow on the packet as we planned, and you'll be back in Hempstead by week's end. Any longer, you know, and your husband might come looking for that grievously ill friend you've been visiting."

"Oh, fah on Heinrick!" Anjelike sniffed disdainfully. "That fat old man wouldn't lift his nose out of his countinghouse if I'd taken myself off to Paris and back in nothing more than my shift!"

Because he'd heard it all before, Gabriel only half listened, staring out again at the fiery glow on the horizon. There, his ears hadn't mistaken it, the sound of a tired horse coming up the long, crushed-shell drive to the front of the house. He wasn't expecting any guests—he seldom chose to entertain, anyway—and Crescent Hill was too far from town for casual visitors. He traced one finger along the lip of the goblet, considering the more interesting possibilities. Perhaps the Spanish had landed in Newport, after all.

He strained to sort out the voices below as Ethan, the old seaman he kept on as a kind of steward, opened the door to the newcomer, argued with him and then slowly climbed the stairs to the upstairs chamber.

"What man is it, Ethan?" Gabriel asked before Ethan, out of breath from the stairs, could announce himself. "Someone with news of the fire?"

The old man didn't answer at first, instead glancing warily at the tall blond woman in the pearls and dressing gown and little else. Self-consciously he wiped his palms along the front of his old-fashioned leather vest. "Not exactly, Cap'n," he hedged, "tho' I told th' party you was engaged."

"Engaged!" Gabriel laughed. "For all love, Ethan, since when did you become so overnice? Give the man a dram for riding out, and double if he can tell me of the fire."

"I'm not a man, Captain Sparhawk," said the girl in Ethan's broad shadow, "and I don't want your rum. I want you."

She spoke without hesitation or timidity, and Gabriel smiled at her boldness. He couldn't help it, not with a girl who sounded so brave. And young. Though her face was still lost in the shadows of the hallway, the light from the candles in the room washed over her small figure, a figure with a ripe lushness that not even her serviceable woolen gown could conceal. So she wanted him. He wondered if she realized how such a request could be misconstrued. Or maybe she *did* know, for all her youth, and his smile widened.

"Send the chit away, Gabriel," said Anjelike peevishly. "The creature should be home with her mother, not shamelessly annoying gentlemen in their homes."

The girl made an abrupt noise of disgust in the back of her throat and impatiently pushed past Ethan. "I'm no chit, ma'am, any more than you look to be the lady of this house to go about giving orders!"

Gabriel could see the girl's face clearly now, black curls beneath her hood, full cheeks, a small chin, blue eyes and thick lashes and brows that arched in perpetual surprise, her whole face so much like Catherine's, *his* Catherine's, that he felt the shock like a sharp, physical blow.

"I'm a greater lady than you'll ever be, you impudent little slut!" Anjelike pulled the gown over her shoulders and drew herself imperiously straight. "I'll see that you're whipped for all your froward airs, see if I don't, and then—"

"Enough." Gabriel's voice cut through the woman's shrillness with all the authority of the quarterdeck. "Ethan, Madame van Riis is retiring now. See that she has whatever she needs in her room. Pleasant dreams, Anjelike. Mind we leave at four bells in the morning."

With a final, murderous glance at the girl, Anjelike swept through the doorway in a rush of satin, followed by a baleful Ethan. Gabriel forced himself to look again at the girl before him. He sought differences now, desperate for anything in her face that would reassure him that he hadn't lost his mind. He was a man who believed in reason, not superstition, and certainly not in ghosts.

"Captain Sparhawk?"

The girl was more nervous than he'd realized, her small, pale hands, still marked from clutching the reins, twisting uneasily in her skirts at her sides. Catherine would never have ridden this far alone at night, and she never would have entered any gentleman's house unattended, nor with splatters of mud on her hem. This girl's coloring was more vibrant, too, her lips and cheeks rosier, her expression more animated than Catherine's languid, hothouse beauty.

Nay, the more he studied her, the more the resemblance faded elusively away, and Gabriel wondered how he'd seen it at all. Perhaps the wine or some trick of the candlelight, or perhaps only his wistful conscience, still longing for another chance that would never come in his lifetime.

"Captain Sparhawk, sir? Are you unwell?"

Damnation, he was behaving like a bloody bedlamite! Swiftly Gabriel shook off the last of his melancholy and held his hand out to her. She hesitated, staring at his outstretched hand before she finally lay her fingers across his palm and let him lead her across the room to the two cane-backed armchairs before the open window. But though she stood before the offered chair, she wouldn't sit, watching him warily like a bird about to take flight.

He sauntered around his own chair and leaned his elbows carelessly across the carved back. He wanted to redeem himself, and with a chair between them for safety she might feel more at ease.

"I am, ma'am, completely at your service," he said softly, and let his smile say the rest. It was usually enough for most women. From Gabriel's father had come that smile, along with his black hair and green eyes and the height and breadth that set him apart from other men. "You say you have need of me?"

"Of your services, yes." She'd blushed prettily when he smiled, the way he'd expected, but her resolute gaze didn't falter, and she held her own with him just as she had with Anjelike. "Two days ago I saw my father buried."

"I'm sorry, I didn't—"

"Nay, I didn't come here for your sympathy!" she said fiercely. Her chin rose a notch higher, enough for Gabriel to see her throat work against the tears she wouldn't shed before him. "My father is—*was*—a shipmaster, Captain Sparhawk, same as yourself, and all my family's fortunes are bound to his vessel. If my mother and sister are not to become paupers, I must find a new captain for his sloop. And I want you, Captain Sparhawk."

"Why me?"

"Because you wouldn't fail me." Her voice became steady again, determined, and impatiently she shoved back the hood of her cloak, letting her unbound hair spill out over her shoulders. "Because you know every thieving Spaniard's lair in the Caribbean, and I could trust you to bring the sloop and her cargo home safe to Newport again."

"A handsome enough arrangement for you, lass, but where's the gain in it for me?" He wanted to run his fingers through that silky dark hair, lift it from her pale throat and kiss her, there, on the softest skin beneath her ear.

"You'll have the standard captain's shares, plus two more of my own, and of course you can add whatever private venture to the cargo you wish."

"Of course," Gabriel repeated dryly. He'd owned his last three commands outright. The only time he'd worked for shares had been when he still sailed for his father. "You're most generous."

Happily unaware, she bobbed her head in acknowledgment. "You won't find a faster vessel in Newport harbor," she said proudly. "She was French built not five years past."

That mouth was made to be kissed, he decided, not to babble on about ships and shares. "You'd trust me with this paragon sloop to go a-chasing after Spaniards?"

"Faith, no!" For the first time she smiled, her small face lit from within, and he was enchanted. "I'd be twenty times a fool to ask you to do that now, when there's scarcely a Spanish ship left afloat!"

So her dead father's sloop was some fat-bottomed merchantman. Did she really expect him to be content with mere trade after the heady cat-and-mouse of privateering?

"Though of course I mean to trust you. I must, if you're to sail for me," she was saying. "And because you're already so prosperous, I could count on you not to cheat me like most of the other swinish masters I could name in Newport."

Gabriel chuckled. She was remarkably forthright for her age, and quite accurate about the other captains.

"Don't laugh at me, Captain, I beg you!" Impulsively she stepped closer to him, near enough for him to smell the salt spray in her hair. Her breasts swelled invitingly above the tight lacing of her stays, and he willed himself not to look down and frighten her away. "The others laughed at me, too, and I know you're not like them. You're not like them at all."

Her dark eyes searched his face for the answer she needed. "I know it's not customary for women to speak of business with men, Captain, but I have no brothers, and my father's death has left me no choice. I hoped you might understand."

Oh, he understood well enough. The pretty child was trying to seduce him.

"Truly, I hoped you might." She lowered her eyes, from modesty or mere uncertainty, he couldn't tell, and her voice slid down to little more than a whisper. "In Newport, 'tis said you are vastly fond of ladies."

"So I am, lass, and vastly fine you are, yourself." Gently Gabriel ran one finger along her jaw to her chin and slanted her face up toward his. "Are you, then, one more reason I should agree to your terms?"

She stayed silent, so still he wondered if she'd forgotten to breathe. Strange how her seriousness seemed more tempting than all of Anjelike's practiced seductions. He tried to remind himself she was a captain's daughter, a girl from a decent family with a maidenhead reserved for the man who married her. He hadn't stayed a bachelor this long without a healthy sense of self-preservation. If he'd any reason at all, he'd send her away now.

Now.

Instead he slowly bent down to kiss her, his fingers cradling her chin. She stiffened with surprise, her hands balling into tight little fists at her sides. She needed time, and he gave it to her, gently coaxing her lips apart to taste the velvety sweetness of her mouth. Gradually he felt her relax, her small hands creeping up to rest against his chest. Her first tentative responses grew bolder, and soon she was answering him, her mouth exploring him and liking what she found. When Gabriel slipped his arm around her waist and drew her closer she leaned into him with a tiny sigh of contentment. Even in his arms she was direct, eager to share the new pleasure he was giving her. How long had it been since he'd kissed a woman as guileless as this one?

Not since Catherine. Not since a lifetime ago.

And his life now had no place for girls like this one. He didn't want to sail in her father's old sloop, trading second-rate rum in the Indies, and he certainly didn't want a wife. Though her father was dead, there were sure to be uncles and neighbors to defend her virtue if he dawdled with her much longer. A girl like this was too dangerous. Reluctantly, almost too late, Gabriel broke away.

"Pretty child," he said softly, stroking the curve of her cheek with his thumb, and she sighed, low and soft. "I don't even know your name."

Her eyes fluttered open as if she'd just awakened, and with a breathy gasp she pulled free of his embrace. As she backed away she touched her fingers to her lips, still moist from his.

"Don't look so scattered, lass." Frustration made him gruff. Damn, he wanted her, and he wasn't used to denying himself where women were concerned. He hoped she wouldn't look down to the front of his breeches and see exactly what she'd done to him. "I've stolen nothing that might be missed on your wedding night."

She flushed clear to the rounded tops of her breasts, and he thought of how much he'd enjoyed those breasts crushed against his chest.

"Your name, poppet. You're asking much of me, and you haven't favored me yet with who you are."

"It's Mariah. Mariah West. And you can stop playacting, Captain Sparhawk." Her smile was unexpected, sharp with regret of her own. "Whatever my name, I'll hazard you're still going to refuse me, aren't you?"

Was he really that obvious? "I'm sorry, Miss West, but it wouldn't suit either of us. I've had my run of luck with the sea, and there's precious little that might tempt me to return. Not even you."

"I know the truth. I don't please you," she said stiffly. "You don't need to explain."

"And you don't need a rogue like me in your life." He smiled, hoping to soften the rejection. "Leastways, not just yet."

"I told you I didn't need any explanations, Captain." She pulled her hood up, stuffing her hair under it, and clutched the sides of her cloak tightly together over her breasts for good measure. "I'll go, and you can return to your—your other pursuits."

She didn't say goodbye when she left the room, and neither did Gabriel. As the heavy front door closed behind her, he dropped into the armchair and stared out at the bay.

Damn, he hadn't even asked her about the fire. She'd made him clean forget about it. Worse yet, she'd made him remember things he thought he'd put behind him forever. Wearily Gabriel rubbed his hands across his eyes. Pretty little poppet. He wished he'd kept her, after all. How bad could a crowd of angry male relatives be, anyway?

"She's gone then, Cap'n?" asked Ethan with surprise, and with the familiarity that made him a better shipmate than servant. "Didn't think ye would be lettin' that one fly away. Not wit' her so favorin' your Miss Langley."

"You thought she resembled Catherine? I didn't see it."

Ethan snorted in disbelief and squinted suspiciously at his captain. "Ye didn't let her tell ye, did ye now, Cap'n?"

Absently Gabriel ran his thumb over and over the chair's curving arm piece. "She told me her father was dead, and she wished me to take his place on his sloop."

"Nay, ye treated her like ye do most ev'ry woman, Cap'n, tryin' so fast to cozen her petticoats o'er her head that ye didn't let her tell ye her news. But she told me, Cap'n, she told old Ethan on account of I'd listen."

Indignantly Ethan seized the used goblet from the sideboard and stuffed it under his arm to take downstairs for washing. "That sloop o' her father's is the *Revenge,* the selfsame *Revenge* you've been cravin' to buy yerself if ye weren't so busy pretendin' ye had set yer rovin' aside. The sleekest sloop for privateerin' ever sailed from Newport, jus' like she says."

"What of it?" Gabriel hid his surprise well. "She also said she wouldn't waste her time chasing the handful of Spaniards left in the sea."

"Ye didn't even let her tell you about them bonfires, did ye?" The look in Ethan's eyes was perilously close to pity. "We're at war wit' the French again, Cap'n, just an' fair an' by order o' the king hisself. That sweet lass says the whole blessed town's gone mad with joy, counting all the money to be had from running after French prizes. The *French,* ye hear me?"

The old sailor turned and contemptuously spat between the andirons into the cold fireplace. "Ye always do prattle on about wanting a second chance to set your mistakes to right, Cap'n. Well, that little Miss West jus' offered ye that chance for salvation. An' ye jus' turned it down.''

Chapter Two

She had made a fool of herself.

There was no other way for Mariah to look at it.
A hapless, helpless, simpering fool. She ripped the
hairbrush through the tangles in her hair, tangles
that had come from riding to that man's house last
night with her hair untied. Because Daniel had always admired her hair loose, she'd been vain—no,
foolish—enough to believe that Captain Gabriel
Sparhawk would like it that way, too.

She winced as the brush caught in a snarl. Because Captain Sparhawk was supposed to be
nearly as old as her father and far more successful as a privateer, she'd imagined him as gray-
haired and fat-bellied and quite safe, despite the
rakish reputation he had among Newport gossips. She had only meant to smile and try to flatter him into agreement, nothing more.

But instead Gabriel Sparhawk was more handsome than any man she'd ever seen, young or old,

so handsome that she'd clear forgotten her reason for coming and let him kiss her instead. Her cheeks burned again from shame. How could she, Mariah West, have let herself forget the fine, noble love of her Daniel for the practiced seduction of a man like Captain Sparhawk?

She started at the pounding at the front door, the heavy, regular thumps that were meant to be heard by every neighbor up and down the street. Swiftly Mariah coiled her hair on her head and tied her cap over it as she hurried down the stairs. In the hallway she passed her mother's tear-swollen face, peeking uncertainly from behind the drawing room door.

"What can they want, Mariah?" her mother asked tremulously. With her words came the strong taint of Geneva spirits, the same solace that had finally killed her husband. "Won't they leave me in peace? Have they no respect for my loss, my grief?"

Mariah glanced at the front door, trying to guess who was on the other side. Duns and collectors were nothing new to her family, and they'd only grown bolder with her father dead.

"I'll speak to the man, Mama," she said gently, touching her hand to her mother's arm. "You rest now. I'll send him on his way."

Her mother was still dressed in the gown she'd worn to the burying two days before, the lace neckerchief soiled and trailing forlornly from her shoulders. Behind her Mariah could see the hangings and blinds drawn against the daylight, and guttered candles across the mantelpiece. Three guineas' worth of the finest spermaceti candles at the very least, thought Mariah with dismay, three guineas that they didn't have now melted into a greasy lump on the woodwork.

The thumping at the front door grew louder, and with it came low, growled threats. Mrs. West's red-rimmed eyes widened with fear, and she scuttled back into the drawing room.

Quickly Mariah closed the room's paneled door after her mother and made certain the lock was latched. She'd have to talk to her mother, and soon, but for now Mariah was determined her mother should have all the peace she wanted. She smoothed her apron over her skirts, took a deep breath to calm herself and with both hands threw open the heavy front door.

"Master Oakes," she said to the man on the step before her, his arm frozen awkwardly overhead in midknock. She knew the chandler from all the cordage and canvas he'd sold to the *Revenge,* and from the bills she'd found with the others that her father hadn't paid. "Master Oakes. Perhaps you are unaware that my father is newly dead?"

"Oh, aye, Miss Mariah, I know it well enough," said Samuel Oakes, his ruddy, jowly face thrust belligerently close to Mariah's. "Whole town knows he died Tuesday night and went into the churchyard on Thursday, and that he's a-laughing with the devil now over all the money he left owing us."

"Mr. Oakes!" Mariah sucked in her breath. "I'll thank you not to speak of my father so, not with him scarcely laid in his grave!"

"Pickled in it's more the truth, girl." Already the summer day was warm, and he swabbed his face with a crumpled blue handkerchief. "Your old man died owing me more'n twenty-five guineas, and I'll not be leaving your doorstep until you pay me, hard money."

Mariah held her place in the center of the doorway. From her experience with other tradesmen, she doubted he'd try to force his way into the house—making the debt public before the Wests' neighbors would be very much more in Oakes's favor—but she still hated the way he was threatening her, standing far closer to her than was proper. Already passersby were beginning to dawdle and eavesdrop.

"You can stand on my doorstep until Judgment Day, Master Oakes," she said firmly, "and I still won't be able to give you what I don't have."

"Sell the bloody sloop and you'll be able to pay us all!"

"Yes, and then where will my mother and sister and I be left? I'll tell you the same as I've told the others, sir, and that's that the *Revenge* is not for sale. Once I've found a master for her—"

"When hell's frozen cold as a whore's heart, you mean!" Oakes snorted. "'Tis common knowledge that every captain worth the name's turned you down."

"Once I've found a master," repeated Mariah stubbornly, "I'll send her out against the French, and I promise you she'll bring back more prizes than any other Newport vessel! *Then* you and every other man can come and I'll honor my father's debts fair. But not now, and not when he's scarce at peace in his grave!"

"Hold your tongue, Oakes! Let the poor lass be!" called a man from the growing crowd, and gratefully Mariah looked to find him. But instead her eye stopped at the flash of salmon-colored skirts and pale gold hair as she recognized her sister, Jenny, her head ducked and her hand linked through Elisha Watson's arm as they tried to hurry by unnoticed.

Mariah slammed the heavy door shut behind her and slipped past the chandler. "Good day to you, Master Oakes," she said quickly, unwilling to let Jenny escape yet again. "Be easy that I'll pay you your due as soon as I can."

Not waiting for his reply, Mariah hurried down the street after her sister. Reverend Dr. Thomas and his wife were invited to dine that evening, and since Mariah had had to turn away the one remaining serving girl last month, she'd need all the help she could to ready both the meal and Mrs.

West for company. And granted, though Captain West was seldom home while they'd been girls, his memory deserved more than this from her sister, running off to do heaven only knew what with Elisha.

And who made you so much more virtuous? whispered Mariah's conscience. With alarming clarity she recalled how willingly she'd slipped into Captain Sparhawk's embrace, how the sacrifice she'd planned to make for her family's welfare had turned instead to a shameful, eager surrender that had been like nothing she'd ever dreamed.

"Out of my path, ye clumsy chit!" The cart full of hogsheads rocked precariously on one wheel, the carter swearing at her as he yanked on the mule's reins. Mariah gasped and darted out of his path and nearer to the houses. "Pull yer head out o' the clouds, hussy, or ye shall end up under my wheels!"

The man was right, decided Mariah miserably as she pressed her palms to her cheeks. She'd lost her wits and nearly her life on account of a man who didn't care a farthing for her. His casual rejection had stung her pride more than she wanted to admit, but at least no one else would ever know. Probably Captain Sparhawk himself had already forgotten she'd even been in his house.

And now she'd lost Jenny, too. With Elisha as her guide, her sister could be anywhere in Newport, and Mariah's despondency grew. She would have to clean the house and cook supper herself and pray that no more angry tradesmen appeared while her hands were covered with flour. She'd have to try to make her mother drink enough tea before supper so she wouldn't weep or fall asleep at the table, and coax her into changing her gown and repinning her hair. The minister's wife had a sharp eye for households that had gone awry and a sharper tongue in the retelling, and Mariah meant to spare her mother as much as she could. Later tonight, after the dishes had been washed and the linens put to soak, she'd go back to sorting through the sea chest filled with twenty years of her father's haphazard records and accounts.

Mariah sighed wearily. Lord only knew it wouldn't be the first time she'd been left to do everything herself. She tried so hard to do what was right, but everyone around her seemed determined to do exactly the opposite. She thought again of Captain Sparhawk and his orderly, handsome house, everything new and shining and, she thought wistfully, paid for.

She squinted at the clock in the tower of Trinity Church. If she hurried, she could still walk by the dock where the *Revenge* was tied. Perhaps Tom Farr, the sloop's mate, had thought of another shipmaster for her to approach. With the new war, some of the other captains might have changed their minds.

It was market day, and the streets around the market house were crowded with empty wagons from the farms clattering across the paving stones, housewives and serving girls with bulging oak-splint baskets on their arms, apprentices on errands and sailors on leave, barking dogs and wailing children, and screeching hens destined for the evening's stew. The acrid smoke from last night's bonfires still hung heavy in the summer air, mingling with the oversweet smell of fermenting molasses from the rum distilleries to the east.

Her steps slower, Mariah turned toward the waterfront. Ahead she could pick out the *Revenge*'s tall, raking mainmast, towering above her moorings, and Mariah's spirits inched higher. Like her father, she had come to love the elegant sloop passionately. With her ocher decks and bright blue sides, the carved flourishes on her bow picked out in gold leaf, the *Revenge* was the handsomest vessel in the harbor, and with the right captain, she'd be the fastest, as well.

Capturing the sloop had been the single piece of luck her father had found in his entire life. Fever had so reduced the *Revenge*'s Spanish crew that Captain West had had to do no more than stop the sloop from drifting aimlessly to claim her as his prize. But the same luck that had given him the *Revenge* had then turned against him, and by the time Edward West had sailed into Narragansett Bay, he was already a dying man. The sloop was his sole legacy, and nothing would ever induce Mariah to part with it.

"You'd never make a gamester, Miss West," said the resonant voice beside her that she'd never expected to hear again. "You underplayed your hand so sadly last night I almost walked away before we'd fair begun."

Gabriel had meant the sloop, but as soon as Mariah turned her small, startled face toward him, he realized the girl herself was the real prize. So it hadn't been the brandy, and she really was as lovely as he remembered. Few women he knew could stand close scrutiny in the midday sun, but this one, now, he could gaze at her until the moon came out and still be charmed.

"Captain Sparhawk." Mariah drew back sharply. He held his laced hat in one hand with a courtier's grace, his long black hair untied and tossing in the breeze off the water. In the bright sun his eyes seemed very green, and she didn't doubt for a moment that the laughter in them was at her expense. "Though I've no notion of what you're saying, I can assure you I don't believe in card play."

He settled his hat on his head and leaned over her the way one would with a child. His height made her feel small, insignificant, and she didn't like it, nor, right now, did she like him.

"La, la, Miss West, such pretty, prissy lady talk!" Gabriel reasoned he could tease her—

there'd be no harm in that. He liked the way her eyes widened indignantly, her brows like inky brush strokes arching higher. "You don't like card play, then, but you do believe in gambling. If I recall, last night you were quite willing to sweeten the pot with your—"

"Good *day,* Captain Sparhawk!" All too well she knew how wantonly she'd behaved. She certainly didn't need him to remind her. With her head down she tried to dodge around him, but deftly he blocked her path.

"Nay, not so fast, poppet." He slipped his hand around her upper arm to lead her along. No one else along Thames Street could know that his fingers held her arm like a trap, that she had no choice but to match his footsteps or be dragged across the paving stones. "Our negotiations have only begun."

"Negotiations!" Indignantly Mariah scowled at him. "You refused my offer last night, Captain, and I accepted that as your final word. I won't beg and I won't grovel, no matter how much you wish to humiliate me. Besides, I've already spoken to another shipmaster this very morning, a gentleman who is more than willing to agree to my terms."

"Liar." He smiled cheerfully. "Tom Farr told me I was your last chance. Powerfully flattering, that. Most ladies would rather place me at the head of their list."

"You've no right talking to *my* first mate!" she sputtered indignantly. "Tom Farr works for me!"

"I've every right in the world to speak with the man, Miss West. Captains generally do talk to their mates."

Mariah glared at him, forced to take two steps to match his every one. She didn't believe for an instant that he was going to sail for her, and his grip on her arm made her uneasy. Like every girl in a seafaring town, she'd always been warned from the waterfront with tales of careless young Englishwomen snatched from the street and sold into Tortuga brothels to serve the lust of pirates. Although Mariah didn't really believe that Captain Sparhawk would do that to her—after all, his mother's family had come down with Roger Williams—she still didn't trust him. Considering the foolhardy way she'd behaved with him last night, how could she?

"Aye, and since I'm to be your master," he was saying, "I've every right to expect a bit of obedience from you, too."

Gabriel saw the panic flicker across her face. He'd only meant to tease, not frighten her, and he relaxed his hold on her arm. With a little yelp of triumph, Mariah broke free and darted across the street and up the *Revenge*'s gangway in a swirl of muslin petticoats.

Gabriel grinned. Beneath her somber dark skirts, her shoes had red lacquer heels and polished buckles, and her neat little ankles wore bright yellow stockings. Too bad she refused to gamble, or else he'd wager she tied those yellow stockings with fancy ribbon garters, and above the knee, too.

Safe on her own sloop, Mariah could hear Captain Sparhawk's heavy footsteps behind her on the planking, taking his time with infuriating confidence. Well, let him follow her, she thought crossly. She'd have the *Revenge*'s crew put him off soon enough.

"Ah, Cap'n Sparhawk, sir, I see ye've found Miss West, after all," called Farr. He tugged at the front of his knitted cap and bobbed his head to Gabriel as if Mariah didn't exist. "Like I told ye, she comes here regular ev'ry morning."

Mariah wheeled around to face the mate. "Tom Farr, you sailed for my father since before you could shave! How *could* you discuss my habits with this man?"

Beneath his weathered tan, Farr's face flushed. "I saw no harm to it, miss, not with ye being th' sloop's owner, an' him being th' new master."

Lightly Gabriel touched Mariah's sleeve. "Come below to the cabin, lass, and we'll sort this out proper."

Ignoring him, Mariah looked from Farr to the other sailors and workmen gathered on the deck, most of them Newport men she'd known all her life. What had Captain Sparhawk told them al-

ready? By the time they repeated it to their wives
and sweethearts over supper there wouldn't be a
soul left in town who wouldn't know she'd kissed
him. Dear Lord, and after all the times she'd lec-
tured Jenny on the importance of keeping a good
name!

With as much dignity as she could marshal, she
turned and fled down the companionway to her
father's old cabin. She didn't pause to look at
Gabriel when he followed her down the narrow
steps, and she stood by the stern windows with her
back to him as he closed the cabin door.

But when at last she spun around to face him,
her skirts swinging and her blue eyes bright with
angry fire, Gabriel realized he'd seldom seen a
woman so angry.

"You're not their captain," she declared, "and
you're not my master, and you've no right to *pre-
sume* to—"

"How many of the other captains did you
kiss?" interrupted Gabriel calmly.

She froze, the fire quenched in an instant, and
she swallowed visibly before she answered.
"None."

Gabriel's brows rose skeptically.

"None, I swear it!"

Gabriel sighed dramatically. "Well, then, perhaps you should have tried it earlier, since it certainly seems to have worked with me."

She stared at him, speechless. Even with his broad shoulders bent beneath the beams overhead, he somehow remained unbowed, his smile far too wicked and knowing for the cramped quarters of the little cabin.

"I didn't whisper a word of it to anyone, Miss Mariah, so you needn't look so fearful," he continued as he hooked his hat on one of the bulkhead pegs. "I'm not some wild African lion, and I've absolutely no intention of devouring you."

But as soon as he'd said it, he found himself imagining how he *would* devour her, in one long, delicious, impossibly sweet meal that would last from day into night. He'd sworn to himself he wouldn't touch her again, but he hadn't counted on her being such a mortal temptation.

"I'm not afraid of you, Captain Sparhawk." She narrowed her eyes at him, her chin low and stubborn like a small bull ready to charge. "You're a wicked man to taunt me like this."

"Nay, poppet, you're the wicked lass to tease me with one kiss. Was that all the favor you meant to grant? I'd wager it was, just as I'd wager you haven't a real notion of what comes next between women and men. A dangerous game, that, for pretty little girls."

He was serious now, his smile gone. Angry or not, she had the same open innocence in her face that he remembered from Catherine's, the kind of innocence he'd avoided ever since. "Even if I were only half the rake you've judged me to be, I never would have let you go until I'd claimed the whole of what you offered. Learn a bit more of the world, and you'll damned well be afraid of men three times your size."

Mariah felt herself blushing again. How empty-headed did he think she was? "You can preach to me all you want, Captain Sparhawk, but I'm still not afraid of you."

"Please yourself, Miss Worldly West." He sighed, shook his head and folded his arms over his chest. "It's this sloop I want, anyway, not you."

"This sloop?" she repeated stupidly.

"This sloop, none other, nothing more." Now look who was lying, he thought wryly. "I've been landlocked too long."

Lightly he traced his fingers across the fluted paneling of the bulkhead, a decorative flourish that no frugal Yankee shipbuilder would ever consider. He liked the idea that he'd take a French-built sloop against Deveaux, especially a vessel so aptly, if a bit broadly, named the *Revenge*. "Having the French in this war changes everything. The richest prizes will be snatched up by the Englishmen with the fastest ships, and in this sloop, I mean to be the first from this colony with a letter of marque in the Caribbean."

As she listened, Mariah absently twisted a loose curl at her nape that had slipped from beneath her cap. He'd expected her to look pleased, even relieved, but instead her expression was curiously guarded.

"So you really do mean to sail for me?" she asked doubtfully.

"Aye, I do. I don't have time to build a ship for myself, and yours is the only vessel in Newport worth bothering with. Since you won't sell her outright, you don't leave me much choice."

"You'll agree to my terms for the division of shares? They're more than fair."

"Fair enough for you, poppet," said Gabriel dryly. "You didn't mention that half the shopkeepers in Newport think they're entitled to a part of this voyage. Your old papa owed more than most men earn in a lifetime."

Consciously she willed her hands to cease their fidgeting. He was right, she would make a wretched cardplayer. "Meaning that you've changed your mind again?"

"Nay, lass, meaning I'll clear your father's debts before we sail so there's no claims on the voyage." The offer wasn't as altruistic as it appeared. Privateering was little more than legal piracy, with all the dangers of any warfare. If he was killed—a possibility that hadn't seemed to have occurred to her—Gabriel didn't want his affairs tangled in the courts with hers. "In return you give me half the shares. Now that's what I'd deem fair."

"Thirty percent." His offer was beyond fair, but her pride wouldn't let her give away half. "I didn't ask you to assume the debts."

"I'll pay them outright, not assume a blessed cent. Forty-five."

Mariah took a deep breath. "Forty. And I mean to pay you back every blessed cent."

"Forty it is." Gabriel slapped his palm on the desk. He would have settled for thirty, but he'd been curious to see how far she'd bargain. She was clever, and he liked that in a woman. "Send your agent here tomorrow with the papers, and then we'll begin outfitting proper."

Mariah told herself she should be grateful. Once it became known that Gabriel Sparhawk was the *Revenge*'s new captain, there'd be no more angry creditors knocking at her front door. With his kind of luck, she and her mother and sister would be free from debt after one, maybe two voyages. She had accomplished what she'd intended to do, even if it had taken one shameless, wanton kiss from a man who'd thought it only a game.

"Thank you, Captain Sparhawk," she said softly, looking at the polished toes of his boots. Better to think of Daniel, his shy smile and the sandy hair that always slipped into his eyes. She remembered her joy when he'd asked her to wed, and felt the too-familiar sting of tears behind her eyes.

Her open face reflected every emotion, and the sadness that Gabriel now saw there baffled him until he remembered her father's death. With her head bent and her hands clasped loosely at her waist, she seemed too fragile for the responsibilities that had been thrust upon her, and he longed to take her into his arms again to comfort her.

"And thank you for leaving me my waistcoat," he said gently. "You're a sharp trader, Miss West."

"You shouldn't be so surprised." Her smile was bittersweet. "In eighteen years I've had to be sharper than most ladies."

Eighteen. Only eighteen. The same age that Catherine had been when he'd lost her.

In the dappled light reflecting off the water, he suddenly saw again her resemblance to Catherine—the shadowy sweep of her lashes across her full cheek, the way her lips were parted, the graceful, curving line of her throat and shoulders. Shaken, he remembered what Ethan had said about second chances and salvation. Without thinking, he swore harshly. Mariah's startled gaze met his, and the resemblance vanished.

To hell with salvation. Mariah West wasn't Catherine Langley, and she never would be. Second chances didn't come to anyone in this life. He hadn't become the man he was now through overnice scruples and preachers' morality. If he wanted something, one way or another he made it his own.

The girl before him lifted her hands to settle her bonnet, unwittingly drawing his attention to the swell of her breasts above her tightly laced waist. Her skin was creamy pale, and he knew it would be soft beneath his touch.

The way Catherine's had been.

Eighteen was young, but old enough. He had the sloop. Why couldn't he have the girl, as well?

"There's one more term to be settled between us." His mouth was too dry for the bantering to come easily, and to his own ear his words sounded forced. "One we won't bother putting to the clerk's paper."

She waited, her brows raised in silent question.

"Before I sail, return to Crescent Hill and dine with me." He smiled, and watched her expression change from surprise to flushed pleasure and then to wariness. Before he was done, he'd make sure she'd feel nothing but pleasure from him. He'd prove to himself that she was no different from all the others. "Supper, that is all."

Mariah hesitated. In the last minutes his face had changed in ways she couldn't fathom. Though his smile remained, the laughter had gone from his eyes, and the lines etched into his cheeks by the sun and wind had deepened. He was right. She *should* be afraid of him.

"I wasn't much of a host last night," he said, sensing her reluctance. Much as he longed to, he wouldn't try to kiss her again. Better to leave her wanting and off-balance. He plucked his hat from the peg and twice tapped the curved brim lightly with his thumbs. "Grant me the chance to make amends. Besides, there's nothing untoward in a shipowner dining with a captain."

"It's vastly untoward when the shipowner's a lady," she said quickly. "I'm sorry, but I cannot accept your invitation."

"Some other place, then? One more agreeable to your...sensibilities?"

She didn't like being teased about her sensibilities. She wasn't even sure what or where they were, and she didn't like granting him even that small advantage. But she could be just as determined. She would dine with him, and prove to him and to herself that that single kiss had meant as little to her as it clearly did to him. "Very well, then. But not your house."

"Not my house. Agreed." Somehow he managed to keep the triumph from his voice. "I mean to clear Newport within a fortnight. We'll name the night soon." With the back of his hand he gently brushed the curve of her cheek, and she prayed he didn't feel how she shivered at his touch. Not until he'd turned to leave did she realize her hands were clasped so tightly that her fingers were shaking.

"Captain Sparhawk!" she called, her voice a little too loud. He stopped and expectantly looked over his shoulder. "I didn't kiss any of the others. Truly. You were the only one."

This time his smile was genuine. "I know, poppet. And I intend to keep it that way."

Chapter Three

"I wish you to know, Mariah," began Mrs. Thomas as she dabbled genteelly at her leek soup with the bowl of her spoon, "that Nan Rhawn came to me this day with the strangest tale. Fancy, she claimed she saw you out walking on Thames Street with Captain Gabriel Sparhawk!"

Mariah forced herself to continue raising her spoon to her lips, to sip and swallow the soup as if what the minister's wife had said meant nothing at all to her. If walking with Captain Sparhawk was so wicked, what would they say about her visit to Crescent Hill? She'd known from the moment the man had accepted her offer that she'd have to explain why she'd asked him. She just hadn't realized the explanations would have to start so soon.

Reverend Thomas clucked his tongue, his jowls quivering against his stiff, starched neckcloth. "Of course Nan was mistaken, my dearest. Mariah would never be 'out walking,' as you say, with a man like Gabriel Sparhawk.''

''Pray, who is he?'' asked Mrs. West with bewilderment. She turned toward Mariah, not noticing how her lace cuff trailed into her soup. ''I don't know this gentleman, do I, Mariah? A captain, you say? Pray, is he a friend of your father's?''

''No, Mama, but he could have been.'' Mariah reached out and carefully blotted her napkin to her mother's sleeve. ''He's another privateer, same as Father was.''

''Don't be cajoled by your daughter's innocence, Mrs. West,'' thundered Reverend Thomas in the same full voice he used for sinners from his pulpit. ''The man's the worst kind of rogue. Because the riches of this life have come easily to him, he gives no thought to his soul in the next. Yet because he has prospered, he is held to be a great fellow, with no regard to the men he has murdered or the women he has debauched!''

''He is a murderer?'' Mrs. West's hand fluttered until it found the reassurance of Mariah's firm grasp. ''In Newport?''

''Oh, aye, ma'am, though *he'd* say 'twas for the king's glory.''

Mrs. Thomas nodded sagely in agreement with her husband. She leaned forward, her face between the candles lit bright with her righteousness. ''You know he comes by his wickedness from the very cradle. Though you yourself are too young to recall the scandal, ma'am, his mother was a Quakeress barred from her congregation for her unlawful, carnal congress with a castaway sailor that she'd found—found, mind you!—washed up on her beach!"

"The sect calls them meetings, my dearest, not congregations." Too late Reverend Thomas had noted Jenny's eager interest, and with self-conscious heartiness he returned to his soup. "And you will recall she did wed the man."

"Oh, aye, and produced a lusty six-month child to prove her guilt!" Mrs. Thomas sighed dramatically and rolled her gaze to the ceiling. "A girl named Sarah, I recall, now grown and wed and as heathen as her mother out there at Nantasket—"

"The young ladies, my dearest, the young ladies!" Reverend Thomas's pewter spoon clattered against his empty soup plate as he nodded toward Mariah and Jenny. "Scandals never improve with age. Suffice it to say that Gabriel Sparhawk is a wicked man, a rakish man, and one quite unfit for ladies' conversation."

"Wicked or not, Captain Sparhawk is the most successful privateer to sail from Newport." Mariah laid her spoon beside her plate, her soup untouched since that single taste. Clumps of carrot floated on the now-cool surface, and she knew she'd never be able to make this soup again, let alone eat it. "I have asked him to serve as the captain of the *Revenge,* and he has agreed."

There, she thought, she'd done it. Telling Mrs. Thomas spread news faster than nailing broadsides to a tree. The whole town would know by noon tomorrow—or at least the few who didn't know already that she'd been walking down Thames Street with Gabriel Sparhawk. Levelly she met the stunned expressions around the table.

"Lud, 'Riah," breathed Jenny. "I'd never countenance *you* knowing Gabriel Sparhawk! Abbie Parker's mother swears he's the most handsomest gentleman on the entire island, and here he is with *you*—"

Mariah silenced her sister with one swift look. But her mother's wistful reproach was much harder to bear.

"Oh, Mariah," Mrs. West murmured, her mouth twisting and her eyes too bright with tears. "Has it come to this, that you must rely on a murderer in your father's stead?"

"The man's no more a murderer than any soldier or sailor in the king's service, Mama. And you know no one can ever take Father's place."

Mariah's smile was forced as she watched the tears spill from her mother's eyes and slide crookedly across her cheeks. She told herself it was grief and the Geneva, not disappointment in her older daughter, but her mother's painful, silent tears were worse than any shouted reprimand could ever be. "Captain Sparhawk will do well with the *Revenge,* I promise."

"With all the decent shipmasters in this town for you to choose from—"

"None of whom would even hear me out." Mariah had twisted the napkin in her lap into a tight linen knot. "Captain Sparhawk listened."

"He'll make his fortune and rob your virtue is what he'll do, miss!" declared Mrs. Thomas. "A woman's reputation should be beyond gold."

Furiously Mariah bit back her retort, knowing she'd gain nothing by making an enemy of the minister's wife. It was easy enough for the woman to preach virtuous poverty when there weren't shopkeepers drumming on her front door. Though Reverend Thomas's living was small, his father-in-law owned a distillery, a business that never faltered in hard times.

"Captain Sparhawk has agreed to sail the *Revenge,* nothing more." In spite of her intentions, Mariah's chin lifted defiantly. "And even a rake as accomplished as you paint him would be hard-pressed to harm me when he is in the Caribbean, and I am here in Newport."

"You would defend him, then?" asked Mrs. Thomas incredulously.

"Nay, ma'am," said Mariah slowly as she rose to her feet. "I only defend myself. Now if you'll excuse me, I must see to the pudding in the kitchen."

* * *

Later, as the night stretched into morning, Mariah sat cross-legged on her bed, her father's papers strewn across the coverlet and a saucer on her pillow to catch the drip from the candlestick. Her only experience with figures and ciphering came from managing the household accounts, but she didn't need to be a clerk to see that her father had left his affairs in shambles. She wouldn't blame Captain Sparhawk at all if he took one look at this mess in the morning and left in disgust.

Why hadn't her father kept ledgers like other captains? She peeled apart two water-stained bills of lading, and between them found another scrap of paper. The ink was faded with water spots, and she had to hold the paper close to the candle to see that it was a voucher from gaming. She whistled low under her breath when she realized her father had risked five thousand dollars on dice in a Barbados rum shop. Five thousand dollars! He must have wagered the *Revenge* herself to meet those stakes. But at least for once he'd won. The voucher was signed with a flourish, a name she couldn't quite make out. Not that it mattered now, thought Mariah. With her father dead and this new war with France, there'd never be a chance of collecting such a debt.

With a long, heartfelt sigh, Mariah lifted the heavy weight of her braid off the back of her neck, sticky from the heat, and stretched her arms over her head. Even with the windows open and the shutters latched back, the air in the room was hot and still. The streets outside were quiet, the town having exhausted itself in celebration the night before. Somewhere to the west a single dog barked forlornly at the quarter moon.

Through the window, over the roofs of the warehouses, Mariah could just make out the top-masts of the ships in the harbor, their furled sails silvery pale in the moonlight. She thought of the *Revenge* and the new master she'd picked for the sloop, how green his eyes had been in the bright sun, how he'd smiled when he called her poppet, and how her heart had thumped against her ribs when he'd stood too close to her in the sloop's cabin.

"Mariah?" The hinges on her door squeaked as Mrs. West slipped into the room, her bare feet making no noise. By the light of the candle in her mother's hand Mariah could see that her hair was neatly plaited beneath her nightcap and that her night rail was clean. Though grief still marked her face, her eyes were clear, and with wonder Mariah realized that for the first time since her father's return her mother was sober, or at least close enough. "Forgive me, child, but I could not sleep, and when I saw the light beneath your door—"

"Nay, Mama, I was done anyway." Hastily Mariah scooped up the piles of papers and smoothed the coverlet for her mother to join her on the bed.

"Is that your father's business?" asked Mrs. West suspiciously, choosing instead to sit in the ladder-back chair. "You shouldn't be doing that, Mariah. You shouldn't have to. Your father wouldn't have wanted his daughter meddling in men's affairs, any more than he'd want you chasing about on the wharves. It's not seemly, Mariah."

Mariah stared at her ink-stained fingers. How could she explain that if she didn't do it, no one would? Even before her father's death, her mother had never understood.

"If you truly wished to help your sister and me, you'd find yourself a husband. A widower, perhaps, an older gentleman established in his trade who would be willing to overlook your—your *seriousness*."

"Mama, no!" Without looking up, Mariah began to shake her head. "I don't want a husband, and I never will. Let Jenny marry Elisha."

"Elisha won't offer for her until he's seen you settled first. No man wants a spinster sister in his household." Mrs. West sighed and rubbed her temples. "Mariah, you really must forget Daniel O'Bierne. There's no use pining away after a man you can't have."

"No!" Mariah's voice shook. "I loved Daniel! No other man could ever mean to me what he does. I loved him, and he loved me, and I'll never marry anyone else, ever!''

Mariah closed her eyes and tried to remember Daniel's face, the freckles on his nose and his shy, uneven smile. Her Daniel, her only love. . . .

But why, instead, did the face in her mind have mocking green eyes and a too-perfect smile against weather-browned skin?

Her mother sighed again and gazed out the window, unconscious of the view and the way she toyed with the pearl on her wedding ring. In profile she was still a handsome woman, not yet forty, with the same golden hair as Jenny, and suddenly Mariah realized her mother meant to remarry. It wasn't Elisha who wouldn't want a spinster sister-in-law underfoot; it was her mother who wished to shed a spinster daughter. Sickened, she wondered if her mother had already chosen the man to replace her father.

"If this Captain Sparhawk has agreed to sail your father's vessel, then clearly he has an interest in you," said Mrs. West without turning. "No man would entertain this sort of agreement with a woman unless he had hopes of an intrigue with her. When you see him again—and you *will* see him again, Daniel or no Daniel—I would have you wear a more comely gown. If you dress like a drab, that's how he will see you."

"Mama, it's not like that between Captain Sparhawk and me!"

"What was his given name again—an angel, wasn't it? Michael?"

"Gabriel." Mariah's voice still shook, and she paused to steady it. "But it doesn't matter, Mama. I'm too young to interest him."

"No man ever thinks a woman is too young for him," said her mother dryly, "any more than they ever judge themselves too old. Besides, I was seventeen when you were born, and you'll be nineteen this autumn, without even the prospect of a husband. Nay, Mariah, you're scarcely too young."

"When Daniel asked for me, you said I was, and now it seems I'm a wizened old spinster," said Mariah bitterly. "What a wonder two years can make in my life!"

"Your age wasn't the only reason the O'Beirne boy wasn't a suitable match for you. You deserve a finer life than some Papist Teague could offer."

Mariah's brittle laugh held no humor. "Oh, aye, we Wests are of the better sort, aren't we?"

"You forget yourself, Mariah." Mrs. West sighed irritably as she retied the bands of her nightcap. "The Wests have been on this island since there was nothing here but mud and Indians. Now this Captain Sparhawk's people—"

"Mama, listen to me. Captain Sparhawk has agreed to sail the *Revenge* for us, and that is all. You heard what Mrs. Thomas said about him at the table. A man like that will likely never marry, and even if he did, he wouldn't choose someone like me.''

"Then it will be your affair to make him choose you." Mrs. West swung around in the chair so she faced Mariah. "Now you listen to me, daughter. You can swear with your dying breath that it's all business between you and this man—knowing you, it likely is—but others won't believe it. I heard well enough what Mrs. Thomas said, and I can guess what she'll say again. Your sister and I will be shamed. You'll be as ruined as if you did lie with him. If you ever want to be regarded as a decent woman, you'll find a way to make the man marry you."

"But *I* don't want to marry him!" wailed Mariah.

"You should have considered that before you meddled in concerns of trade. Prowling round Thames Street, looking for privateering captains!" Her voice softened. "I'm sorry, lamb. The world can be a harsh judge for a woman."

"Then the world is full of sharp-tongued gossips! I—*we*—had no choice, Mama, else be tossed out on the street! All these papers, all these bills. Can't you understand that Father didn't—"

"Don't speak ill of your father, Mariah. It grieves me sorely." She pressed the tips of her fingers to her temples and closed her eyes. "There is a pitcher of limewater on the claw-foot table in my room, if you'll but fetch it for me."

"Oh, no, Mama, please." Mariah knew the pitcher, just as she knew the thin-sliced limes that floated in the Geneva. "You don't need that now. You're better tonight, I can tell."

"I *was* better, but you have vexed me so that my poor head aches worse than ever. Even now, when I'm ill, you're bent on crossing me." Her hands were trembling as she took up the candlestick again and rose to her feet, clutching the back of the chair for support. "You've been strong willed and obstinate from the morning I brought you into this life, Mariah. God knows I've expected little enough, but you never try to please me, do you? You never have, and you never will."

To please her mother, Mariah borrowed Jenny's second-best day gown, ice-blue sateen looped over a striped petticoat. But Mrs. West's head ached too much for her to notice what Mariah wore, and she kept to her bed with the hangings drawn against the daylight. Mariah gathered the withered lime rinds from the top of the claw-foot table and took them away with the empty pitcher.

By the time she'd reached the *Revenge*'s wharf, Mariah wished she'd changed back into her old dark wool. Jenny was smaller, and Mariah had had to lace her stays tighter to make the pale blue gown fit. She had tied a scarf around her shoulders to hide the way the lacings pushed her breasts up above the gown's low round neckline, but from the suggestive invitations she received along Thames Street she realized the scarf was a failure. Beneath her wide-brimmed straw hat her face was red with embarrassment, and she was nearly running, her eyes steadfastly on her feet, when she finally reached the sloop's gangway.

"Here now, sweetheart, what's your hurry?" A bare male arm snaked around her waist and nearly lifted her off the deck. Mariah twisted around to see the man's face, shiny from the sun and work and rimmed with a curling red beard. "Couldn't bear to be away from me, eh, love? And brung me supper in a willow basket, too!"

"Let me go!" cried Mariah indignantly, but the man's grip only tightened, pulling her face close enough to his that her hat brim bent up against his forehead. She swung the basket up to strike his chest, but the man only laughed and swatted it away. All around them other men were laughing, too, and as Mariah struggled she wondered furiously who they all could be on board her sloop. "Let me go, you great oaf!"

Suddenly she was yanked free and set down on the deck so sharply she almost tumbled back from the impact. She shoved her hat brim up in time to see Gabriel Sparhawk's fist strike the bearded man's jaw and send him sprawling against the railing as the other men scattered out of the way.

"Why'd you go putting your dirty hands on the lady, Duffy?" demanded Gabriel as the other man held his jaw. "Don't you know who she is?"

"Sorry, Cap'n," he mumbled thickly, "I never would've touched her if I'd known she belonged t'you."

With his hands on his waist, Gabriel glared down at him. "That would have been bad enough, you great randy fool. But it's worse than that. She doesn't belong to me. This sloop belongs to her."

"Th' owner?" repeated Duffy weakly. "Ah, damn it all, Cap'n, how would I know?"

But Gabriel had already turned toward Mariah. "Did he harm you, lass?"

Mariah shook her head, clutching the basket with both hands before her. By now she should remember the man's sheer size and presence, but still she caught herself inching upward, striving to make the most of her own diminutive height before him.

"But who is *he,* Captain Sparhawk? And these other men, too. Only the *Revenge*'s crewmen have any right to be on board."

"Then they belong here and no place else," declared Gabriel, wiping his shirtsleeve across his brow. In this heat he longed to peel off the shirt and the satin waistcoat over it and work bare chested like the men, but not until after he'd met with this blasted clerk, wherever he was. He looked past the girl, wondering if the man had come with her. She didn't have any other reason for being here, and her presence was one more irritation in a morning full of them. "If the logbook below's to be believed, your father sailed with barely enough men to trim his sails. A vessel this size needs eighty good hands to make a privateer out of her, men for sailing and fighting and taking prizes into port."

A wild, whooping cheer rose up from the men at the mention of prizes, a cheer that Gabriel silenced with one black look over his shoulder. Best to let them know early on what kind of captain he was. Enthusiasm was one thing. Raving like jackals was quite another, and he was in no mood for jackals, or, for that matter, pretty, rosy-cheeked little girls like this one before him.

"I left word at several taverns that I was looking for men, and these were the best of the lot. Of course the ones that sailed with your father still have a place if they wish it. I'll be shipping a surgeon, too, Andrew Macauly of Tiverton. Most of them have sailed with me before, but speak up if there's any you'd like to naysay."

"Oh, no, as long as they suit you." She glanced around the circle of eager faces. So many men to find in so short a time, and the unimaginable luxury of a surgeon, too! Her father had always been among the luckless captains forced to delay voyages until he could muster a crew, and there'd never been enough money to offer the bounties that some captains did. Though she should be pleased, it stung Mariah for her father's sake to see how readily Captain Sparhawk's reputation alone could draw more men in a morning than her father had attracted in his whole career.

"Have you any word from your warehouse man?" asked Gabriel. "It's halfway to noon, and the fellow's yet to show his face with your accounts."

Mariah cleared her throat. "He won't be coming because he doesn't exist. My father kept his own accounts. He said clerks were landlocked cheats and scoundrels, and he didn't trust them."

"They're also a mighty useful way to keep other, bigger cheats and scoundrels out of your pockets." His shoulders worked uneasily beneath the sticky linen. No clerk to impress, but he couldn't very well strip down before the girl, and his irritation grew. He wished he hadn't had to strike Duffy. The man had only done what he wanted to do himself, and all of his resentment fell on her doorstep. "So is that what you've got in that basket? Your father's ledgers?"

"Not precisely." Lord, why had her father made this so hard for her? "He didn't have much use for ledgers, either."

Gabriel stared at her for an endless moment, dumbfounded. "So your father didn't believe in clerks or ledgers, and he didn't keep a crew large enough to keep his sloop afloat. He let his gunnery turn foul from disuse, and he didn't keep enough dry powder to light his pipe. There are no stores on board to speak of, leastways not that I could find. This suit of sails is worn thinner than the linen in your shift. And then, of course, there's the size of the bills his three ladies have managed to accumulate with every sempstress and bonnet maker in town.''

To Mariah the only sound on the deck came from the gulls overhead. She knew to her shame that the entire crew was openly listening. How could she blame them when the flaws of her entire family were being laid out one by one like the dirtiest laundry?

"Captain Sparhawk," she said, her temper simmering. She wouldn't give them all the satisfaction of one more scene to add to their gossip. "Captain Sparhawk, I believe this conversation is better suited to the privacy of the cabin."

She headed for the companionway, her heels clicking briskly on the holystoned deck. He lunged after her, covering four of her steps with two of his own.

"Come along, Miss West, let's see what other secrets your father didn't take with him to the grave." Impatiently Gabriel reached out to take the basket from her, but Mariah pulled it away.

"Nay, I'll share nothing more with you until you apologize for insulting my father!" Bunching her skirts to one side, she started down the narrow steps with the basket looped over her arm.

"Your father!" Gabriel thundered after her. "Sweet Jesus, woman, I'd warrant that most would say I'm the one who's been insulted! Not one thing about this whole rotten deal's been true, and if there was another ship that would suit me, I'd leave now and consider myself a fortunate man!"

Gabriel grabbed for the basket again, and again Mariah managed to jerk it out of his reach. But as she did she lost her balance on the steep, narrow companionway ladder and toppled backward with a shriek to the lower deck. Layers of petticoats broke her fall, but the basket flipped off her arm and upended. All around her drifted the precious bits and scraps of paper with her father's handwriting, all her careful sorting destroyed.

"Miss West!" In an instant Gabriel was beside her, his brows drawn with concern as he offered his hand to help her to her feet.

"Dear God, how could you do this to me?" Ignoring his assistance, Mariah scrambled to her knees to gather the papers. "How could you?"

She was weeping stupid, sloppy tears as she clutched the papers in her fists. "I swear I didn't know about the guns or the powder or any of the rest, or I would have told you. My poor father only did his best. Can you understand that? He wasn't lucky like you. This last cruise he was so ill

that Tom Farr and the others had to carry him
ashore. All he wanted then was to die in his own
bed, and thank God he did. So if he let the
wretched guns turn foul or whatever they did
that's offended you so mightily, well then, I'm
sorry. Damn you, I'm *sorry!*''

Gabriel crouched beside her, his hands resting
loosely on his bent knees. Weeping women seldom disarmed him like this, perhaps because most
of the women he knew had little real reason to cry.
He felt sure this one did and, oddly, he cared.

"You loved the old man that much?" he asked
quietly.

"Of course I did." Mariah sniffed loudly. "He
was my father."

"It doesn't always follow like that." He took
her hand and gently began to pry her fingers open
to free the crumpled papers, and to his surprise she
let him. With great care he smoothed each one out
across his knee before he put it back into the basket. "At present I doubt my own father cares
whether I'm alive or dead."

"You can't mean that!"

"I wouldn't have said it if I didn't. We're too
much alike, my father and I. The old Turk looks
at me and sees himself, and he doesn't much like
what he finds." He held her small hand in his a
moment longer. Her palm was slightly moist, like
a child's, and her fingertips were raw where she'd

bitten her nails. "I'm sorry I dishonored your father's memory."

She dipped her head in confused acknowledgment. Apologies wouldn't come easily to a man like this. She drew back her hand, closing her fingers into a little fist in her lap. Overhead she heard the footsteps and shouts of threescore men at their work, but for her everything had narrowed to the single man before her.

She sat in the square of sunlight made by the open hatch. Her hat had fallen back over her shoulders, the ribbon a black band across the white column of her neck. Strange how his eyes were drawn to the vulnerable little hollow there at the base of her throat. There he longed to press his lips and feel the quickening of her blood, and then trace lower, to the tantalizing fullness of her breasts. But he wouldn't kiss her again. Not here, not yet.

"That color blue becomes you." His voice was low, meant for her ears alone. "I approve."

"The gown, you mean." She wasn't comfortable with compliments, especially not for a gown that made her feel trussed up like a plump little hen for roasting. "It's Jenny's. Blue becomes her more than me, on account of her eyes. She has blue eyes, too, you know, but brighter, blue eyes and pale gold hair, like Mama. The mantua makers all like Jenny because she knows what favors her and what will please Elisha, and she never shilly-shallies the way I do, or decides it's better to do without. All those bills—from Madame Lambert's and the other shops—those are Jenny's, not mine. And Mama's, too, of course.''

Miserably she knew she was chattering, but she couldn't help it. He was listening, really listening, as if what she said was of the greatest importance, and that disconcerted her even more than the green eyes that never left her. She stood quickly, before he could offer his hand again, and brushed her skirts as she looped her wrist through the basket's handle. "If we're going to review my father's records, Captain Sparhawk, we should begin soon. I did my best but—"

"So Jenny's the pretty one, then." As Gabriel rose before her, his wide shoulders blotted out the sunlight. "Your parents' favorite."

"I didn't say that," said Mariah, shaken that he'd so easily put into words something she'd never dared think herself.

"You didn't have to." His smile spread slowly across his face, the warmth from it more intense than the sun behind him. Lightly he touched two fingers to her lips, and with a startled little gasp her lips parted, her breath warm on his fingertips. "But without having met her, I can tell you your parents were wrong to prefer Jenny."

She was certain he was going to kiss her, and even as she waited, the anticipation so sharp it was almost painful, she knew she shouldn't let him do it. To kiss him again would make a lie of everything that she'd said to Mrs. Thomas and her mother.

His fingers slid slowly from her lip and around her chin, his touch lighter than a feather along her skin, down the length of her throat. For an endless moment he paused there, and she felt her heartbeat wild beneath his fingers. He leaned closer, his eyes half-closed and his smile lazy, and foolishly she wondered how a man had come by such long eyelashes.

"Pretty poppet," he said softly. "Don't forget it."

He took the basket from her hands, turned and headed toward the cabin, leaving her to follow.

She closed her eyes, her mouth dry, her heart still pounding. They had all warned her against seduction, and she believed she could withstand it. His wealth and his well-practiced charm might entice other ladies but she'd sworn they meant nothing to her. She'd promised herself she'd stay true to Daniel, and after that one mistake at Crescent Hill she meant to stand firm.

But simple kindness could be her undoing.

Chapter Four

"I don't care what you swear to, Talbot," said Gabriel as he leaned across the counter, his temper barely held in check. "That rum in the wagon out front is mine, bought and paid for, and the sooner you deliver it to my sloop, the better for you."

"Nay, Cap'n, I told you it ain't yours." Although his words were belligerent, instinct still made the distiller shuffle back beyond Gabriel's reach. "That out front belongs to Cap'n Reed. War's good for my business, same as yours. Like I told you, you ain't the only shipmaster eager t'light off after the French."

Gabriel swore and pounded his fist on the counter hard enough to rattle the tin lantern. "And I tell you, Talbot, I mean to put to sea day after tomorrow, and I mean to have that rum with me!"

"And mebbe you won't be first out o' the harbor, Cap'n Sparhawk," said the other man peevishly. He was fat, with breasts like a woman's that quivered now with his indignation. "Mebbe this once you won't get what you want. Mebbe you'll be thinking twice afore you go unbuttonin' yourself."

"I don't see what the devil—"

"Betty Millar, that's what. 'Cepting now she's Betty Talbot." His eyes narrowed to mean-spirited slits in his doughy face as he jerked his thumb in Mariah's direction. "You don't want me saying any more afore the lady, Cap'n, now do you?"

With both hands flat on the counter, Gabriel sighed with exasperation. Without Talbot's rum, the *Revenge* couldn't clear Newport, at least not if Gabriel expected to get an ounce of work from his crew. He could barely remember Betty Millar beyond her name and a single inebriated night on a straw-filled mattress upstairs in a third-rate Greenwich tavern, it was so long past. Why hadn't the silly strumpet been wise enough to keep her past to herself when she'd finally landed a husband?

"You should be ashamed of yourself, Cap'n," said Talbot righteously. "A fine gentleman like you, claiming a poor maid's innocence for your own selfish pleasure!"

Gabriel choked on his disbelief. Betty's innocence had been long gone before he'd met her, at least two times with his own acquaintances earlier that evening. But how much more flattering for her to lay her ruin on his well-used doorstep!

He heard the rustle of Mariah's skirts beside him as she joined him at the worn wooden counter. God in heaven, why did all this have to come out in front of her?

"Mr. Talbot, you are, I know, a wise man," she began, her voice so soft and gentle that Gabriel glanced at her sharply, wondering what was coming next. In the two weeks she'd been by his side, she'd reserved that voice for recalcitrant coopers and difficult chandlers, and each time that gentleness had gotten her what she'd wanted. "My father always said so, and that was why he chose to bring his trade to you."

Mariah smiled winningly, and the man leered in return. No wonder Betty Talbot still thought of Gabriel Sparhawk if she had to lie with this awful man beside her in bed each night!

"You watch yourself, miss, and think on your poor father. My Betty can tell you the sorrow of trusting the likes of Cap'n Sparhawk."

Mariah nodded primly and sighed. "I've no complaints of my own about Captain Sparhawk, but I wouldn't dare come between the two of you in your quarrel. If you say he's not to have your rum, well, then, that is your right. Of course, my family must suffer, too, since the *Revenge* belongs to us, but that's how it must be."

She folded her hands neatly on the counter and studied them with what she hoped seemed like maidenly indecision. Her day had begun before dawn, and now it was after sunset, and she was hot and tired and she knew her hair needed repinning, and her dark woolen gown was filmed with dust. But she was determined not to leave until she had gotten the rum Talbot had promised for the *Revenge,* and she forced herself to smile at him again.

"I've heard your younger brother is seeking a berth on a privateer. I'm certain a sailor of his gifts has many offers, but if he wishes to consider the *Revenge,* you might ask him to come to our mooring on Long Wharf and see Captain Sparhawk. You may fault this gentleman's morals, but you can't dispute his skills for privateering."

She saw the greedy spark in Talbot's eyes. No matter how—or even if—his wife had been dishonored, Mariah was certain he'd rather have his brother's shares from the *Revenge.* She placed her fingertips on Gabriel's arm, ready to leave. "Good day to you, Master Talbot. Forgive us for keeping you from your wife and your supper."

"How bad is this brother?" asked Gabriel as soon as the door closed behind them.

Mariah wrinkled her nose. "He's even fatter, and I doubt he'll ever earn his keep on any crew, let alone be rated able." She grinned at him. "But I'll wager you'll have your rum in the morning."

Gabriel groaned as he smoothed his hair from his forehead and settled his hat. "I'd rather have cudgeled the rascal's head from his overstuffed shoulders, but it wouldn't have brought that rum any closer to my hold. But you, Miss West—ah, once again you've shown me how to catch more flies with honey than vinegar."

"Or rum with greed instead of a cudgel."

The laughter between them was comfortable, and Mariah let her fingers stay on the sleeve of his coat. The breeze from the water had cooled the summer evening just enough to make it pleasant, and though the first stars glittered overhead, the sky still kept the deep, velvety blue of twilight. She hadn't meant to stay out this late, but nights like this were rare. Another day, another night, and then Gabriel—for that was how she'd come to call him in her thoughts, if not to his face—would be gone. Tonight, for once, Jenny could fix supper.

Her fingers tightened a tiny fraction on his arm, enough for her to be aware of the hard muscle beneath the soft wool. In the last two weeks he had involved her far more in the sloop's preparations than she'd ever imagined. He'd argued that it was only proper for an owner to see how her investment stood, and though bewildered at first by all she didn't know, she'd been thankful for the education that would keep her from being cheated the way her father too often had been.

At Gabriel's side she had been able to go where women seldom went. With him she'd haggled with chandlers, surveyed the length of a ropewalk and climbed the narrow steps to a sail maker's loft to feel the different weights of canvas for different weather sails.

In the same process she'd learned as much about Gabriel, how he could talk as equals with journeymen carpenters and gentlemen in carriages alike, how he was as quick with figures as he was with a jest, how his two sisters were married with children and his two brothers weren't. She'd come to know the way he cleared his throat while considering a question, the cowlick on his crown that he hid beneath his hat, and how pale his green eyes became in the sunlight.

And she'd learned how little he cared for her as a woman.

Oh, his manner with her was scrupulously respectful, and he teased her gently the way a brother might. But since that first night he hadn't tried to kiss her again, and though she reminded herself over and over that this was how she wanted it to be between them, her conscience whispered otherwise, and fed her guilty disappointment.

Sometimes, when her back was turned to him, she felt certain she could feel his gaze upon her, and with it the hunger she remembered like another presence between them. But when she turned around, she'd find his expression no more than cordial, and chide herself for foolish imaginings. She'd tasted the brandy on his lips that first night when he kissed her; that was explanation enough. To him she was Miss West, owner of the privateering sloop *Revenge,* and nothing more.

Together they walked slowly, Mariah lost in her thoughts and Gabriel unwilling to disturb her. Crossing the empty marketplace, two well-dressed matrons pointedly turned their faces rather than acknowledge them, and Gabriel felt Mariah stiffen beside him.

"Has that happened to you before?" he asked, defensive anger in his voice.

"It's not the first time," she admitted forlornly. "Most often it's the wives of the tradesmen we hadn't paid. When I was a child, they'd forbid their daughters to play with me until my father settled his accounts, though of course then I didn't know why. It doesn't hurt so much now, because I know the reason."

"I don't want to see you hurt at all," he said gruffly. He hadn't planned on caring what others thought of her, and it made him uncomfortable. "I feared it was from your connection with me."

She sighed and looked at the tips of her shoes, afraid to meet his eyes and let him see the truth. "I can't deny that there's been talk. My own mother, for one." She tried to smile. "But I have the eighty-two men in the *Revenge*'s company to speak in my defense, and their women with them."

In silent agreement they turned from the marketplace to the smaller streets that led to the water, where they would walk alone. Twilight had deepened into night, the shadows black between the locked warehouses. With a skittering of gravel two cats chased across their path, and from a tavern's summer kitchen rose the smell of frying bacon.

Mariah looked at the stars overhead, seeking and finding the North Star. "Two nights from now, Captain Sparhawk, and that will be your guiding light," she said softly. "I'll pray you come back safe."

"Pray I come back with a string of prizes behind me, or none of this will matter."

She wanted to say that he could come back a pauper and it still wouldn't matter to her. She wanted to say that and a hundred other things before he left, before she lost her courage.

But the two men who lunged at them from the shadows wouldn't let her.

"Gabriel!" she screamed as the shorter man grabbed her by the waist and pulled her tight against his chest. Before she could scream again he stuffed a dirty rag into her mouth, and when her hands flew up to pull it away he grabbed them by the wrists, wrenching them behind her waist.

Struggling with pain and fear, she tried to twist around to see Gabriel and the second man. In that fraction of a second she saw two figures rolling over and over in the street, the glint of moonlight on the long blade of a sailor's knife, before her face was thrust against a rough brick wall. His breath sour on the back of her neck, the man trapped her beneath his body as he dug his hand into her pocket, groping for the few coins she carried there.

Twelve shillings, she thought wildly. She and Gabriel would be killed for twelve shillings and her household keys. . . .

The man grunted with satisfaction as he stuffed the coins into his pocket, then slid his hand up the front of her bodice. She shuddered and tried to struggle free as his fingers thrust into her neckline beneath her shift to grope the bare skin of her breast.

She heard Gabriel swear behind her. The man who held her was suddenly gone, torn away so abruptly that she staggered backward from the wall. She heard him grunt again, this time with surprise and pain, and then the scraping of his pewter buttons as his body struck the paving stones.

"Are you unharmed, poppet?" demanded Gabriel as he gathered her into his arms.

She was shaking, but he made her feel safe. She closed her eyes, listening to the rapid beat of his heart beneath her ear.

"Jesus, Mariah, if they hurt you—"

"Nay, I'm fine." *He had called her Mariah.* When he thought she'd been hurt, he'd called her by her name instead of Miss West, and though she told herself she was a fool, it comforted her even more than his arms around her shoulders. She forced herself to stand away from him, modestly tugging her bodice back in place. Her smile was as shaky as her legs. "I swear to it, Gabriel. I'm fine."

In the moonlight he searched her face, his untied hair flopping disheveled around his face. Gently he touched his fingers to the bruise already swelling along her cheek from where she'd struck the bricks, and she winced. "That's not fine."

"It's well enough." She'd forgotten what it was like to stand this near to him, or maybe she'd only tried to forget. She took a deep breath that was more a shuddering sigh. "Are they gone now?"

"Nay, but they won't bother us." Hoping that she wasn't going to faint without his support, Gabriel returned to the still bodies of the two men in the street. Roughly he rolled the first one over onto his back, and Mariah gasped at the dark splotch of blood that covered the man's chest. His lifeless hand fell open and his knife clattered to the street.

"Clumsy fool," said Gabriel, shrugging. "Falling on his own knife like that."

Uneasily Mariah looked from the dead man to Gabriel. For the first time she noticed the blood-stains on his shirt, blood that had clearly not come from any wounds of his own. Though her own experience with knives and fighting was nonexistent, she doubted the man had been quite as clumsy as Gabriel wanted her to believe.

Gabriel saw the skepticism mingled with the uncertainty in her eyes.

"Mind why you hired me, Miss West," he said harshly, angry with himself. "There's only a scrap of paper from the governor between me being praised as a patriotic man and me being hung for a pirate. You didn't want an angel, and you didn't get one. Be thankful for what you got instead, else we'd both be lying dead instead of them."

"They're dead?"

"Can't be much more dead, by my lights."

Mariah stared at the two bodies. She tried to think of it the way he did, that they'd have killed her if they'd had the chance, but she couldn't. The comfort she'd found from Gabriel seemed to fade away, and the summer night seemed suddenly chilly.

"We should go find the watch." She rubbed her hands along the goose bumps on her bare forearms. "We'll have to tell them what happened."

"What, and miss our sailing on account of swearing this and that before a magistrate? Nay, we'll just let the watchman find the pair of 'em on his own, and mark it down that they killed one another.''

Gabriel squatted down beside the second body and turned the man's slack jaw up toward the moonlight. Gabriel frowned, striving to place the face in memories of the past. How long had it been? Five, six years, since he'd last crossed paths—and swords—with Deveaux and his men?

He bent closer, lifting the crudely carved bone crucifix that hung from a thong around the man's neck. Enough to mark him as a Papist, no Newport man, but not enough to satisfy Gabriel. With both hands he tore the man's shirt open, ignoring the blood that still seeped from the jagged knife wound.

"Gabriel?" Mariah couldn't keep the quaver from her voice. She didn't know what he was doing, but she wasn't sure she really wanted to know, either. "If you don't want to meet with a watchman—"

"Hush, lass, I'm just—" He stopped abruptly when he saw the neat black fleur-de-lis tattooed over the man's still heart, the brand Deveaux demanded from all his men. Only two weeks had passed since he'd learned of the new war, only two weeks since he'd decided to go back to sea to fight again. Yet already Deveaux knew, and now, in turn, so did he. Slowly he stood, wiping the blood from his fingers onto his handkerchief.

"Gabriel?" In the moonlight it was impossible for Mariah to read his expression. "Captain Sparhawk?"

He had almost forgotten her. She looked pathetically small there in the dark street, small and vulnerable. Being her savior didn't sit comfortably with him. That wasn't what he wanted from her. He told himself he was accustomed to women who knew how to take care of themselves, trying to overlook how he'd been the one who'd put her at risk in the first place. Fleetingly he regretted the plans he'd put in motion, then angrily thrust his guilt aside.

She smiled uncertainly, and he felt something twist deep inside. Hell, when would he be able to look at her and stop thinking of Catherine?

"Come along," he said gruffly, holding his hand out to her. "It's high time I saw you home."

Furiously Mariah swept the ashes from the kitchen fireplace, soot swirling around her skirts. No matter how many times she'd explained to Jenny how to lay a proper cooking fire, her sister still put far too much wood on the flames too soon, and after last night's effort they were all fortunate the house hadn't burned along with the chicken, charred black on the outside and bloody raw within. Here it was the day before the *Revenge* sailed, with a thousand little things left for her to do, yet first she must clean up the mess that Jenny had made.

She glanced around at the whitewashed walls, smudged black from the smoke, and shook her head. She'd sent Jenny to fetch water to scrub them down, but knowing her sister's doleful housewifery, by now Jenny had likely fallen into the well.

"Miss West?"

The broom in her hands, Mariah turned, brushing her hair from her forehead and unconsciously streaking her face with soot. Her eyes widened when she saw the beautifully dressed woman waiting at the open kitchen door.

"Oh, Madame Lambert, forgive me for not hearing you!" she began, anxiously wiping her hands on her apron. The mantua maker had always made her uncomfortable, looking down her long nose at Mariah as the dark, difficult sister, the one who cared more about what ribbons cost than how they looked. She'd rather face a dozen angry tradesmen than one Madame Lambert. "I thought our accounts had been settled."

"They have, Miss West, and I thank you for your patronage." She dipped her white-powdered head graciously and smiled, the first real smile Mariah could remember receiving from her. She stepped into the kitchen, lifting her chintz skirts clear of ashes. She clapped her hands in their black net mitts, and one of her seamstresses followed, a bundle wrapped in muslin draped gingerly across her outstretched arms. "We've come, you see, with a gift to deliver."

She took the bundle from her assistant and with a flourish swept away the muslin. Mariah caught her breath, for in the woman's arms was the most beautiful gown she'd ever seen, the pale pink silk, brocaded with a pattern of darker pink carnations, shimmering against the sooty walls. Below the deep, square neckline the stomacher was embroidered with more carnations to match, and attached to each of the elbow-length pleated cuffs were deep openwork flounces of linen so fine as to be nearly transparent.

"Oh, madame, what perfection!" With a thump Jenny let the bucketful of water drop onto the stone doorstep and rushed inside, her eyes bright with covetous appreciation for the gown. "Oh, I can't wait for Elisha to see me in this!"

With a hiss Madame Lambert lifted the silk out of the reach of Jenny's wet hands. "No, no, Miss West, this color would be wrong for you. Quite wrong. But that is of no matter, for the gown is for your sister, not for you."

Mariah shook her head. "You're mistaken. I would never have ordered such a gown."

"That is what the gentleman said, too. The silk, the fashion—his choices for you, and wise ones, too. He has an eye for beauty, that one." Madame Lambert plucked at one of the sleeves, her smile smug. "It is a gift, Miss West, a gift to you from Captain Sparhawk. The letter, Amity."

With a tiny bob of a curtsey, the seamstress handed the folded sheet to Mariah. Carefully Mariah slid her finger beneath the wax seal, wishing she did not have to read the message before the others.

My Brave Mariah,

Surely you will wish yr. Captain well before he sails in yr. Name against France. Dine with me this Night at my home, & tho' yr. Beauty like Lilies needs no Gilding, accept this my poor Gift & wear it to Honor me.

Yr. Devot'd Capt.
G.S.

"It's from your captain, isn't it, Mariah?" asked Jenny, stretching as she tried to read over Mariah's shoulder. "He's the only gentleman in Newport who'd do such a grand thing for a lady. Oh, 'Riah, to think you've caught *his* eye!"

"I can't accept it." Mariah stared at the bold, elegant handwriting. He thought she was brave, and he thought she was beautiful, and again he'd called her Mariah. *His* brave Mariah. Likely he meant nothing by it, of course, only conventional gallantry. But after last night, she was painfully aware of how dangerous his life was going to be, and she wanted to believe that gallantry. Tonight might well be the last chance she'd have to be with him alone.

"If you'll but have us fit the gown, Miss West," coaxed Madame Lambert, stroking the silk with the side of her hand, "then you shall realize how wise the captain's choice is. Though of course every stitch was made with you alone in mind, Miss West. Such a lovely gown for a lady like yourself!"

But lovely or not, Mariah knew a gown like this was a wildly inappropriate gift for any gentleman to give to a lady he respected, too personal and costly, equally as inappropriate as his invitation. Her reputation had survived one visit to Crescent Hill, but now this supper, at his bidding— No, Madame Lambert would see to it that all of Newport knew.

She gazed longingly at the gown. She'd never had anything half as fine, and he'd been right, the color would suit her. But if she accepted it . . .

"No," she said with a firmness that surprised herself. "I told him before I couldn't dine with him at his house, and I can't keep the gown. You must take it away, madame."

The older woman shook her head so sharply that a fine dusting of white powder fell from her hair to the dark lutestring shoulders of her pelisse. "No, Miss West, the gown is yours, and I cannot take it back without risking Captain Sparhawk's anger," she said firmly. She motioned for

Amity to lay the muslin wrapper on the kitchen table and then very carefully spread the gown on top of it. "Good day, ladies."

Mariah stared at the gown on the table. "I can't keep it, and I can't go to his house for supper," she said wretchedly. "I told him when he'd asked me before that I couldn't. To do so would be madness."

"To do so would be heaven, 'Riah!" declared Jenny. "All along you've sworn there's nothing between you and Captain Sparhawk save boring countinghouse matters. If that's true, then why are you so frightened of him?"

"I'm not frightened of him!"

"Then you're frightened of yourself, and that's worse." She smiled indulgently, delighted for once to know more than Mariah. "What harm could come of it? All you do is work, 'Riah. Even when you were with Daniel O'Bierne, the pair of you were as serious as old sticks."

"That's not fair, Jenny," said Mariah resentfully.

"Well, it's true enough, and I'll wager that Captain Sparhawk wouldn't be an old stick with any lady. If you don't wish to go to his house— and even I'll grant that that might be seen as passing bold—then meet him elsewhere for supper, the way you said. He is sailing *our* ship, 'Riah. He wouldn't dare dishonor you. Though he might call you a blind ninny for walking into walls. I vow you look like you've been brawling in a tavern.''

Self-consciously Mariah touched the bright, swollen bruise on the side of her face. She hadn't told her mother or sister the real cause, not wanting them to worry, and though it did look like she'd been brawling in some rum shop, Gabriel would understand.

Gabriel. Since when had she come to think first of Gabriel instead of Daniel?

Watching Mariah waver, Jenny continued, clapping her hands before her for emphasis. ''You might as well keep the gown, too. Likely Madame Lambert's already told everyone who's passed through her shop this week about it and you and Captain Sparhawk. Go ahead and enjoy the gown since you'll suffer her gossip regardless.''

Mariah looked from her sister's dimpled face to the gown and back again, surprised to find Jenny's logic worth considering. She'd always been so busy watching over Jenny that she hadn't realized her younger sister might have an opinion or two herself.

''Can you imagine what Father would say?'' said Mariah, trying to smile. ''He'd double damn me for a brazen hussy.''

''Oh, no, he wouldn't, 'Riah, any more than Mama would, if you asked her.'' Jenny's smile shrank, her pretty face taking on a bitterness that Mariah would never have expected. ''Captain

Sparhawk is rich, and we are—well, we are something quite other than rich, aren't we?''

"Oh, Jenny," murmured Mariah, resting a hand on Jenny's shoulder. She couldn't argue with her sister, not about this. Too well she remembered the awful conversation she'd had with her mother the night the Thomases had come to dine. "I suppose they just want us to be happy and not to want."

"I won't credit the happiness part, not from Mama," said Jenny vehemently. "She doesn't like my Elisha any more than she liked your Daniel. If we let her, she'll marry us off to whichever shriveled old men offer her the most. Don't try to say otherwise, 'Riah, you know it's true!"

She sighed with frustration, and reached out to trace one of the satin-stitch petals on the embroidered carnations. "Captain Sparhawk may be old as blazes, but at least he's still handsome, and he has all his teeth. *And* he wants to please you, if he sent you this gown. He must find you passing fair."

"I'm not sure he thinks of me that way at all, fair or not. As a lady, I mean." Unconsciously Mariah touched the bruise on her cheek, remembering all that had passed the night before. "He calls me poppet."

"Poppet?" Jenny wrinkled her nose. "That's not very gallant of him, is it? But I still think you should go to him tonight. If you cross him in this,

you know, he could still throw us all over and refuse to sail Papa's ship."

"I don't know if you're right or not, Jen."
Mariah sighed deeply. "But if I go, swear you
won't tell Mama."

Impatiently Gabriel glanced again at the tall
clock in the corner of his bedchamber. Where the
devil was Ethan with his hot water, anyway? He'd
no intention of greeting Miss Mariah with a jaw
bristling like a hog's, but Ethan had scarcely left
him time to shave, let alone dress, before he had to
leave to meet the girl. Swearing under his breath,
he thundered down the broad stairway, striking his
fist on the top of the newel post so hard that the
carved wood rattled. Already the chairs in the
hallway were shrouded with sheets to protect them
from dust and sunlight while he was away, and his
packed sea chest sat waiting beside the front door.

Still swearing, Gabriel threw open the door to
the kitchen. Beside a steaming kettle on the
kitchen table stood Ethan, his leather waistcoat
dusted with flour and dabbed with grease spots.
His lips pursed in concentration, he held a long
pewter ladle out to the woman across the table,
waiting for her reaction to the sauce that she was
tasting.

"Sister Sarah." Gabriel made no effort to hide
his irritation. "I should have known you'd be
here, meddling in the order of my kitchen."

"Perfection, Ethan," said Sarah Sparhawk Tillinghast. "You're a better cook than any woman in Newport." She scooped another dollop of the red cherry sauce onto her finger and licked it off, then turned and smiled beatifically at Gabriel. "And good day to you, Brother Gabriel. I should have known you'd offer me such a warm welcome into your home."

"Stop it, Sarah," said Gabriel. "I'm sailing with the morning tide, and we're in uproar enough here without you to add to it."

Belatedly he went to his sister and kissed her on the forehead. Oldest and youngest, they were the only two of the Sparhawk siblings to inherit their father's black hair and green eyes, and his temper, as well. The other three were fair and mild like their mother, and as a result Gabriel had always felt a peculiar, irascible bond with Sarah alone.

"I heard you're bound for the Caribbean, and I brought you letters and a package to take to Mother and Father." Her eyes narrowed, and she put her hands on her hips. "You will, I trust, take a few hours from chasing Frenchmen to go to Barbados and see them?"

Gabriel made a noncommittal growling noise deep in his throat and bent to check the water heating on the fire.

"Gabriel, it's one thing for you not to come to John and me at Nantasket. Though Lord knows we're near enough to Crescent Hill, at least we'll be waiting when you change your mind. But Father's nearly seventy, and if you keep dawdling with your pride, you might not have another chance in this life."

"Preach to the old man about pride, not me," began Gabriel, then sighed and shook his head. Even talking about his father made him edgy. "Damnation, Sarah, of course I'll see them, though when Mother learns I'm back to privateering, like as not she won't have me in the house."

"She'll forget all about the privateering when you tell her you've taken to ruining virginal young ladies instead." She waved her arm at the pies and pasties and other made dishes Ethan had set to cool on the table. With an incomprehensible grumble of disapproval, Ethan glared at Gabriel's back, then hoisted a wicker basket from the table and stalked from the room. "She must be a very pretty little morsel to merit all this, Gabriel. A hungry one, too."

Gabriel dropped into the old rush-bottom chair and propped his stockinged feet on the edge of the table, tipping the chair onto its rear legs. "She's very pretty and very clever, and she's none of your damned business."

Sarah's eyebrows rose with interest. "Clever, Gabriel? That's something new for you in ladies. But I'd watch yourself with this one. I've known her mother, Letty, since we were both girls, and she's pretty and clever, too, when she's sober. Very, very clever. You tumble little Mariah's petticoats, and Letty West will have the first banns read from the pulpit the following Sabbath.''

''You sound like you're standing in the pulpit yourself, Sarah. The girl's of age, and God knows I am.'' He made a tent of his flexed fingers and looked over it to his sister. ''You know the little minx came here at her own will? Bloody well seduced me into taking over her dead father's sloop.''

''I'd believe that from some of the doxies you traffic with, Gabriel, but not this girl.'' Sarah came to stand before him, leaning against the table with her arms folded over her chest. Her expression softened, her smile tinged with sadness. ''Ethan says she's the very image of Catherine Langley.''

''And I say both you and Ethan should keep your interfering noses from what I do, and with whom I choose to do it.'' Abruptly he rocked the chair forward with a crack on the floorboards and rose to his feet. ''I've much to do before tomorrow, Sarah. Forgive me if I don't see you out.''

Sarah didn't move. ''Ethan also told me the watch found two sailors, marked with fleur-de-lis, cut to death on Water Street. He said when you came home last night he found blood all over your coat and shirt, and nary a scrape on you.''

She reached up to tousle his black hair. "Whatever happened to you before is beginning again, isn't it, little brother?" she said, her eyelashes spiky with tears as she searched his face. "Here you haven't even sailed, yet this time I'm so afraid you won't return. Be careful, Gabriel, for me if no one else. Watch your back, and guard your heart."

Chapter Five

"Heaven take me, what a sight you be, Mariah West!" called Allen Welsh at the passing shay. From his unsteady walk and the jug cradled in the crook of his arm, the gunner's mate of the *Revenge* was obviously enjoying his last night ashore. Belatedly his brother Will tugged his hat off for him, but Allen was too enthralled with Mariah to notice. "Bound for th' gov'ner's great house, are you?"

On the seat beside her, Ethan answered before Mariah could. "Nay, you drunken booby, the lady's dining with the cap'n, as is right an' proper before a sailing."

Allen flashed Mariah a mooncalf smile as the shay rattled past him. "Ah, Miss Mariah, you'll set Cap'n Sparhawk arse over ears rigged out like that, you will!"

"Mind the lady's good name, Welsh!" bellowed Ethan over his shoulder. "Else you'll have the cap'n hisself to answer to!"

Her cheeks burning, Mariah stared down at the folded ivory blades of her mother's fan in her hand, wishing she was safe again in her kitchen at home.

"You shouldn't've had to hear that, miss," huffed Ethan. "Not that it isn't true, o' course. You look better'n any lady in this colony tonight, and you'll turn the cap'n's head. No doubt o' that, not a pretty little maid like you."

He sighed with a mournfulness that puzzled Mariah. For what Madame Lambert had likely charged for her gown, Gabriel had every right to be pleased. Lightly she smoothed her skirts, delighting in the feel of the ribbed silk beneath her fingers. Though she still doubted the propriety of accepting such a gift, the gown did make her feel like a lady bound for the governor's house.

As the mantua maker had promised, the gown had been made to Mariah's measurements, and the style—the rosy pink silk that heightened her coloring and the simple, graceful lines that flattered her small, rounded figure—had obviously been chosen with her in mind. Mariah wondered how much of this was due to Madame Lambert, and how much she might credit Gabriel himself. Neither her father nor Daniel had ever shown much interest in women's finery. But Gabriel was different in so many ways that it wouldn't surprise her if he knew as much about *engageantes* and lappets as he did spars and shrouds.

Ethan flicked the whip over the horse's back, and the shay turned onto High Street. With the long, straight road out of town before them, the horse eagerly quickened his pace. Clutching at the side while her ribbons fluttered from her hair, Mariah turned uneasily toward Ethan's hawk-nosed profile.

"We are on the road to Crescent Hill," she began, not quite certain what to say to convince a man to stop a trotting horse and turn back toward town.

"Aye, that we are," agreed Ethan. "But we don't be bound there. You wrote the cap'n 'tweren't proper for you to go there, an' you was right."

Expectantly Mariah waited for him to continue, and he didn't.

"So we're not going to Crescent Hill?"

"Nay, we're not," said Ethan amiably. "Cap'n Sparhawk's as good at followin' orders as at givin' them."

Mariah tried again. "So where shall I meet him?"

"Where I'll be takin' you."

With a sigh, Mariah looked out across the open fields and the bay to the mainland, and the bright orange ball of the setting sun on the edge of the dark horizon. Red sky at night, sailor's delight. The *Revenge* would have a fair morning for her departure.

Rounding the curve of a hillside, Ethan drew the horse to a halt. At the gate of a crumbling field-stone wall stood Gabriel, a lantern wedged into the wall beside him. From her seat in the shay her eyes were nearly level with his, and she felt a sudden wave of shyness sweep over her. She had never seen any gentleman dressed so elegantly, and though she, too, was dressed in silk and lace, though she employed him and not the other way around, the gulf between their ages and stations seemed somehow in that minute to widen into a chasm. He was of the world, and she was only from Newport, and with a little chill she remembered how callously he had killed their attackers the night before. She felt miserably tongue-tied and childish, only able to gawk like a country maid.

And he was worth gawking at. His suit was dark green velvet, tailored to set off his broad shoulders and narrow hips, and the lantern's light glittered on the elaborate silver embroidery that faced the edgings of his coat and the matching waistcoat beneath. He was hatless, and his black hair was sleeked back and clubbed with a silk bow. Flemish lace spilled down his shirtfront and from his cuffs. On any other man, the affect would have been foppish, a macaroni's indulgence. But on

Gabriel, all the lace and embroidery only made him seem by contrast stronger, more aggressively, unsettlingly male.

"Good evening, my lady shipowner," he said as he stepped away from the wall and made a leg to her, his sweeping bow in the tall grass worthy of a courtier. "I'm honored that you've come, and relieved, too. When you didn't appear at the sloop today, I worried that you'd suffered more last night than you'd let me know."

"My mother was unwell, and I couldn't leave her." Mariah lowered her eyes to her lap, praying he hadn't heard the stories that said her mother belonged in the madhouse in Boston. Too much Geneva had set her to weeping inconsolably, huddled on the floor beside the bed while Mariah had held her shaking shoulders.

Too much Geneva, but only more had brought the insensible peace her mother had craved, and reluctantly, Mariah had given it to her. These last weeks she had left her mother too much alone while she'd played at being a shipowner, just as now she was playing at being a lady. Her mother's teary accusations were right. She *was* a selfish, undutiful daughter.

Yet still Mariah bargained with her troubled conscience. *Just a little longer. Just this last night....*

"Mariah." Gabriel said her name softly as he swung open the door to the shay. By the lantern's

light he'd seen the bright eagerness in her eyes fade
away when she'd spoken of her mother. He hadn't
needed his sister to warn him about Mrs. West.
Despite her artless omissions and evasions, Mariah had already told him more than enough about
her dismal home life. Had the old witch read her
a sermon on sin and wickedness? If so, he'd make
her forget every word. Tonight he'd make her forget everything she'd ever been taught about sin,
and forget himself as he gave her a rich new world
of memories. "Welcome, my pretty poppet."

She smiled shyly, glad the twilight would hide
how easily he could make her blush. She'd rather
be called poppet by him than a thousand more
gallant endearments by anyone else. She rose as he
swung open the door to the shay, but instead of
offering her his hand he spanned her waist with his
hands and lifted her, light as thistledown, to the
ground.

"You are, you know, really quite lovely," he
said softly, his face above hers.

"Oh, but you are much more beautiful!" she
blurted out, then gasped at her own idiocy. She
realized his hands were lingering too long on her
waist, and she slipped free. "Dear Lord, I didn't
mean that!"

"I'd rather hoped you did." Her honesty delighted him as much as her beauty. Her waist had
fit so neatly between his palms, but he wanted to
feel the softness of her flesh, not silk over whale-

bone. "I'm not averse to compliments. I do, you know, mean to please you."

Behind them Ethan, forgotten, coughed loudly. "I'll be waitin' in the usual place, Cap'n Sparhawk," he said, and again Mariah heard the inexplicable unhappiness in his voice. "Waitin' and ready to take the young lady home."

She caught the look that passed between the two men, but not its meaning, and the shay slowly rattled off down the road, leaving her alone with Gabriel on the Newport Road. Night had fallen, and the three-quarter moon was rising, and the crickets were loud in the tall, dewy grass. Gabriel lifted the lantern from the wall, casting the wavering light onto a path that led up the hillside.

"Because you accepted my hospitality but not my home, I'm forced to bring you here," he explained. "It's still my land, but free, I trust, of whatever taints my house for you."

"Your 'here' appears to be nowhere, Captain Sparhawk." If he could tease, so could she. Pointedly she ignored his offered arm, unwilling to risk even that slight physical contact with him, and he laughed.

"You'll see where here is soon enough. And no more Captain Sparhawk, mind? My mother called me Gabriel, and I always liked the sound of it better on a female tongue."

She smiled reluctantly. Though she'd called him by his given name before without any thought, she sensed an intimacy behind his request that had nothing to do with names. Swiftly she turned and started up the path, lifting her skirts clear of the tall grass on either side. In some way she knew she was running away, and she wondered if she should be running farther, clear back to Newport.

Swinging the lantern as he followed, Gabriel smiled at her skittishness. To protect her skirts, she was showing him a good deal more of her ankles and calves in their pale pink stockings than she likely intended, but he wasn't about to complain. Pretty poppet, he thought fondly, indulgence mingling with desire. He was glad the gown had pleased her. He hadn't exaggerated. In it she *was* beautiful, and far more woman than girl. Who would have guessed that that silly provincial seamstress would keep silk of that deep rose on her shelf, the same pink that Catherine had always favored?

"A windmill?" asked Mariah as they neared the crest, the disappointment keen in her voice. The mill was no different from all the others that dotted the hilltops on the island, eight-sided, three-storied, and shingled, with the long blades turned to catch the wind from the water.

"Now don't go scoffing at my mill, lass," said Gabriel as he pushed open the door and let her go first. "There's precious few people I trust with its secret. If dukes and lords can have Roman temples as follies on their lands, why, then I can have a windmill.''

Still dubious, Mariah climbed the narrow, twisting stairway, feeling her way in the shadows. She came to the top floor, and gasped with delight.

The mill's hopper and works had been taken away, and though the square-cut timbers that framed the octagonal walls remained unplastered, the oak had been rubbed and polished until it gleamed like the finest drawing room paneling. Candles in brass sconces flickered from the beams and were reflected in the framed mirror that hung over a bench, cushioned with checkered red pillows, built into one corner. Set before the bunk was a small supper table with places for two, a ham on a platter waiting to be sliced and a porcelain bowl filled with fresh strawberries.

Gabriel hooked the lantern on a timber and tapped a finger on the gleaming service plates. ''Spanish silver from some grandee's table, taken out of a ship bound for Cadiz in forty-one,'' he said proudly. ''I hope you don't mind dining with the enemy?''

''How could I mind any of this?'' She circled the table, her eyes shining as she trailed her fingers across the pressed linens. It wasn't the lavishness of the silver or the porcelain that impressed her. It was the thought that had gone into it, the care he'd taken to please her, just as he'd promised he would. She looked up at him through her lashes and smiled shyly. "No one has ever done anything like this for me before."

The vulnerability that she let him see surprised him even more than her admission. Even when they'd been set upon by Deveaux's men, she'd kept her feistiness. "How could anyone know you, poppet, and not want to do things to make you smile?"

Instantly she raised her guard again, aware of how much she'd inadvertently revealed. "I mean that at home I'm the one who cooks, and I've never had anyone else cook for me. Not that you've cooked all this yourself, of course. I know that!"

She grinned suddenly, imagining him bending his broad shoulders in green velvet over a kettle on the hearth. "But this, this night, and the gown, and how much you've taught me about the *Revenge,* and how you've never made me feel as foolish as I likely seem to you, and—and thank you. Thank you, Gabriel."

Could she know how neatly she'd just turned the tables on him? If no one had ever cared enough for her to indulge her, then no one had ever thanked him so genuinely for something he'd done, either, not even Catherine. Lord, she was a match for him, and as his gaze wandered from her face to her high, round breasts rising from the low-cut bodice, he felt his body tighten with anticipation.

There, thought Mariah miserably, she'd gone and said more than she'd intended, and certainly more than poor Gabriel had expected. She could tell that from the odd expression on his face. Desperately she tried to lighten the mood.

"But I am willing to wager," she said as she plucked a berry from the bowl and bit into it, "that you haven't brought any of the other shipowners you've sailed for here for strawberries."

"The only other person I've ever sailed for was my father," he said lightly, "and no, I never brought him here."

She frowned, incredulous. "No one else? Then why me?"

He smiled at her over the table, his chin tipped down so that he gazed at her from beneath his brows, his eyes as green as the velvet of his coat. No man had ever looked at her like this before. With a start she realized that to him, tonight, she really was as beautiful as he'd said, and it had nothing to do with the gown, and nothing at all to do with her owning the *Revenge*.

"Why will I sail for you?" he repeated, musing. He chose the largest strawberry from the bowl, shifting it back and forth between his thumb and forefinger as he gazed at her. "Perhaps because you dared to come to my house and then . . . then asked me so nicely."

She watched as the dark red berry disappeared into his mouth, gone in a single bite. He hadn't touched her since he'd helped her from the shay. He didn't need to. The way he was watching her, the half smile on his lips, was enough. In these few moments everything was changing between them, and she felt as if she'd been tossed from a dock into water far beyond her depth.

With a swirl of her skirts she turned and crossed the tiny room to the open window, her fingers grasping at the wooden sill as she tried to steady herself. Below her the hillside fell away to the ocean, and the breezes that once had fueled the mill now cooled her cheeks, grown hot from the intensity she'd found in those green eyes.

With a deep breath she struggled to regain her scattered composure. Just because she'd put on a silk gown didn't mean she'd left her wits behind with her old clothes. He was the same man he'd always been with her, and she was the same woman.

Or was she?

She tried hard to think of Daniel, and all she could remember was the night he'd left, a night like this one, and what had happened between them. She'd sworn to never love another, but she knew that when Gabriel kissed her tonight—not *if,* but *when*—she would let him, and the certainty of her response appalled her.

Oh, Daniel, love, why did you leave me?

"Do you see that sail, there, to the sou'east?" Gabriel asked, coming to stand behind her, his arm brushing against her shoulder as he pointed out the open window. He'd taken off his coat, and the lace on his cuff blew across his wrist. "That's Richardson's *Felicity,* bound for Bridgetown with her hold filled with ponies and mutton. Though I told him I'd see him safely down the coast beneath my guns, the hasty fool decided he'd rather clear Newport tonight."

A hasty fool, thought Gabriel with satisfaction, but a useful one. Not that he'd pay the man a shilling until his consignment was safe in Bridgetown. Would Mariah still be grateful when she learned what else he'd done to please her this night? Nay, not her alone, but the two of them together.

The breeze from the water tossed the loose tendrils across the nape of her neck, and though she stared out toward the departing ship, Gabriel was quite certain she didn't see it. In the moonlight her skin was ivory pale, her eyes dark and liquid. He touched her neck below the shell of her ear, and though she didn't flinch or draw away, he felt her pulse quicken beneath his fingers.

"You really aren't frightened by anything, are you?" he asked, his voice dark and low over the distant rush of the breakers on the beach below. Her skin was like silk velvet, her pulse warm and insistent beneath his touch. Gently he pressed his thumbs deeper into the back of her shoulders and felt the tension slip from her muscles as she relaxed. He marveled at her trust, remembering how boldly she'd come to Crescent Hill that first night. Not so long ago, yet it seemed like he'd wanted her all his life. "My brave Mariah."

Her mouth twisted wryly. "Not so very brave."

"More so than any other lass I've known."

"That's because you believe I'm too young to know fear. But last night, with those men..." Her words trailed off when she remembered her terror as the man pinned her to the wall, not knowing what had become of Gabriel, if he lived or had been killed. Unconsciously she swayed back against his chest, seeking to share his strength against her weakness.

"Those men had nothing to do with you," he answered, his hands sliding down the length of her arms and around her waist, pulling her closer. "They wanted me, and your only misfortune was to be at my side when they found me. You'll be safe enough now."

Safe enough, that is, if she stayed in Newport. He'd told so many women what they'd wanted to hear that the meaningless reassurance came readily enough to his lips, but the angry bruise on the side of her face was an uncomfortable reminder he couldn't ignore. Once again he fought the odd need to protect her. What he'd set into motion couldn't be undone, he told himself, and one night would no more satisfy Mariah than it would him.

There were no certainties to be found anywhere in life, not in Newport, not on Barbados.

But misfortunes—how could he ever forget that it had been Catherine's misfortune, too, to come between him and Deveaux? He breathed in the fragrance of Mariah's hair, lowering his mouth to her ear. What he felt for her was desire, nothing more complicated than that.

"When I'm gone," he whispered, "you'll be safe enough."

"Gone?" His breath was warm in her ear, his hands around her waist pressing her closer against him, moving her in a way that made it impossible to think.

"Aye, my sweet poppet, gone with the morning tide, as well you know. You and I will share only this last night ashore, and then I'll be gone."

Gone. The finality of the word dropped like a stone into her consciousness. She closed her eyes, fighting the sense of loss that was already beginning. Of course she'd known he would leave, but part of her had fought the reality and all that his sailing signified.

Gone. Dear God, not again!

"You'll miss me, then, poppet?" How many times, he wondered cynically, had sailors asked that of the women they meant to leave? "Say you'll miss me for at least a night and a day, pretty Mariah, and I'll go content."

"Miss you!" she cried with real anguish. She twisted about in his arms to face him, her tear-filled eyes searching his. "Oh, Gabriel, you aren't even mine to miss, and already I feel like part of me has been torn away!"

Swiftly his mouth closed over hers, and with a ragged sob she welcomed him, her hands linking around his neck to pull him closer. She opened her lips to his, seeking the same magic she remembered when she'd kissed him before, but what she found this time was different. This went far beyond those pleasurable sensations. This time, when his tongue swept into her mouth, she thought she'd swallowed fire itself, the heat racing through her entire body to center low in her belly.

His hands slid lower, over the stiff boning of her stays to the soft swell of her hips, caressing her through the layers of fabric, lifting her against the hard muscle of his thigh pressed between her legs. Hungrily he deepened the kiss, and she felt herself slipping farther into the fire. Light-headed with the first rush of desire, she clung to him for support, for she doubted her legs would hold her. Dear Lord, what was happening to her?

Fighting for breath, for sanity, she broke away and stared at him. Captain Gabriel Sparhawk, the most successful captain and the most notorious rogue in Newport, a man nearly twice her years in age and a hundred times that in experience, yet one look at the guarded wonder in his eyes, and she knew he'd felt the same fire that had seared her.

Shaken, Gabriel reached down to slip his fingers into her hair, letting the curve of her cheek fill his palm. Her lips were parted and swollen from his kiss, her eyes dark with passion. So much passion for such a little maid! He couldn't fathom it, or her. If she could rouse him this much with only her kiss, what kind of heaven would he have found with her by daybreak?

With Mariah's hands still linked around his neck, Gabriel swiftly gathered her into his arms and lay her across the pillows on the bunk, the rose silk shushing as her skirts fell around her body. She didn't speak, and neither did he, unwilling to break whatever spell it was they'd created between them. Shyly she reached up to touch his face, her fingers traveling from the rough beard of his jaw to the curve of his lips. He caught her fingers in his and pressed them to his lips, savoring her touch as he kissed her captive fingertips. By the candlelight he would have noticed if she blushed, and she didn't. How much knowledge did she have of what would come next?

"Sweet Mariah," he murmured as he bent to kiss her throat. "My own sweet poppet."

Mariah closed her eyes as his lips found her pulse in the hollow at the base of her throat, the tantalizing sensations of his warm, wet mouth on her fevered skin. She tangled her fingers in his long hair, the bow slipping off as his hair slid, untied, around her wrists. She didn't realize he'd unpinned her bodice until he eased the silk from her shoulders, his fingers teasing along the edge of her shift. When his tongue found the soft bud of her nipple, she gasped, her back arching against the pillows as he held her steady. Her fingers clasped convulsively into the velvet of his waistcoat as he suckled her soft flesh into firm arousal. She whimpered and dragged his mouth back to hers, her body twisting beneath his with her need, a need she still didn't truly comprehend. She only knew the fire came from Gabriel, and only Gabriel could show her its meaning.

His breathing harsh, he shoved back her skirts, his hand sliding up the length of her leg beneath her shift, to the warm, bare skin of her thigh above her stocking. Lord, his hands were shaking like a green boy's! She moved restlessly beneath his touch, and when he found her she was wet and ready for him. He moved his hand against her, and she gasped with pleasure and surprise, curling her legs around him as she strived to draw him in. The womanly scent of her, her small, breathy whimpers, the sight of her pale legs tangled in the rose silk, her dark red garters against her white skin, her head pressed back into the pillows, the flush of desire already dark on her throat and breasts—all of her more enticing, more erotic, than anything he could ever imagine. With every one of his senses on edge and his arousal painful from its intensity, he tore at the buttons on his breeches.

Salvation, that's what Ethan had called her. Fleetingly Gabriel thought of the war that lay before him, of slaughter and destruction and the screams of mutilated men. *Salvation.* And now Gabriel knew if he didn't have her, he'd be damned forever.

He kneeled between her legs, and instinctively she welcomed him, shifting her body to accommodate him, and again he marveled at her rare combination of innocence and passion. But for all her willingness, she was still a maid. Even as he lay hard and ready against her, for her sake, he could not forget that.

"Mariah, sweet, mark what I say," he said, his voice rough with the effort it took to restrain himself. "I don't want to hurt you, but this first time I must. Then I swear to you I'll never give you anything but pleasure."

Her eyes flew open, stunning Gabriel with the pain already there, and she pressed her hand to her mouth to stifle a sob.

"No weeping, now, poppet," he said as, bewildered, he wiped away the tear that slid across her cheek toward the pillow. "I'm sorry, but since Eve in the garden there's been no help for this—"

"Nay, but you *will* hurt me, no matter if you mean to or not!" she cried, her words breaking with emotion and anguish. She covered her eyes with her arm. "You'll go, and I'll be left with nothing save the right to mourn you!"

"Mariah, listen to me—"

"I loved Daniel, and I promised to wed him when he returned, promised against the wishes of my mother and father because I *loved* him, and he loved me!" She rolled away from Gabriel and curled herself on her side, lost in misery. She hadn't wanted to remember Daniel, not now, but once she'd begun she couldn't stop. "I wished him fare-thee-well and waved until I could see his ship no more, and then I waited and lived on my hopes and his promise. He was second mate on a Jamaican schooner, and their run was fast, but two days from Newport he was lost in a squall in the dogwatch.

"And I did not know. I waited and waited on the dock while all the other men came ashore, and then at last the captain came to tell me, almost like he'd already forgotten Daniel had ever lived, and I wanted to die from the pain of it. My poor, sweet, forgotten Daniel!"

Gabriel was known as a ruthless man, one who had made his way in the world by taking what we wanted. But as much as he desired the sobbing girl beside him, he knew he'd let her go. For once his conscience left him no choice. He had lost her this night to the ghost of a drowned boy, lost her to a heartbreaking grief that excluded him.

He watched her as she wept, her dark hair wet with her tears, her fingers digging into her folded arms. Gently he smoothed her hair from her face. With a sigh he lay down beside her and pulled her close, holding her and murmuring her name until her sobs finally died away and she lay still in his arms.

He listened to waves on the beach below and held Mariah, just held her. He thought of Catherine, and wondered if she would have mourned him if he'd been lost, instead, as fiercely as Mariah did her Daniel.

He had never felt more alone in his life.

The house was dark when Mariah returned home. In the kitchen she took off her shoes, unwilling to wake her mother or sister on the stairs, and in her stockinged feet she padded through the hallway. She felt desolate and empty inside, loneliness already echoing within her soul, and though she would go to bed she knew she'd find no sleep or comfort from her misery.

She was halfway up the stairs before she saw the dark mass of the figure huddled on the landing and the empty pitcher on the top step.

"You don't love me, neither of you do," said Mrs. West hoarsely. In her hands was a folded paper, and over and over her shaking fingers smoothed the crease. "The truth's written here, where I can't deny it."

"Come, Mama, I'll take you to bed. It's very late, and you're tired."

"Read this, daughter, and learn how a mother's love's repaid!" Pulling herself unsteadily to her feet, Mrs. West thrust the paper toward Mariah. "Jenny's run off with her precious Elisha."

Chapter Six

All that morning during the final hectic preparations before the tide turned and the *Revenge* sailed, Gabriel both dreaded and anticipated Mariah's appearance. He didn't doubt she would come—he'd left her little enough choice—it was only *when* that kept him wondering, that and what mood she'd be in when she finally appeared.

He had driven her to Newport himself, and for the entire trip she had been miserably silent and withdrawn, and clearly shamed by what they'd done. Or hadn't done, by his reckoning. She'd no notion that she was the first woman in his life he'd sent home unsatisfied, and that questionable distinction rankled at his pride. But worse than that was realizing that he cared less about his own disappointment than about hers. He *cared* that she was unhappy, even if the source of her unhappiness had nothing to do with him.

The sorry truth was that in the past weeks, while he thought he'd been giving her the chance to come to trust him, instead he'd been the one who'd come to know and like her for more than just her lovely face. He liked the way she bantered and bartered with tradesmen, how quickly she'd learned to cope with the thousand details of outfitting the *Revenge,* even how, when faced by her father's obvious incompetence, she'd remained devoted to his worthless memory.

This small, dark-haired lass with the rippling laugh was beyond all his experience. There'd been plenty of women whose company he enjoyed, and one—Catherine—whom he'd loved dearly, but Mariah West was the first that he had ever *liked* as much. It was the damnedest thing, and it did absolutely nothing to improve his temper this morning.

He scowled at the sloop's long, red pennant waving languidly against the slate gray sky. He didn't like the heavy look of the clouds, a sure sign of foul weather to come, and the air was too hot and still to suit him. Already his shirt was stuck to his back beneath his coat, and tide or no tide, it was high time they headed out to the deep water, where the winds would fill his sails and clear his wits. This morning he had no patience with the crowds of laughing, cheering townspeople come to the docks to see them off, and though he suspected they were counting on him to make some sort of patriotic, death-and-confusion-to-the-French speech, he had absolutely no intention of obliging them.

Once again he scanned the milling crowds on the dock. Where the devil was she, anyway?

He turned and tripped over a small, towheaded boy coiling a line around a pin. "What the thundering hell d'you think you're doing," he began as the boy cowered before him, "you fumble-fingered little son of a—"

"You needn't swear at the boy, Captain Sparhawk!" said Mariah warmly. "From where I stood, you were the one who was clumsy, not he!"

Gabriel swung around to face her, his feelings at seeing her again decidedly mixed. She stood with her balled fists on her waist, and beneath her wide-brimmed straw hat her eyes were narrowed and her face flushed with anger. Oh, they were a righteous pair this morning, he thought grimly, trying to remember how differently he'd planned this reunion.

Ignoring her for the moment, Gabriel cuffed the boy lightly on the side of his head. "Off with you, puppy. Find Mr. Farr and tell him I said to put you to more useful work out of my sight."

"You've no right to strike him!" declared Mariah indignantly. "He's scarcely more than a child!"

"I've every right in the world, and if he's in this sloop's company, he's not a child." He didn't really expect her to back down, and she didn't, her little chin raised stubbornly and her black brows tugged down low over the bridge of her nose. "If you were a man, I'd seize you up for backtalk and have the bos'n give you a dozen lashes to take the bile out of your tongue."

"Then perhaps you'd best prescribe two dozen for yourself, Captain!" This wasn't going at all as Mariah had expected, though in a peculiar way it was easier. Easier to be angry at Gabriel than to let him know how hard it was for her to come to him after last night, better to have him berate her for interfering than whisper honeyed lovers' words that confused and shamed her. All better than having him kiss her and caress her and make her world turn upside down with the sweetness of his touch. "I'm quite certain your bos'n would be willing to oblige."

"What in God's name are you doing on board now, anyway?" he demanded, as if he didn't already know. Against his best intentions he pictured how she'd looked last night, her eyes seductively half-closed and her lips parted as she'd arched back against his pillows.

Some things, it seemed, hadn't changed one bit between them.

"I'm coming with you." The determination in her eyes dared him to object. "My sister has eloped with a young man, and I must go after them to bring her back. They sailed last night with your friend Captain Richardson. I would have been here earlier, but I had to make arrangements for someone to stay with my mother while I'm gone.''

He looked at her closely, wondering from her mention of Richardson if she'd discovered his role in Jenny West's flight. If he could, he would have undone it in an instant. He'd wanted Mariah with him when he thought she'd be only a pleasant, cooing diversion until they reached the Caribbean and then he'd send her home. Now that she wasn't his mistress and most likely never would be, he didn't want to be laden with the responsibility of having her on board.

''Then you can go right on home and unmake your arrangements, because I'm not taking you with me.'' He waved his hand toward her in a gesture of dismissal. ''I'll find your foolish sister for you and ship her home myself.''

''I'm the owner of this vessel, and I can give you orders if I want. It says so in your commission from the governor. I've every intention of sailing in this sloop to Bridgetown, and nothing you can say will dissuade me. And there's another consideration, Captain Sparhawk.''

She lowered her head and her voice so that he had to bend over to hear her. ''I wouldn't trust you to walk my sister across the street, let alone fetch her back to Newport.''

Before he could answer she turned and scurried toward the companionway, leaving him to follow.

"Mariah, come back here!" None of the crew dared to comment or even notice that their captain was chasing their owner down the companionway, but Gabriel knew that later, between decks, they'd laugh and talk of nothing else, and his fury grew. He dropped to the lower deck without touching a single step. "Mariah, you're going ashore if I have to carry you off myself!"

She was sitting perched on her sea chest in the middle of his cabin when he charged in after her, grateful that she'd had the foresight to have her few belongings already brought below.

"I'm staying, Gabriel," she said, struggling to sound calm. Deliberately she untied her hat and set it on the chest beside her, smoothing the satin ribbons into two straight, overhanging lines. "Here, I mean. I'm going with you."

"The devil you will, Miss West." He wanted to throttle her and her gracious, mannerly airs. He could see in her eyes that she was every bit as angry and full of fire as he was himself. What else could he expect after last night? All that heated blood still swirling around inside them both with no release. "There are other ships bound for Bridgetown. One of them will suit you fine."

"The *Revenge* is the only ship fast enough to catch Captain Richardson, or arrive at Bridgetown first."

"We're on a privateering cruise, Mariah, or at least that's what my orders say. We're out to chase Frenchmen, not flibbertigibbety young females."

"Jenny is my sister. And I'm your owner, and if I say we go first to Bridgetown, that's what we'll do."

"Have you forgotten that we're going to war? The long guns firing, boarders clambering over the sides, and you'll be looking for your tea."

She lowered her chin, reminding Gabriel again of a baby bull with ridiculously long lashes. "I don't drink tea."

"Well, then, chocolate or coffee or santagree or whatever blasted potable you do drink. You won't be able to find it when we're fighting for our lives against five score of French bastards."

"I know how privateering's done. You make sure to chase merchant ships without any guns of their own, fire a shot or two over their bows to frighten them, and then down comes their flag and up goes yours." She knew this was an oversimplification, but she needed to retaliate after that nonsense with the tea. *Tea* drinking, as if she was some completely empty-headed miss! How much she'd love to toss his handsome, arrogant self out the stern windows! "Likely you won't see five score of French bastards total in the whole cruise."

"Damnation, Mariah, you know that isn't true!" In his frustration he snatched her hat and threw it down on the deck. If she kept up this maddening line of argument, she would be next. "Can't I be concerned about what becomes of you? Can't I want you to be here in Newport where I'll know you'll be safe instead of worrying that you'll be blown to bits with the rest of us? Or was all that canting concern last night only reserved for those lucky enough to be dead?"

Instantly he regretted his words. He watched as the antagonism vanished from her eyes and the color drained from her cheeks, and he cursed himself for his thoughtless cruelty.

"I must find Jenny. My mother says I must," she said softly, bending down to retrieve her hat, "and no matter how you wish to fault me, I'd rather accept the risks than be left behind again."

"Mariah, no." Yet he couldn't help thinking of all the times she must have felt abandoned, first by her father, leaving her over and over again to look after her mother, then by the boy Daniel. Some women married to sailors welcomed the time alone while their men went to sea. Mariah wouldn't be one of them. "You can't come."

She turned away from him so he wouldn't see the bright tears in her eyes, and crossed the deck to hang her hat on a bulkhead peg. Even if he'd stoop to such effortless cruelty, he wouldn't dare have her carried off the sloop and down the gangway for all the town to see.

Gabriel's gaze followed her, watching how her skirts swayed as she walked and remembering the shape of her pale legs. Damnation, what had she done to him?

"What would your father say to see you now, the only woman on board, and sharing my cabin, too?"

"We won't be sharing the cabin, thank you. Once we've fairly set sail, I'll thank you to have your things removed," she managed to say with surprising evenness. She could well imagine what her father would call her, and how he would have beaten her, too, if he'd been drinking when he learned of it. But he was dead, she reminded herself sternly, and guessing games like this were meaningless. "You can send Ethan to pack for you, and I'll keep my own chest packed until he's done."

Incredulous, Gabriel stared at her straight back in the dark blue linsey-woolsey. "This is my cabin, Mariah, and I'll be damned if you think I'm going to leave it to you. There are nigh on eighty men packed onto this sloop, and that doesn't allow an extra hairsbreadth for special accommodations. If you stay, you'll stay in this cabin, and you'll have me for company."

She looked over her shoulder at him, the disbelief now hers. "I can't share this cabin with you," she said, clearly appalled by his suggestion. "A gentleman like yourself must understand that much!"

For the first time she noticed that Gabriel had had her father's bunk replaced with one considerably longer and wider and more appropriate to his size and, perhaps, another occupant besides. In spite of what he'd just said she blushed furiously, remembering the intimacies she'd shared with him on similar checkered pillows.

His smile became perilously close to being a smirk. Perhaps if he made the threat to her reputation dire enough, she'd be convinced to go ashore. "I thought, poppet, after last night there wasn't much question about my being mistaken for a gentleman, not even by an innocent like yourself. Or less than fully innocent this morning, eh?"

"Oh—*oh!*" Mariah grabbed the heavy logbook from the desk and with both hands hurled it at Gabriel, the empty white pages fluttering as it thumped to the floor short of her target. "I pray you did lie with Betty Talbot, and that the slatternly cow poxed you rotten!"

God in heaven, she was jealous, and jealousy meant she cared. Cared for *him*, Gabriel Sparhawk, regardless of how much she mourned her Daniel. He told himself he didn't need such concern, that he hadn't sought it and didn't want it. But still he couldn't quite suppress the unfamiliar, tentative flutterings around his cynical, well-guarded heart, feelings that had no more place on a privateering sloop than the girl did herself.

"Oh, I did lie with fair Betty, sure enough," he confessed with a show of hard-bitten relish he certainly didn't feel. "But though her linen was grimy, I do recall her own sweet self was quite, quite clean, and not at all slatternly, though of course that was before Talbot got his greasy fingers on her bum. Still, if you're worried about taking the French pox, it won't have come by Betty."

"You would know about that, wouldn't you?" she said bitterly. "But if you think that's enough to make me run back home like a frightened rabbit, you are most mistaken. I don't run, Gabriel. I'm coming with you, and I'm staying in this cabin whether you do or not, and nothing, *nothing* you can say will change my mind!"

"Then stay, you little fool!" His patience was gone, and he was through arguing with her. If she wanted to come along so badly, he would take the chit with him. He'd done his best to dissuade her. If any ill befell her now, it would be her own damned fault, not his. "But not one tear, not one sigh, or so help me I'll toss you over the side and let you swim back to Newport!"

He slammed the cabin door so hard that her hat bounced off the bulkhead peg and dropped to the deck. For a long moment Mariah didn't move, letting the anger drain away and despair replace it. Slowly she replaced the hat on the peg, then sank down onto the chest again and buried her face in her hands.

She had what she wanted. So why did she feel so wretched? No matter how much she tried to please the people she loved, she always failed. First her father and mother, then Jenny, and now Gabriel, too. Maybe Gabriel worst of all.

She had managed to keep her father's beloved sloop from creditors, but then had tumbled into the captain's bed with a readiness that would have earned her every inch of her father's fury and disgust. She had taken over all the housekeeping and cooking and family accounts when her mother seemed unable to cope with them any longer, and in return her mother had called her a dull, stingy drab who would never attract a husband.

Mariah squeezed her eyes shut, trying not to remember all the hateful words her mother had poured onto her like scalding oil as she'd made her hurried preparations to go after Jenny, beautiful, gold-haired Jenny, the only hope her mother had for an auspicious match. To her mother, there was nothing improper about her being the only woman on board the *Revenge,* for Mariah, she'd said scathingly, was so hopeless with men, such a confirmed, pathetic spinster, that she'd be perfectly safe. Perfectly safe, thought Mariah bitterly, and wondered why her mother hadn't noticed the rumpled pink silk gown with the bodice still half unpinned.

And then, finally, there was Gabriel. His bluster and swearing just now hadn't fooled her for an instant. She could recognize the pain of rejection because she'd felt it so often herself.

She realized that he had brought her to the windmill last night determined to seduce her with his customary, calculated ease, while she had blithely gone to dine with a man she believed had not the slightest interest in her as a woman. Strange how they'd both been so confounded, and at precisely the same moment. He had kissed her, and she had kissed him, and the spark that passed between them had shocked them both with its unexpected intensity.

For that single moment he had dropped the barrier of world-weary, cynical charm that kept the rest of the world at bay and let her see a vulnerable unhappiness that no practiced rake would ever admit. Fleetingly she'd wondered why—he was wealthy and handsome, respected by every man who knew him and adored by women—until his mouth had found hers again, and she forgot everything else.

She couldn't remember it without setting her heart to racing all over again. The few embraces she'd shared with Daniel, the kisses stolen in the kitchen and behind the stables, hadn't prepared her for Gabriel. Yet whatever his intentions had been, Gabriel hadn't seduced her. He'd made love to her. Even in her inexperience she'd sensed the difference. The magic he'd wrought with his hands, his fingers, his mouth, had been beyond imagining, raising her higher and higher so that she'd forgotten all modesty as she'd arched beneath him with her legs spread like some common dockside trull. All she'd wanted was more of the same unbelievable pleasure he was giving her, and the part of himself that he was giving her with it, giving so freely that the one worthy thing she could offer in return would be her heart and her love.

And then, for her, the pleasure had turned to fear. No matter if she loved him, he still would go, the same way Daniel had. If she'd accepted the brilliant promise of pleasure that Gabriel was offering, if she'd soared so high with him to find the completion her body begged for, then the inevitable loss would have been that much more unbearable. She had tried to tell him about Daniel to explain what she felt, but instead of understanding she'd seen only the pain her words caused him, and then it had been too late. All he'd heard was Daniel's name, the name of another man spoken as she lay in his arms.

He spoke so often of her courage, but last night she had been an abysmal coward. He had offered her, if not quite his love, then his trust, and she had been too afraid of losing him to accept. And without question a man like Gabriel Sparhawk would never, never repeat such an offer.

Slowly she became aware that the sloop was moving, and she could hear the last frantic farewells called from the dock mingled with the shouted orders from the deck. Through her tears she looked out the open windows in the stern, watching Newport swing gently past her as the sloop began to make its way through the harbor to the bay and the open sea beyond. This would be the first time she'd ever journeyed from the island on which she'd been born.

All her past was being left behind. She wished she knew what lay ahead to replace it.

"Tell me the part about our wedding again," begged Jenny, her smile full of contentment as she gazed up at Elisha. To stand here at the *Felicity*'s rail, with Elisha's arms around her and the moon and a skyful of stars overhead, far from her mother's whining and weeping and nagging, was as close to heaven as she had ever imagined. She wished she'd been able to tell Mariah. Mariah might have scolded at first, but her sister would have understood why she had to leave, especially now that that wicked old captain had taken such a liking to her. "I like the flowers best."

Elisha cleared his throat and flipped his blond hair from his eyes. "In Jamaica there're flowers like you've never seen in Rhode Island. Big red and yellow and white ones, bigger'n your two hands together, and they climb like beans all over every house. I mean to pick a whole bunch for you to carry when we stand before the minister, as many as you ever could want. And when he says we're wed, you'd best toss them all up in the air, because you'll need your arms to hold me tight when I kiss you proper as my wife.''

Jenny snuggled against his gingham shirt. "It sounds grand, dearest, excepting that Captain Richardson says we're bound for Barbados, not Jamaica.''

"Don't vex me, lamb!" growled Elisha, kissing Jenny behind her ear until she giggled. "I know where we're bound, same as you. But I've never been to Barbados and I have been to Jamaica, and I warrant since they're both in the same sea, they'll be of a piece. The flowers will, anyways. You won't find nothing to fault.''

"I haven't found anything to complain of yet." She turned in his arms and lifted her lips to his, kissing him eagerly. With a little purr of happiness, she rested her cheek over his heart. "It's still a wonder to me that your aunt gave you the money so we could leave together. You've never mentioned her before, and now, la! She gives you thirty gold guineas, and Captain Richardson sells us passage, and here we are, next to being husband and wife.''

Knowing his limitations with untruths, Elisha kissed her again instead. He hoped he'd never have to explain that his aunt was really Captain Gabriel Sparhawk. He'd sworn to the captain he wouldn't tell Jenny until they were wed, and an oath like that, to a man like that, meant something to Elisha. He'd be seventeen in less than a fortnight, a man by anyone's standards, but he'd felt like such a snotty-nosed boy before Captain Sparhawk that he hadn't even had the sense to ask him why he cared so much—thirty guineas' worth—about Elisha marrying Jenny West. But he had Jenny, his beautiful, sweet, teasing Jenny, and that was what mattered most.

"I love you, Jen," he said softly, stroking her hair as he marveled at the good fortune that had given him the prettiest girl in Newport to be his wife.

"I love you, too, Elisha," whispered Jenny, almost overwhelmed by sheer happiness. "I love you more than anything."

Stripped down to his shirt and breeches as he stood on the quarterdeck with the setting sun at his back, Gabriel stared at the pocket watch clasped in his hand and swore. Even the gun crews out of earshot could tell the captain was unhappy with them, and to a man they stared out the gunports or over the side at the four empty barrels lashed together to make their target, a target that dipped and bounced merrily in the choppy water off Block Island and refused to be hit by even one ball of the *Revenge*'s ragged broadside.

"A pack of boys shooting peas through reeds could do better than that," said Gabriel sorrowfully. "Piss poor, that's what it was. Nigh on six minutes to load, and then not a one of you found the mark. Why, your aim's so bad the Quaker ladies on Nantucket will likely be scooping your balls out of their kitchen gardens, wondering at what sorry articles they be."

A few of the younger men chortled nervously at the double meaning before their older mates silenced them with swift, murderous looks. Many of the seamen had shipped with Captain Sparhawk before, and knew his humors well, just as they knew they deserved his disappointment with their lackluster performance, and his anger, too, if he cared to show it.

"Now I know it's but the first night, and you're all still soft from too much fine drinking and dining and playing hide-and-seek between the trollops' thighs." Gabriel's voice rose, and his dark brows gathered together. With his jaw stubbled dark and his black hair tossing wildly like a madman's in the wind, not a sailor dared meet his eyes. "But any day now we could meet a French flag, and they won't sit there waiting for us to say *bonjour*. Not merchantmen, either, but King Louis's navy, and I don't want them to see what sad, sorry excuses for English fighting sailors we are. Nor do I have any particular wish to be blown into a thousand tiny fragments by French gunnery, which is exactly what will happen unless you blasted lubbers learn enough to hit them first. So do it again, damn your lazy hides, and do it right!''

"Is he always this mean to his crew?" whispered Mariah to Ethan as they sat on the top step of the companionway. "He's so hateful I don't know why any sailor would sign on with him."

"Because he'll make their fortunes, that's why." Ethan looked at her pityingly, disappointed that such an almighty truth had to be stated. His station in an engagement was to see that wounded men were carried quickly below. In a practice like this one, he had nothing to do except explain the exercise to Mariah. "Besides, cap'n's supposed to be *mean*. If he ain't, then no one minds, each thinkin' they could do better, an' then, like he said, we'll all end up dressed in Frenchie garlic cloves an' feedin' the fishes."

Mariah considered this as she took another bite of the cold chicken leg in her hand. At least she'd been given supper, thanks to Ethan. The crew wasn't going to get theirs until they hit the target. This morning, once they'd reached deep water, she'd watched them run up and down the rigging, taking in and setting out sails over and over before Gabriel had finally given a halfhearted nod of approval. In the afternoon they'd been set to mock hand-to-hand battles among themselves with cutlasses and boarding axes until her own arm ached in sympathy. Now they'd toiled at the guns for at least an hour, with no end in sight that she could see. As the owner of the *Revenge*, she should be delighted with her captain's thoroughness. As another first-time sailor, she was appalled.

She studied how the wind blew Gabriel's fine linen shirt taut against his chest and shoulders, how he'd rolled his sleeves over forearms dark with curling black hair and thick with a sailor's muscles and ...

No, she ordered herself sternly, she'd no business at all looking at him that way. That kind of admiration would bring her only trouble later, when she'd need every ounce of resolution to keep him from the cabin, and from his bed, now hers. She was sure he was still too angry with her to repeat the tenderness he'd shown her last night, but she wasn't at all certain that same anger might not tempt him to try taking her by force. Quickly she turned along with everyone else to stare at the floating barrels.

Each gun crew was firing in turn, and Mariah watched the one nearest her, captained by Allen Welsh. Welsh had served in a king's frigate before he'd jumped ship for a woman in Boston, and though he was reputed to be one of the best gunners on board the *Revenge*, Mariah recalled how drunk he'd been last night, and she wondered how he'd survived this day. Welsh levered the handspike that eased the black-barrelled gun into the final position for firing, barking anxious, single-word commands to the three men in the crew to haul on the training tackles. Mariah covered her ears with her hands, knowing what came next. The *Revenge* rolled gently with a swell, Welsh touched the linstock to the powder in the base ring, and abruptly the gun came to life, flames shooting from its mouth along with the ball, acrid white smoke from the explosion enveloping the crew, as close to a ton of hot black iron hurtled back against the ropes.

On the quarterdeck above the smoke, Gabriel was the first to see the barrels splinter when the ball hit its mark, followed by the white plume of water and spray rising high against the setting sun. A ragged cheer began as soon as the smoke began to drift away, growing louder and louder as more men realized what had happened, finally becoming a unanimous roar nearly as deafening as the explosion itself.

Gabriel grinned. It had been a sad, sorry excuse for a drill, one that would have made Deveaux dance with joy, but it had begun the task of bonding eighty disparate men into a crew who could work together, a crew he could trust. Fine enough work for the first day.

With his hands clasped behind his back, he turned for'ard toward the companionway. He wanted a clean shirt and his supper, and the chance to lie down with his eyes closed. God only knew how many peaceful evenings like this one he had left.

But he stopped when he saw Mariah. She was bouncing up and down with excitement, clapping her hands and cheering along with the others. There were gunpowder smudges on her cheeks and on her white ruffled cuffs, but her face beamed with an open, giddy happiness that he himself could never hope to inspire.

"Mariah!" As he headed across the sloping deck toward her, wariness replaced her smile and she braced her shoulders as if preparing for a physical battle. Damnation, what did she think of him? He held his hand out to her, the gesture more imperious than he'd intended. He was too aware of the men watching him, from curiosity and lechery both, and he hated how just by her presence she'd subtly changed the entire balance of the *Revenge*'s company.

"Mariah," he said curtly. "Come. I am tired, and it's high time I found my bed."

Chapter Seven

"How dare you speak to me like that before your men?" demanded Mariah as soon as the cabin door was shut behind them. Her fingers shook so much with anger that she fumbled with the ribbons beneath her chin. Furiously she tore her hat off without untying the bow and dashed it to the deck between her and Gabriel—a braided straw gauntlet he couldn't miss. "I saw how they all winked and guffawed and jabbed their elbows at each other, believing me to be—to be your *mistress*—because of what you said!"

"You made the decision yourself when you forced yourself onto this sloop." Gabriel poured himself a tankardful of water, deliberately drinking it slowly. He'd do better in this argument if he could stay calm, especially since her temper was so wildly out of control already.

"You insist you want to share my cabin," he continued, striving to be the ideal of reason.

"What else are they supposed to think? There are more than eighty of us packed into fifty feet of oak walls, Mariah, and precious few secrets—even yours—won't become common knowledge in the space of one watch. I tried to tell you that before we sailed, but you wouldn't listen. You thought you knew better, and now you're howling because you've just realized how wrong you are."

"Oh, you're a fine one to speak of the value of my reputation!" She stalked back and forth, unable to stand still in the face of his infuriating calm. "You were the one who invited me to that windmill with every intention of tossing me onto my back!"

Gabriel clucked his tongue. "Oh, Mariah, such a genteel expression! As I recall, you came first to Crescent Hill and rather flagrantly tried to seduce me into sailing for you."

"I never intended to seduce you!" sputtered Mariah. "I only let you kiss me because I thought you were going to say yes!"

"Only a matter of degree, poppet. And there wasn't much 'letting' involved. As I recall, you were as willing then as you were last night." He poured more water into the leather tankard, swirling it gently before he brought it to his lips. "I've done nothing to your name, Mariah. No one save Ethan knew you were with me at my house or the windmill, and Ethan's silent as the grave. Any tattering of your virtue is your own doing."

"I'm not—" She halted abruptly, her mouth staying open longer than she realized. "What are you doing, Gabriel?"

"I'd think that was fairly obvious, Mariah." He tugged his shirt free of the waistband of his breeches and pulled it over his head, wadding the linen into a rough ball to wipe his face and chest before he tossed it onto the bunk. "If we are to share this cabin, you'll have to accustom yourself to the sight of me changing my clothing. As, I warrant, shall I with you, unless you mean to wear that selfsame bodice and petticoat for the next month or so."

She gasped, speechless at the possibilities she hadn't considered. Shame stained her cheeks as she stared at his bare chest and arms, the planes and bands of lean muscle so clearly delineated beneath the whirling pattern of dark hair. Raised without brothers, her father often away at sea, her experience with half-clad men was nonexistent. Certainly she'd never seen Daniel stand before her the way Gabriel was doing now, and even if he had, Daniel had been slight and wiry, with none of the physical presence that seemed so much a part of Gabriel.

The evening was still warm, and he made no move to dress. He was as comfortable in a pair of old duck trousers and nothing else as he was in a London suit of embroidered velvet, while she was a lass from a good family who'd likely no notion of what Adam had looked like in the garden. He expected her to blush. He would have been disappointed if she hadn't.

But what he hadn't expected was her sudden look of concern and the way she pressed her fingers to her mouth to stifle—stifle what?

"That scar," she said finally, her eyes concentrating on the jagged pale line that ran diagonally from his right collarbone to his waist. "How did you ever survive a wound so grievous?"

"I'm sure the man whose sword gave it to me wonders that as well." He tried to be light, dismissive. He'd been in enough fights that his body was peppered and crisscrossed with scars, but he'd known at once which one she meant, and he had no intention of discussing it with her.

In his mind's eye he saw again the terror on Catherine's face as they'd seized her, the shrill sound of her screams....

"You were so fortunate you didn't die," said Mariah softly.

"Was I now?" He shouldn't be so harsh with her. How could she know the truth? If she did, she wouldn't waste her concern on him. He didn't need it, and he didn't deserve it.

"Aye, you were." Slowly, she took her fingers from her lips and reached out to touch the scar. "'Tis always better to live than die."

Gabriel swore and jerked beyond her reach, turning away so he didn't have to meet her eyes.

She wasn't thinking of him. All that sweet concern was meant for a man past caring in return. Damnation, she wasn't thinking of *him*.

Startled by his reaction, Mariah swiftly pulled her hand away, curling the fingers into a tight little fist before she tucked it behind her back as if to punish it. "I'm sorry, I didn't mean—"

"If your darling Daniel drowned, then he died clean," he said roughly. "No blood, no scars, nothing to mar the pretty memory of a pretty boy."

"You're wrong, Gabriel," she began miserably. "I never wanted—"

"Why the devil are you here, Mariah?" he demanded, swinging round to face her. "Is it really your sister you want, or have you come after my soul?"

Shaking her head, she backed away, intimidated by the raw emotions on his face. Relentlessly he followed, until she felt herself bump against the bulkhead. He took her face in his hands, his fingers sliding along her jaw, disarming her with his unexpected gentleness. He rubbed one callused thumb along her lower lip, stroking the soft flesh as he searched her small, serious face, drinking in her innocence from the dark blue pools of her eyes.

"What do you want of me?" she echoed, her words bold though her voice trembled. He hadn't even kissed her, and already the strange weakness that came with his touch was there, making her body yearn for more.

"What do *you* want, Mariah?" he asked hoarsely in return. "Do you want what I can offer? I can give you fire in your blood and pleasure so hot it'll scorch your soul. There'll be no going back, no returning to how it was, no way to undo the past. Aye, then, my sweet innocent lass, *then*, you can tell me if 'tis always better to live than to die."

He lifted his hands from her face, holding his cupped fingers above her jaw like a man shielding a spark from the wind. She stood unmoving, her face upturned toward his as if he held it still. Her lip quivered, and reflexively she licked the spot he'd touched with his thumb.

He swore softly beneath his breath, turned on his heel and left her before he lost his mind.

When Gabriel returned, the moon was sliding low in the night sky, the glow of the first dawn not far away. Mariah had let the candles in the gimbals gutter out, and moonlight reflected off the water in silvery ripples along the cabin's bulkheads. She lay curled on the bunk asleep, her face pillowed in the crook of one arm. He smiled sadly when he saw she hadn't undressed. She was wise not to trust him when he doubted he could trust himself. She slept with one knee drawn up, the other thrust out beneath her skirts. He longed to kiss the curve at the back of her knee, there above her half-untied garter, one more place where he might feel her heart beating beneath his lips.

Instead he unbuckled her shoes, sliding them carefully off her feet so as not to wake her. He set the shoes on the deck, heels neatly together, and pulled the coverlet over her. She murmured in her sleep and pushed her face into the pillows with a drowsy sigh.

Then he slung the sailor's hammock from the beams across from her and climbed into it to wait for dawn. But not, he knew, for sleep.

"He won't speak to me, Ethan. Not, of course, that I wish him to," said Mariah a week later as Ethan cleared away the dishes from her breakfast. After the first days of bickering with Ethan over who should carry the tray from the galley, and whether he judged her too frail to do even that much for herself, Mariah had at last given in and let him fuss over her as he wished. At least then she had one person who spoke to her on board. "You can just put aside your little matchmaking schemes right now. Captain Sparhawk spends as little time in my company as he can, and then he won't look at me squarely or say more than five words, and that only if he must."

"Ah, miss, the cap'n don't hate ye like that," scoffed Ethan. "He be in one o' his moods, that's the truth. Once we takes us a prize or two, he'll come round."

Mariah wasn't sure if she wished him to come round or not, and she sighed deeply, stroking her fingers along the barb of her pen. She sat at the table with her little pocketbook of notes and paper before her, writing—or trying to write—a letter to her mother. Any prizes the *Revenge* took would be sent to Newport to be condemned by the court there, and dutifully Mariah planned to have at least one letter to send along home. Her mother would expect it. But the sea was so rough this morning that while Mariah held the ink pot steady on the tabletop, the ink inside slopped out across her fingers with each roll of the sloop. Finally she gave up, corking the pot and wiping the worst of the ink from her hand with a napkin.

"I can't help it if he thinks I forced myself on the sloop and into his business. I did, but I didn't have much choice myself. My sister—"

"Aye, miss, ye don't have to be telling me that tale again, any more than you should be worryin' about what the cap'n thinks." Ethan cocked the lid of the pewter coffeepot to see if Mariah needed more from the galley. "Miss Jenny be your sister, an' that be that. The cap'n, now, he'd run clear to China if one of his sisters needed rescuing, an' clear to the moon if *his* mama asked. Ye be doing exactly what he'd be doing hisself. So stop your frettin', mind?"

Mariah shook her head. She couldn't imagine Gabriel going clear to China for anyone, especially not at his mother's request. If any man had cut his leading strings, she was certain it would be Gabriel Sparhawk. Strange how he'd never mentioned her. She'd assumed his mother was dead. "You're probably the only man on board who thinks so."

"There's plenty o' them that do, miss. Only cap'n's orders be that no men are to speak to you, th' way he always wants it."

Mariah's brows rose with surprise. "You mean he's brought other women with him before me?"

Ethan frowned, realizing too late that he'd said too much, and concentrated on buffing an invisible smudge from the side of the coffeepot.

"The cap'n does like his ladies," he admitted. "But the others weren't nothing like you. They be fancy, gaudy bits, married, most o' them, bent on givin' their poor husbands an extra set o' horns. But ye be a good girl, a cap'n's daughter yerself, an' not one out to make mischief on a feather bed. Now to my mind th' cap'n's dishonored ye some, talkin' bold like he does, but I told them 'tween decks that he's been sleepin' apart, and I told 'em about that hammock, an' set things right for ye."

"Oh, Ethan, you didn't—"

"Nay, hear me out, miss! I felt bad about takin' ye to that wicked old mill that night, knowin' what the cap'n was expectin', but I knew from his temper next morn that he hadn't gotten what he wanted. Right ye was, miss, to cross him like that! But like I said, I've done my best to set things right for ye there, miss. Them 'tween decks listen to me in such concerns. So ye don't fret about that either, miss, hear me?"

"I hear you, Ethan. And I thank you, more than you'll ever know." She smiled so warmly at him that he blushed all the way to the bald circle on the top of his head. He lifted the tray with a clatter of crockery, glancing over Mariah's shoulder at the papers spread on the table.

"What ye be about there, miss?" he asked, squinting at the papers. "I thought ye was done all that before we sailed."

"I was. These are others of my own, letters and such." She shuffled them together in a neater pile, self-consciously covering the gambling voucher of her father's that lay on top. She'd brought it on a whim, a whim that she'd rather Ethan didn't share with Gabriel. "Nothing of importance."

Ethan shrugged. "I couldn't tell ye if it be important or not, seeing as how I went t'sea before I learned my letters. I can make my mark alongside my name, an' that's all I need to know."

Mariah relaxed, smoothing the water-wrinkled sheet with her fingers. "I have difficulty with this one myself. Half of it's in French, and it might as well be Greek for all I can make it out."

"The cap'n can read an' speak their lingo clear as day," said Ethan proudly. "'Twill be powerfully entertaining to see how he fights 'em. Won't be like the Spanish, though. Bead-telling bunch o' superstitious Papists, Spaniards. Them be scared senseless by th' cap'n on account o' his size, him comin' after them with his sword swingin' an' those green cat's eyes o' his all afire. It were a pleasure to see, miss! But with the French—eh, things will be different wit' the French this time."

"This time?" She'd learned soon enough when Ethan wasn't telling her everything he knew. "We haven't been at war with France for years and years, and Gab—I mean, Captain Sparhawk's not that much older than I."

Ethan scowled at the tray, working his tongue behind his lip around the few teeth he had left in his mouth. "Years don't always tell the story of a man, lass, nor do kings make all the wars. Our cap'n, now, he's seen things that made him older than the lot of us stowed together. That's why I know he'll come round about you. You can make him forget what needs forgettin'. An' that's all I be sayin' on *that*."

That might be *that* for Ethan, thought Mariah, but his riddles about years and French wars certainly weren't the end of it as far as she was concerned. She remembered the two Frenchmen Gabriel had killed in Newport, all his allusions to her being safe once he was gone, then the way he'd avoided telling her how he'd come by the awful scar, and now this from Ethan. She didn't like secrets or mysteries, especially ones that somehow seemed to involve her. They were trying to protect her, and she didn't like that, either. No matter what Gabriel wanted to believe, she wasn't a child. There wasn't one whit of childishness in how she felt when he kissed her, and she'd wager he felt the same. So why didn't anyone trust her with the truth?

She was still trying to sort it out that night as she lay alone in the middle of the oversize bunk. She listened to the wind thrumming in the standing rigging, the rush of the waves along the sloop's sides, the constant creaks and groans of the timbers, all sounds she'd become so accustomed to that she nearly stopped hearing them. She counted the bells—four—that marked the end of one watch and the beginning of the next. She sighed and turned over, looking across at the empty place where Gabriel's hammock usually hung.

Though he never spoke to her at night, coming into the cabin only when he was certain she would be sleeping, and leaving before dawn, she always sensed his presence and silently lay awake in the dark, staring at the shadow of his body in the hammock and unconsciously pacing her breathing to match his until she, too, would finally sleep. On the nights when the loneliness became too much, when she would have given the world in exchange for a kind word from him, she muffled her weeping with her fist and let her tears trickle unheeded into the pillow.

She pushed herself upright in the bunk and tossed back the coverlet. Ethan said they were off the Carolinas, and tonight the wind smelled of the land. Too hot by half for sleeping, Mariah decided as she quickly dressed without bothering with petticoats or stays, determined to go up on deck for air. And to see that all was right with Gabriel—she wouldn't lie to herself. Just a few minutes to reassure herself that only the sloop's sailing had kept him away from the cabin and that no harm had come his way.

He stood alone as far forward on the starboard side as he could without climbing out onto the bowsprit, in his shirtsleeves with his waistcoat unbuttoned and flapping in the wind. The *Revenge* sliced through the black waves, her deck canting sharply beneath the force of the wind stretching the ghostly pale canvas overhead. Carefully Mariah made her way forward, moving from one handhold to another. The slanting deck was slippery with spray, and on such a dark night she wasn't certain she'd be rescued if she fell overboard.

To her surprise, Gabriel turned as if expecting her, grinning wildly as he shook his hair from his face. He held his hand out to her, the way he had so many times before in Newport, and tentatively, unsure of what would follow, Mariah took it. His fingers curled around her wrist and he drew her in to stand before him, one arm around her waist to hold her steady.

He told himself he shouldn't touch her again, and again he paid no heed to his own warnings. Already having her here beside him felt right, just as all the days and nights he'd kept apart from her had felt so miserably wrong. Tonight he had reason enough to forget the vows he'd made about her. He had to share this moment with someone, and he thanked whatever god of sleeplessness had sent him Mariah.

"Look, poppet, there," he said into her ear, holding his brass spyglass steady for her. How had he forgotten how neatly she fit beneath his arm, against his chest? "Do you see the tiny silver triangles, there on the horizon? Will Allen up top should've seen 'em first, and he'll be powerfully sorry he didn't, and not just because I mean to stop his rum for a fortnight for nodding off on watch. Those little bits of silver mean gold for you, Mariah, you and me and all the rest of us, for they're French sails above a French ship."

"A French ship!" repeated Mariah, his excitement contagious. No wonder they were charging onward as if the devil himself snapped at their heels!

"Aye, a French ship," he said, his breath hot in her ear. "And I mean to take her by dawn."

She didn't miss the second meaning to his words, and she found she didn't care. As the sloop raced ahead, the wind and spray whipped into her face, molding her gown against her body as Gabriel's arm pulled her closer to his chest. The night sky and the sea were inseparable, as inseparable as she felt standing here with Gabriel. She realized she was grinning, too, and she laughed with her head back, the exhilaration beyond words, as she dug her fingers into his sleeve. She had never felt more intensely alive.

Beneath his hand he felt how her heart pounded, not with fear but with the same wild spirit that surged through him. God, he'd missed her. He lowered the glass and kissed her swiftly, roughly, his teeth nipping at her lower lip as she hungrily opened her mouth to his, her taste mingled with the salt from the spray.

Mariah tried to tell herself that what she felt was no more than the excitement of the chase. But no chase could bring that twisting, tightening sensation so low in her body, that curious heat that made her long shamelessly to twine herself around Gabriel. Only Gabriel made her feel like this.

"Stay with me, Mariah," he ordered, his breathing harsh. "Swear you'll stay with me!"

Mariah stared at him, wild-eyed. He wanted her to stay with him. Not go away or be left behind. He wanted her with him. *Swear you'll stay with me!*

Before she could answer, the excited cry finally came from the lookout above them. The deck was suddenly filled with men, the whole crew willingly roused from their sleep for the first sight of their good fortune, the fortune that came with Gabriel Sparhawk as their master. The *Revenge* was gaining fast, her speed no match for the overburdened merchant brig that now showed clearly before them. The men shouted and pointed and pounded each other on the back with eager pleasure as they parted a path for Gabriel, pulling Mariah along with him, to reach the quarterdeck.

There Mariah's skirts whipped in the wind around her and her hair streamed from her face as she stood beside Gabriel, his arm possessively around her waist. She saw the wild anticipation in the faces of the men turned up to them, and she knew it must mirror her own. Spontaneously someone began to cheer Gabriel, and the roar was soon picked up by the others.

"Nay, lads, not so soon," cautioned Gabriel, though his grin was as eager as theirs. "Wait until she's under King George's flag and headed to Newport. By breakfast, say, when we've put this little business behind us. Then you can cheer yourself hoarse as you count the gold that will drop into your pockets like rain!"

The cheering began again, and Gabriel let himself savor it, knowing too well how fleeting such moments could be. This was the best part of any chase, when every man was eager for glory, when every battle promised to be an easy one, every prize full of gold, when there were yet no wounded to tend or dead to mourn. And with him to share it all was Mariah, his eager, fierce little poppet. He tightened his arm around her waist, relishing how soft and pliant she was against him. She was as intoxicated with the chase as he was, her face flushed from the wind and excitement, her eyes dancing. Every other woman he'd known would have been shrieking with anxiety, begging to go below to shiver with fear. Not Mariah, not his brave poppet.

He was sorely tempted to carry her below now, before they captured the other ship, and put an end to all their foolish spitting and scraping and toss her on the bunk and give her what they both craved. Soon, he promised himself, very soon, when he made this capture, he'd take himself another prize. For now he'd content himself by keeping her with him as long as he dared before it became too dangerous.

Not that she would have gone even if he'd ordered her to. Gabriel had asked her to stay, and nothing would persuade Mariah to do otherwise. Heedless of the hours that stretched through the night and into early morning, she stayed beside him as he gave the orders that closed the gap between the sloop and the hapless French ship, and then the last careful advice to the gunners as the decks were finally cleared for action.

Through Gabriel's spyglass Mariah could see the panic on the French ship, the tiny figures of crew members running aimlessly about as the captain, the only one in a cockaded hat, gestured with both arms. Gabriel had been right, the little brig was heavily burdened, wallowing in the same choppy water the *Revenge*'s sharp lines cut through so neatly, and Mariah caught herself making the same greedy speculations on the French cargo as everyone else did on board. Rice, most likely, since they were so near to Charlestown, or maybe indigo. Either one would bring a good price in Newport. The only guns that Mariah could spot were a pair of old stern chasers that none of the French sailors seemed to know how to load or fire, and from the amount of handwringing she could see through the glass she guessed that the French had no intention of putting up any sort of defense.

This was, she decided merrily, almost too easy, and she let herself think of what lavish gift she'd buy for her mother. Her mother liked presents, complaining that they too seldom came her way. Gold and coral beads, perhaps, or maybe even a sapphire ring....

Far too easy, thought Gabriel, and that alone was enough to make him doubly wary. This early in the war, odds were that this French captain had scurried out to sea, hoping to run for home before any Englishmen put to sea in pursuit, but experience had taught Gabriel that suspicious men tended to live the longest. He studied the brig's sides for disguised gun ports, and he scanned the horizon for another ship that might claim this one as wandered from a convoy. Although he was nearly certain the French captain would strike to him without a fight, he decided a well-placed shot across their bows wouldn't hurt.

"Cover your ears, poppet," he said to Mariah, settling his hat more firmly onto his head. Earlier he'd had Ethan fetch his coat and a silver-laced hat along with his sword and a pair of Spanish-worked pistols. Cutting a stylish figure was good for his reputation. Clean linen with lace, he'd found, could be every bit as daunting as a sword to a harried captain forced to surrender. "We'll give them a taste of our fireworks, just so the lads can keep their hands in it."

Mariah's eyes widened with joyful, childish delight. "You're truly going to shoot at them?"

"Truly, you bloodthirsty creature." They'd swung round parallel to the brig, not one hundred yards away, as pretty a shot as any gunner ever had. "Allen Welsh, there! When you're ready!"

The gun fired instantly, the explosion echoing across the open water. The brig's bowsprit shattered and crumpled into the water in a trailing tangle of lines and canvas. Immediately the blue flag with the white lilies dipped and jerked as the French captain himself pulled down the color. In less than a minute, with only one shot fired, the *Revenge* had made her first capture.

The Englishmen exploded in frenzied rejoicing. Gabriel grabbed Mariah by the waist and swung her, shrieking with surprise, high in the air, and as he lowered her to the deck he gave her a loud, boisterous kiss that made her giggle as she shoved him away.

"I told you how easy this privateering was!" she teased, tossing her hair from her face. "You sailors only brag about your dangerous exploits to keep away the competition from farmers!"

"Any landsman's welcome to try his hand," Gabriel answered, wondering if she'd any idea how delectable she looked with her hair loose around her sunburned cheeks. Soon, very soon… "Or hers. Yours. I give you joy of your first prize, my lady owner."

Laughing again, she dipped in as neat a curtsy as she could manage on the rocking deck, and only with heavy reluctance did Gabriel turn away from her and to the business of securing the captured brig. Already the *Revenge*'s boat was heading across with a party to bring the French sailors as prisoners and jury-rig the bowsprit for sailing. He handed Mariah his glass so she could watch, and headed below decks to make arrangements for the prisoners. He'd lose a dozen of his own men for the prize crew, but the space below would still be tight. Oh, Lord, and then he'd have to suffer the company of the French captain, too, until he could be put ashore, when he'd been counting on having Mariah to himself.

Alone at the rail, Mariah idly watched the Englishmen repair the French brig. Her brig now, once the court had condemned the prize. Strange to think herself the owner of two ships, and stranger still to think of what was happening between her and Gabriel. *Swear you'll stay with me.* She smiled happily. Tonight she was quite sure he would still be speaking to her.

She swung the glass along the deck of the brig. Farr and two other Englishmen stood by the rail, each with drawn cutlasses. One by one the sad-looking French sailors were being herded over the side and into the longboat. The French captain waited, his logbook and a strongbox under his arm, his face long beneath his cocked hat. He kept trying to speak to Farr, who steadfastly shook his head, refusing whatever favor was being asked. Suddenly the French captain dropped his strong-box and rushed across to the companionway. Mariah frowned, wondering what kind of mischief the Frenchman planned. She'd heard they were wily, the French, not to be trusted.

But all he did was bend to help a woman up the steps, a young woman with bright gold hair so much like Jenny's that Mariah's fingers tightened around the polished brass. Leaning heavily on the arm of the captain, her movements cautious, the young woman was clearly with child, and in her arms was a small boy, his face buried against his mother's shoulder. They were followed by two more French sailors hauling a large trunk and several smaller bundles to the deck. Farr took one look at the trunk, shook his head first at the sailors and then, when the woman turned to him, he shook his head at her, as well, his arms folded sternly across his chest. Her shoulders drooped with dejection, the woman pulled a stuffed toy rabbit from one of the bundles and handed it to her son. She hesitated for a moment before pointing to the second, smaller bundle for the French captain to carry, and then resolutely turned her back on all her belongings.

Slowly Mariah lowered Gabriel's glass. Somehow, for her, the joy of privateering had just vanished.

Chapter Eight

Standing on the quarterdeck with his hand resting on the hilt of his sword, Gabriel frowned down at the little French captain twisting his cocked hat anxiously in his hands. Once Capitaine Cherault, late of the brig *Marie-Claire,* had learned that the enormous English pirate spoke French, he had launched into a high-pitched torrent of complaints, the words streaming so indignantly from his round little mouth that Gabriel could only grasp every fifth one. Not that it really mattered to Gabriel. Long ago he'd learned not to become too involved with the woes of the men whose livelihood he'd just seized. The fortunes—and misfortunes—of war didn't encourage empathy.

He glanced over the Cherault's stiff brown wig, still marked with the circle of his hat, to the *Marie-Claire*'s crew, looking sullen and betrayed and not particularly loyal to Cherault. Though they didn't know it yet, Gabriel had every intention of releasing them in Bridgetown, where he wagered not a one of them would sign on again with Cherault. But whichever ship they joined, they'd carry tales of the ruthless Captain Sparhawk and the justly named *Revenge* and, men's pride being what it was, how each one of them had fought for his very life—exactly the sort of polishing that Gabriel knew his reputation needed after two years hidden away on shore.

And then there was Deveaux. He wanted to be quite, quite sure that Deveaux knew he'd returned.

The little boy in the woman's arms began to cry, a long, mournful wail that his mother frantically tried to quiet, and Gabriel's frown deepened. Lord, they probably both believed he ate French infants for breakfast. He heartily wished the *Marie-Claire* hadn't been carrying any passengers. Women and children complicated captures immeasurably, and though he tried to tell himself to be unsentimental, he still didn't like knowing he'd fired on them.

"Who are they?" asked Mariah softly beside him. "The woman, I mean."

Cherault broke off abruptly and glared at her for interrupting. Gabriel let his fingers tighten on his sword just enough for Cherault to notice, his eyes widening anxiously.

"The woman is the captain's cousin," explained Gabriel. "Her husband died of a fever, and now she is returning to her family in Bordeaux. Or she was, until we came along."

"Oh, Gabriel, that's so sad! What will become of her?"

"They'll come with us to Bridgetown. There they can make any arrangements they like." With growing apprehension Gabriel saw the sympathy fill Mariah's eyes.

"We've taken everything she has left then, haven't we? All you'll let her keep is what she can carry?"

Damn her for having a tender heart, or at least for having one right now!

"Mariah, I'll treat them civilly enough, but they're my prisoners." He hoped she heard the warning in his voice. "I'll warrant Cherault here wouldn't be treating you so genteel if our places were reversed."

Nor had Deveaux been genteel with poor Catherine....

The boy wriggled tighter against his mother, and the stuffed rabbit tumbled to the deck. At once the boy began to scream, pointing and waving at the dropped toy. To Gabriel's dismay Mariah was the one who darted forward to retrieve the rabbit and place it in the child's chubby hand. The Frenchwoman smiled timidly at Mariah, who smiled warmly in return.

"*Mariah.*" His voice was icy cold with anger. He wouldn't have any ship of his turned into a she-house. Already he could sense the change in the French sailors, clearly wondering if they'd misjudged the Englishmen, and his own crew, too, was shifting uneasily where they stood, worrying and doubting about whether their captain had turned soft. What kind of faith could they put in a man ruled by a woman's niceties?

Mariah turned toward him, her eyes full of wounded surprise, but she didn't come.

"Mariah, remember that you are a loyal subject of King George," rumbled Gabriel, "and bring your English backside over here now!"

Her chin shot up defiantly, but thank God she came. Gabriel could tease her all he wanted about flogging her for disobedience, but he wasn't sure what he'd have done if she'd flagrantly crossed him before his men.

He looked across to the *Marie-Claire,* where the carpenter and the others had finished their repairs and were rowing back to the *Revenge.* He beckoned curtly to the first mate.

"Farr, you'll give up your quarters to m'dame until we reach Bridgetown. Take her and Captain Cherault below and make them as comfortable as possible. Parker, you—"

"No!"

Stunned, Gabriel stared at Mariah, her fury a match for his. The first moment they were alone he'd turn her over his knee and thrash her like the obstinate child she was.

"No, Gabriel, I won't be party to *stealing* from that poor woman," she declared, her eyes narrowed and each word clipped. "She can stay on her ship with her baby and her belongings and go to Newport. I don't care how the French would treat me. All I know is how I'd feel if someone came and ordered me out of my cabin and stole every last precious thing that my poor dead husband had given me! I won't do it, Gabriel, and neither will you, because I own this sloop and I won't allow it!"

Jesus Christ, the little fool was trying to pull rank on him! Before she could make it any worse, Gabriel bent down, grabbed her around the knees and flipped her over his shoulder. Awkwardly she dangled down his back, her small, bare, pink feet kicking furiously against his chest.

"I've changed my mind, Rawson," he said over Mariah's outraged shrieks, loud enough for the whole gawking, grinning company to hear. "One bitch's yapping is enough for me. Send m'dame and her brat and a Frenchman of her choosing to tend her, back to the *Marie-Claire*. Stow Cherault and the rest of them below wherever you can."

"How dare you call me a bitch, you cowardly, blackhearted, thieving rogue!" With one hand Mariah struggled to hold her hair out of her face while with the other she clung to his coat, worrying that he might dump her with as little warning as he'd plucked her from the deck. She kicked at him again. He began down the companionway, the narrow steps swaying dizzily beneath her. "Damn you, Gabriel, put me down now!"

"Once I set you down, you foolish chit, and you see what I've in mind, you'll be begging me to pick you up again." He shoved open the cabin door with his shoulder and tossed her on her back onto the bunk.

Mariah landed with an indignant yelp, skirts and hair flying. She yanked her skirts over her bare knees as she scuttled against the bulkhead, her eyes glowing with rage. "Begging you, indeed! I wouldn't waste my wind begging you to do anything decent or gentlemanly!"

"Then you won't be disappointed, will you?" Breathing hard, he unbuckled his sword belt and let it drop clattering to the deck, then pulled his arms free of his coat and let it, too, fall into a heap. "You with all your orders, wagging your finger at me like some kind of preacher in petticoats! You'd unman me before my own crew!"

She watched as he tore off his waistcoat, buttons spinning across the deck. No doubt his breeches would be next. Deep down beneath her anger she realized she'd pushed him too far, and she didn't care. No, more than that—she was glad. She'd rather have him shouting at her than more of that awful, icy silence. "Since when has basic kindness become such a sin?"

"Sin, for all love! I'll show you sin, Mariah, and by God, I'll make you thank me for it!"

He lunged across the bunk and grabbed her ankles. She twisted and fought to free herself of his grasp, but he easily jerked her over the coverlet in one rough motion, leaving her with her skirts rucked up and her legs sprawled over the edge of the bunk.

"Let me go, Gabriel!" As she struggled to wriggle past him, he swiftly trapped her beneath his body.

"Nay, Mariah, no more orders. There's only one master on board this ship, and it's not you."

Unable to move, she lay still beneath him, her heart pounding, his face so close above hers that she felt his breath hot upon her face. He made no effort to hide the raw hunger in his eyes, hunger that she knew was mirrored in her own, just as her own lips were already parted, waiting for him to take her surrender.

"Cap'n Sparhawk, sir, Cap'n, there be another ship bearin' down on us two points t'the—ah, Mary, Joseph and all the saints!"

In an instant Gabriel was on his feet, shielding Mariah as best he could from the gaping eyes of Israel Talbot. Damn him ten times for a fool for not taking the time to shut and latch the cabin door!

"What is it, Talbot?" he demanded, shoving his shirt into his breeches. "This had best be the message of your lifetime or I'll see it's the last."

The fat sailor's chins worked convulsively as he tried not to look at Mariah, scrambling to smooth down her skirts as she clambered off the bunk. "Beggin' pardon, sir, I didn't know, else I never—"

"Spit it out, Talbot!" roared Gabriel.

Talbot took a deep breath, swelling his cherubic cheeks further. "Mr. Farr said tell the cap'n that there's some frigging French bastard—beg pardon, Miss West—bearing down on us two points on the larboard, south-southeast. Said he's sure as he be of his own mother that the Frenchman be a frigate bent on taking back the *Marie-Claire,* and that you'd best come directly."

Swearing to himself, Gabriel snatched up his sword belt again and rushed past Talbot, taking the steps to the deck two at a time. There was the *Marie-Claire,* only just beginning to make sail and bring her nose around north toward Rhode Island, the red-and-blue flag of King George flying proudly over King Louis's fleur-de-lis. But to the south was the ship Farr had guessed was French, as well, and Gabriel didn't even need his glass to see the first mate was right. She was bearing down on the *Revenge* and the *Marie-Claire* with every bit of canvas set, and the double rows of black squares along her sides each framing a gun.

He knew his first capture had been too easy. To face a French frigate with such a green crew would be madness, but if he ran, they'd retake the *Marie-Claire* and he'd lose both the prize and her crew— not an auspicious beginning to any cruise. Gabriel's brows drew together. He didn't like giving up anything that was his, and he'd never yet run from a fight. And it didn't have to be a real engagement, anyway, only a few disabling shots, a few quick dodges here and there, to buy the *Marie-Claire* time to escape before he, too, turned on his heels and fled. He had the wind in his favor, the sloop was lighter, faster than any frigate afloat, and he had more daring than any Frenchman he'd yet to meet.

His gaze swept across the *Revenge*'s immaculate deck, imagining the carnage and destruction there that could follow his decision, and what might become of the men who trusted him with their lives. Damnation, he *was* getting soft! Every man who'd signed on with him knew the risks and had weighed them for himself against the possible gains.

Every man had, but not the single woman.

Mariah stood with her back to the mainmast, her hands holding tight to the pin rack. Against the dark tangle of her hair her face was pale in the bright sun, her mouth tight-lipped and her eyes wide, and all the fire of her anger and desire had vanished. She looked very small and very young, and for the first time he could remember, very frightened.

"You're going to fight a frigate," she said, a statement, not a question.

"You can't stay here," he said, avoiding answering what she wasn't asking. "You must go below, not to the cabin, but lower, into the hold. I'll have one of the men take you if you wish."

She clung a little tighter to the pin rack as her body swayed unconsciously toward him. "You're going to let yourself be killed."

"You'll be safe enough below." Gently he pried her fingers free, noticing how cold her hands were. "Go now. I'll come to you when it's done."

"If you still live." She pulled her hands free of his. "You're a fool, Gabriel Sparhawk."

Unexpectedly he smiled, the warmth of it twisting into her heart. "I'd never have brought you with me otherwise, would I? Take care, poppet."

She turned and left him before she wept, before she became the fool and told Gabriel Sparhawk how much she loved him.

Mariah sat deep in the hold, huddled on the broad, curving side of a water cask. The lantern with the single candle gave little light and less comfort as she tried to imagine what was happening two decks above her. She had lost count of the times the long guns were fired, each broadside sending a shudder through the sloop that she could feel clear down here, and she was sure they'd been hit, in return. There had been explosions of a different kind, and screams of pain mingled with the shouting. She squeezed her eyes tightly, wishing she could close her ears, as well. She'd never thought of men screaming, especially not any of the men she knew on the *Revenge,* some she'd known all her life.

And Gabriel. God in heaven, what had become of Gabriel, standing so proudly on his quarterdeck, his height and size an easy mark for any Frenchman? He wouldn't scream. He would swear, spending his last breath cursing. No, she wouldn't think of it. He couldn't die. He wouldn't. He was too large and strong and full of life and he'd survived worse than this before. And he'd promised her he'd come for her.

Just as Daniel had promised he'd come back....

She forced her thoughts away. She guessed from how the sloop's speed had been cut that she'd been hit at least once up high, with a mast or some of the standing rigging carried away. More crashes, more shouts and the sharp crack of splintering wood, and then, suddenly, no sounds beyond the usual creaks and groans of the timbers around her. Whatever had happened must now be done. The relative silence proved that.

Her heart was still pounding, and she didn't realize how tightly she had curled herself until she tried to stand and every tensed muscle screamed in protest. She had no idea how long she'd been hidden away—one hour or six, a day and a night? They were still afloat, and they were still moving through the water, so she guessed that they'd escaped the way Gabriel had hoped.

But where in God's name *was* Gabriel? He had told her to wait here until he came for her, but what if he couldn't? What if he was wounded, delirious from pain, dying while she hung here below, doing nothing but waiting? He'd always called her brave, his brave, fierce poppet. Hot tears stung behind her eyes as she remembered how he teased her. She wouldn't disappoint him by being a coward now, when he might need her most.

Carrying the lantern, she slowly felt her way across the stacked barrels to the ladder. With her skirts looped over one arm and the lantern in the other, she climbed clumsily up the rungs through the gloom to the berth deck, and nearly collided with Dr. Macauly. She gasped as she saw by the lantern light how his coat was rusty with blood, his hands stained bright red as he thrust a basin of dark water at one of the ship's boys for him to carry away.

"Och, Miss West, is it finally! Come along, lass, I've need of another pair of hands." He grasped her by the shoulder with no regard for the bloody fingerprints he left on her gown and steered her aft along the passageway. "You know well as I that Captain Sparhawk ships no idlers."

"Where is the captain?" she asked breathlessly.

"I've not seen the man this day, lass." In the heat he had left off his wig when he'd been called to quarters, and the bristly stubble of his close-cropped hair gleamed as he shook his head. "Rejoice that he hasn't come across my platform, but that's not to say they haven't tossed him over the side. The butcher's bill today is as steep as ever I've seen on a Sparhawk ship."

Mariah's heart refused to accept the possibility of Gabriel dead, Gabriel's body unceremoniously thrown overboard, Gabriel never to be seen or held or kissed or loved again in this life.

He had promised to come for her....

Numb, she let Macauly lead her from the passage to the makeshift surgery in the cable tier, made bright with thick candles. With a little cry of horror Mariah recoiled, backing into Macauly's chest. The surgeon's mate was sluicing down the bloody planks laid on barrels that served as the platform for operations, and spread along one side were saws and hooks and needles that looked more suited to mending furniture than men. Two seamen gently laid a third onto the planks, a young man writhing in pain, his face dead white and beaded with sweat, his left arm hanging from the elbow at an unnatural angle, and all of him soaked with blood.

"Big splinter caught 'im, sir," said the first seaman, his face twisted with apprehension. "'E be a topman, sir, so 'e begs ye special not t'take 'is arm."

Wearily Macauly stepped forward, ripping off what was left of the man's sleeve and ignoring his screams while his two companions held him still. The mate tried to pour the draft of rum to deaden the pain into the young man's mouth, but weakly he twisted his head away.

"Come now, laddie, drink up," coaxed Macauly as he held the man's jaw steady.

"No, don't force him!" said Mariah, stepping forward to look down at the wounded man. "He's a Quaker, a Friend, and it goes against his faith to drink spirits."

Macauly snorted. "Queer sort of Quaker that's too nice for a tot of rum, but takes to killing his brethren on a privateer. You know the poor lad, then?"

"George Clarke's his name, and yes, he lives on the next street from mine." Mariah looked at him and saw Gabriel's face instead, Gabriel's body lying broken and bloody. Lord, she'd seen more spilled blood in the past few minutes than in her entire life.

"Then come sit here near his head and talk pretty nonsense to him to take his thoughts from the pain. If he won't take the rum, you're all he'll have. Be lively at it, lass, the man's suffering!"

Mariah swallowed hard, forcing herself to turn her back to George Clarke's mangled arm and concentrate instead on his face. His eyes were closed, his mouth working convulsively, wordlessly.

"George, it's Mariah, Mariah West from Water Street. I played dollies with your sister Sara." She thought he might have shifted his head toward her voice, and she plunged onward. "Mr. Macauly here is going to do everything he can for you, George. Most privateers don't have a surgeon, but Gabriel wanted the best for his men. Gabriel will see that you're well looked after, no matter what happens."

The tears were sliding down her cheeks now, falling on the stained planks beside George Clarke's pale face. She wept for him, and for Gabriel, and for Daniel, and for herself. Dear God, look what had become of them all!

"Mariah, I ask thee, do not tell my mother I sailed for thee—for thee and Gabriel Sparhawk," gasped George. "Thee—I—would not give her that sorrow."

As she touched her hand to his cheek he stiffened suddenly, his face contorted and then relaxed. Behind her Macauly grunted with satisfaction as the splinter pulled clear of the muscle.

"There now, I've but to bind up the break and then back to his hammock he'll go," he said as he dropped the foot-long splinter into the bucket beside him. "Though it's best that he's lost consciousness before I set the fracture."

"No, Mr. Macauly," said Mariah, her voice wavering upward. "He's dead."

She took her hand from George's cheek and pressed it across her mouth as the doctor searched for a pulse and found none. As if from a great distance she heard Macauly sigh with resignation, and explain sorrowfully to the others that the shock to his heart had carried the poor lad off. She closed her eyes, searching for the strength to pray, to hope, to be as brave as Gabriel had told her she was.

"Mariah!" At once Gabriel's exhaustion and grief vanished, forgotten in his concern for her. She was sobbing, huddled on the deck at Macauly's feet, and she was covered with blood. "Lord, Mariah, are you hurt? I've gone mad trying to find you, but I didn't think to look here."

Swiftly he raised her up into his arms, and she stared at him with disbelief before she buried her face against his chest, clinging to him as if she'd never let go.

Macauly snorted. "Don't go looking like someone tried to drown your kitten, Cap'n. The girl's fine. More'n fine."

"Then why the devil is she here?"

"I found her wandering 'tween decks. The blood's poor Clarke's, not hers, and she brought a sight more comfort to his dying than I could."

Gabriel swore softly as he looked down at the young man's body, his arm tightening protectively around Mariah. He'd meant to spare her this. He loved the exhilaration of battle, the wild excitement that came when he'd bettered another, but even after so much fighting, so many ships captured, he'd never become hardened to the sight of men, young men like George Clarke, who'd died because they'd followed him. What must an innocent like Mariah make of this kind of slaughter?

"How many others, Macauly?"

The surgeon began wiping his instruments clean with a rag. "Six brought down dead, two died under the knife—nay, three, including this one, six I've kept below and eleven more sent back to their hammocks."

Gabriel nodded grimly. Thank God it wasn't worse. "I've already visited the wounded. I thank you, Andrew, for all you've done for them."

"The shares mean more to me, Cap'n." Shrewdly he glanced at Gabriel from beneath his bushy eyebrows. "I'll warrant you took the day? Saved that pretty prize?"

Trust the surgeon to be the most mercenary man on board. "Aye, the *Marie-Claire*'s safe enough, and we left the *Macedonia* licking her wounds, foremast and mainmast gone and a ball through her side. I'll warrant her captain won't be tempted by another Englishman any time soon.''

Mariah's sobs had stopped, but still she kept her face hidden, and he could feel how she trembled in his arms. He'd kept her waiting long enough.

"Give me a full report on the wounded in the morning, Andrew," he said as he bent down to lift Mariah, one arm beneath her knees, and cradle her. She lay there limply, with none of the fight and fire she'd shown when he'd carried her over his shoulder earlier. God, had it really been this same day?

Macauly shrugged. "Och. There's nothing I can't tell you now, if you—"

"In the morning," repeated Gabriel firmly. "Not before."

He took her to the cabin and sat her on the bunk, and this time, he remembered to close and latch the door after them. He poured her a glass of rum and placed it firmly in her hands.

"Drink this now, poppet," he ordered, and as he stood over her, hands at his waist, she did, coughing only once at the bite of the liquor. He took the glass and bent before her so their eyes were level. Gently he smoothed her hair from her face. "Are you certain you're unharmed, Mariah?"

She nodded, breaking her gaze from his to look at her clasped hands, letting her hair fall on either side of her face like a curtain to hide behind. She had been so certain he'd died that the relief of having him back, alive and touching her so gently, was almost overwhelming.

With a sigh, he rose and pulled his filthy shirt over his head. Mariah watched as he bent over the washbowl, his legs spread wide against the sloop's roll, pouring pitcherfuls of water over his head and shoulders as he scrubbed away the black smudges of gunpowder and the blotches of other men's blood. The water highlighted the pattern of his muscles, droplets glistening in the dark hair of his chest and arms and on the pale crisscross of the old scars. How had he managed to escape unmarked today while others around him had been maimed or killed? She thought again of the surgery and shuddered, the rum churning uneasily in her empty stomach.

"I thought you were dead," she said so softly that he turned expectantly, waiting for her to repeat it.

She lifted her chin and shook her hair, her hands twisting in her lap. "When you didn't come, I thought you were dead."

"But I did come, didn't I, poppet?" He smiled, coaxing her to trust in him. "As soon as I could. And I most certainly didn't die."

With the bowl in his hands, he came again to kneel before her. He dipped the towel into the water and carefully began to wipe away the grime from her tear-streaked face. The water was cool, his touch gentle, and she felt the tension and fear that still coiled within her begin to slip away.

"We won, you know," he said. He trailed the damp cloth down her throat and lower, across the tops of her breasts, and she shivered from the mixture of sensations, the cool water on her warm skin, the roughness of the cloth. "You haven't asked, but as owner, you should be pleased. We had to jury-rig the foremast, but we're only a few days from Bridgetown."

He took her hands in his and lowered them into the water. With bayberry soap he washed away the blood from the surgery, forcing her hands to relax as he slid the soap between her fingers, working them between his own. In his hands her own looked like a child's, tiny and pink, the tips wrinkling from the water.

"This whole long day, you were always in my thoughts," he said quietly. "I missed you. Though I knew you had to be safe, when I couldn't find you I nearly finished what the French had begun and tore the sloop apart."

"You came for me." She smiled slowly, the first time since he'd found her. She lifted her hand to touch his face, water trickling down her wrist. "You said you would, and you did."

"Aye," he whispered hoarsely, turning his lips to meet her soft, moist palm. "Now try to keep me away."

Chapter Nine

"How could I ever send you away?" asked Mariah softly, smiling shyly as his lips nibbled at her palm, his beard rough and his mouth gentle, and her heartbeat already beginning to quicken. She had always thought of kissing as a pastime confined to lips, but with Gabriel she was rapidly learning how little she knew about what passed between men and women and how much he could teach her. "You've never yet given up your cabin to me."

She turned her hand to stroke his jaw lightly, with just her fingertips, too unsure of herself to dare more. With the gunpowder soot cleaned away from his face, she could see the lines of weariness etched deep into his features, the grief for the men he'd lost that tugged his mouth downward even as he smiled at her in return. What she had seen today was nothing compared with what had been a part of his life for years. Too many years. He had first made war on the Spanish when she was scarcely more than a baby, and again she felt the gap in their ages yawn between them.

"You tried to warn me before we left Newport that we'd be in danger," she continued. "I didn't want to hear it. You were right, I did behave like a spoiled child."

"Ah, poppet, you're not so very wicked." He liked how she touched his face. He wanted very much for her to touch the rest of him the same way, but he didn't want to frighten her. "Though I've given much thought to flipping you over my knee with your skirts turned up."

Her fingers stilled on his jaw. She frowned, trying to look stern even as she blushed. "*I* may not be very wicked, Gabriel, but you are."

"True enough." His smile faded and the teasing left his eyes. Pleasurable though it was, he owed her more than banter. "I'm sorry, Mariah, for Macauly and the surgery, what you saw and all the rest. I'd meant to spare you that. If you'd only stayed in the hold—"

"I couldn't." By the candlelight, her eyes were troubled, so dark beneath the lashes they were almost black. "I feared for you. If you'd been hurt, I wanted to be there with you. That's why I was there with poor George Clarke."

"Few men are so fortunate to die with a lady's hand on their cheek to bring them peace."

She shook her head sadly. "No, Gabriel, you don't understand. I'm not that *good*. I was looking at George, and I saw you. I told you I feared for you."

She saw *him,* not her Daniel, and he discovered that he cared that she had, cared a surprising, alarming amount. The plain truth, if he'd admit it, was that he cared for her and everything about her.

"We're quite a pair, Mariah West," he said softly. He took both her hands in his, rubbing her palms with his thumbs before he drew them forward and placed them on his chest. He watched as she swallowed, her serious gaze following her hands to his chest. "Fighting and worrying seem to be all we're capable of doing together."

"Not quite." Beneath her fingers she could feel his heart racing at the same insane pace as her own. She scarcely noticed when her lips parted on their own as her breathing grew ragged, or how the cabin seemed to have grown warmer and warmer despite the stern windows open to the evening breezes. She only knew that touching him, learning his body, fascinated her. Still trapped beneath his hands, her fingers flexed against his chest and tangled in the dark, curling hair. Slowly she slid her hands free of his and upward, across his shoulders, exploring his body even as she wondered at her boldness.

She lowered her eyes, reluctant to let him see her uncertainty. Though she longed to show him how much he meant to her, the memory of how badly she'd blundered with him that night at the mill haunted her, the painful politeness he'd shown to her as he'd driven her back to Newport. She didn't want that to happen again. Miserably she thought of the tall, beautiful Dutch woman in the amber dressing gown who'd so clearly been Gabriel's last mistress at Crescent Hill. *She* would have known how to please him.

"Oh, Gabriel, forgive me," she said forlornly, her chin dropping lower against her chest with shame. "I don't really know what comes next."

"If it's any solace to you, sweetheart, neither do I." Could she truly have so little notion of how potently charged her inexperience was to him? He could think of nothing beyond how he wanted to lose himself deep in all that blessed innocence, deep in her small, lush body. He wanted to forget who he was and what he was and the death he'd brought today with his orders, forget everything except his pretty little poppet.

"Would you please hold me then, Gabriel?" she asked in a whisper. "Hold me and—and kiss me like you did before?"

His body tensed and hardened with the unspoken promise in that tiny plea. But as he rose to his feet and lifted her with him, her hands still linked trustingly around his neck, he couldn't help but wonder if she realized the extent of what she was offering.

He lay her on the pillows beneath him, her face small and serious against the dark cloud of her hair, her cheeks already flushed with a desire he was sure she didn't yet fully comprehend. But he did. Though she couldn't know, his experience told him this was going to be different from what he'd shared with any other woman. Very, very different, and he couldn't wait.

"This time I won't stop at kissing, Mariah," he said, the shaky control he had on himself making his voice harsh. "Not now, not after today."

"What makes you think I'd want you to?" Carefully she traced one finger back and forth across his chin. His wet hair slipped forward across his face. A single droplet of water fell on her cheek, and she smiled crookedly. He had barely touched her at all, yet already she felt the warmth building in her body. "I could have lost you forever today. Tomorrow's no more certain. Now, here with you, is the only sure thing I have."

"Now?" He kissed her lightly, his lips barely brushing over hers as his wet hair grazed her cheek.

"*Now.*" Impatiently she arched up to claim what he'd so teasingly offered. At once his mouth crushed down on hers, the hunger they'd held back for so long too fierce to deny any longer. The fire she remembered returned to burn in her blood, and the dizzying heat only increased as his tongue swept deeper into her mouth. She clutched at his shoulders, her fingers digging deep into the hard muscles as she twisted beneath him. He was so much larger than she was, so much stronger, and she loved the feel of the length of his body pressed against hers.

She threaded her fingers through the wet black silk of his hair and pulled him closer, savoring the taste of him. She felt his hand slide along her side to find her breast, cupping her fullness through her gown. He made a growling noise deep in his throat before he lifted his mouth only a fraction from hers to whisper, "You've too many layers for me, love." He shifted his weight to one side and began to unlace the front of her bodice, his long fingers deftly tugging the cording free of the eyelets.

"You've done this before," she noted breathlessly, faintly accusing, her eyes never leaving his. She shrugged herself free of the sleeves and shoved the bodice off the bunk, then wriggled out of her skirt once he'd untied the waistband for her. "You're more accomplished than most ladies' maids."

"A useful skill for an impatient man," he murmured as he ran his tongue lightly around the pink shell of her ear. "And I *am* impatient."

In her hurry to dress earlier she'd left off her stays, and now only the thin linen of her shift lay between her breasts and his chest. Gently he rubbed his palms across the darker tips of her breasts through the linen, feeling how they tightened and peaked at once and how the pulse at the base of her throat quickened. The girlish simplicity of her shift, with her initials cross-stitched neatly at the neckline, touched him, so much at odds with her passion-clouded eyes and lips swollen from his kisses. In Bridgetown he'd buy her a shift of the sheerest, finest cambric he could find, trimmed with lace and silk ribbons, a shift fit for the woman she would this night become.

He hooked his thumb in the shift's neckline, easing it farther down over her breasts as he let his nail brush across her skin. She shivered with the sensation, sighing restlessly. "That's not fair, Gabriel. I can be impatient, too."

Feeling impossibly daring, she trailed her hands along his chest, down lower across his belly until she reached the buttons at the fall of his breeches. She grinned with gleeful triumph, but her fingers lacked his expertise and he soon was forced to complete what she'd begun. As he turned and stripped off his breeches, Mariah pulled her shift over her head, swiftly, before she lost her nerve. She'd never been naked before anyone, woman or man, since she'd been a child, and she'd never in her life seen a man without his clothes. But when he turned toward her, she forgot her shyness, lost instead in the sight of him. Nowhere on earth, she decided as she held her arms open to him, could there be a more beautiful man, and tonight he was hers to love.

Now when he lay with her, there was nothing between them, no barriers to dull the sensation of her breasts against the rough hair on his chest or to hinder his hands as they roamed the length of her body. Everywhere he touched she felt her skin burn and the ache low in her belly grow, and when he kissed her now there was only a raw urgency that made her cling feverishly to him. When he moved between her thighs her legs parted naturally for him, and when he touched her, sliding across her wet, swollen heat, she gasped, her eyes wide as she arched against him. Swiftly he lowered himself to meet her, and instinctively her legs curled around his back, drawing him deeper.

With his last bit of conscious thought, Gabriel prayed her pain would not be great then drove deeply into her. She whimpered and hugged him tighter, while he forced himself to be still so she could accustom herself to him.

''There, poppet, it's done,'' he gasped, kissing her quivering, closed eyelids. ''My fine, brave Mariah.''

She was so hot, so sweet around him, that long moments passed before he realized her whimpers were from pleasure, not pain, and the subtle rocking of her hips was urging him onward, not struggling to escape.

And that though innocent she always seemed, there'd been no maidenhead, no final barrier to block his way.

Then he felt her thighs tighten around his waist, and he thought of nothing beyond the incredible need she raised in him. His thrusts were as relentless as her passion as she moved with him, her small body as fevered and fierce as his own as together they reached for the pleasure each could only give to the other. When the peak came and he felt the unbelievable intensity of his release, she was there with him, her wild, broken cries the most beautiful sound he'd ever heard as she twined herself around him. In that moment he could pretend that nothing else mattered in the world except Mariah West, and that that world was the finest he could ever imagine.

Afterward he rolled over onto his back, pulling her with him. She lay peacefully sprawled over his body, her cheek over his heart and her breathing regular. Only the way she rubbed her left thigh gently over and over against his hip in a caress that he found incredibly erotic told him she was awake. Because the edge was gone from his hunger he could savor her touch and know that next time the pleasure would be all the greater for waiting. He wasn't in any particular rush. The whole night lay before them. Drowsily he wondered what the men would think if he kept to his cabin until they reached Bridgetown.

She sighed, and her leg stilled against him. "You knew, didn't you?" she said softly, her words muffled against his chest.

He sighed, too. Of course he'd known, but he hadn't expected her to feel obliged to ask. "Daniel?"

"I'm sorry." From the way she kept her cheek plastered to his chest he suspected she was crying, and trying to hide it from him. He didn't know which was worse, that she was weeping after she'd brought him the most intense response he'd ever experienced, or that she didn't trust him enough to see her tears.

"Ah, sweetheart, what's there to be sorry for?" He tried to stroke her hair to comfort her, but she shook his hand away.

"I'm sorry because I let you believe I was—was otherwise than I was."

"Believe me, Mariah, when I say it doesn't matter." She might not have been a virgin, but he'd stake his life that he'd given her her first taste of pleasure, and to him that seemed the greater gift. "I haven't exactly come to you blameless."

"But for gentlemen it's different!" she cried with anguish. "It was only once, Gabriel, I swear, and only Daniel."

"I'd guessed that, too, sweetheart." Gently he rubbed his knuckles along her spine, and she sighed, a great, shuddering, heartbroken sigh. "That first time wasn't like tonight, was it?"

"Daniel isn't—wasn't—you," she said sorrowfully. "He had asked my father for my hand, and Father and Mama both said he was beneath me, that I was too young besides, and forbade me to see him. But I did, because I loved him. I promised I'd marry him, no matter what my parents said. The night before he sailed away for the last time, I let him do what he wished. I thought if he got me with child, then they'd have to let us wed."

Mentally Gabriel cursed himself. The women he usually took to his bed were a worldly lot who knew enough to protect themselves. Mariah wouldn't. He fondly called her his poppet, but she was old enough to share his passion, old enough to conceive his child. Next time, for her sake, he'd have to be more careful.

"I liked the kissing well enough," she continued, "but after that..." She trailed off, unwilling to be faithless to Daniel's memory. God knows she'd betrayed him badly enough with Gabriel already without sharing every detail of their brief intimacy.

Not that there was so much to tell. She had met Daniel behind the hedgerow in back of the Baptist Meetinghouse. When she showed herself willing, he'd been so eager she hardly realized what was happening until she was on her back in the wet grass with her skirts crumpled and Daniel crushing her, hurting her, and there'd been splotches of blood on her petticoats along with the grass stains.

The best part had come afterward, when he'd held her and told her about the house he planned to buy them once they were married. Then he'd left with the tide and taken all her dreams with him.

But her few terse words told everything to Gabriel. "Ah, poppet, lovemaking is definitely one of the things that improves with practice," he said gently. "Despite what the poets say, the first time's seldom sweet for the lady."

"With you it probably would have been." She smiled wistfully, wary enough not to mistake his lovemaking for any sort of declaration. "No wonder the ladies are so fond of you."

"There's only one lady I want fond of me now." He took her by the shoulders and pulled her up along the length of his body to kiss her, and the sound that rose from deep in her throat was filled with contentment.

He was so much older, so much more experienced. Perhaps every woman he'd been with had felt the same fire when he'd kissed her, the same delirious fever from his touch. For her, with Gabriel, everything was different and new. He hadn't hurt her the way Daniel had, even though he was so much larger. Instead he'd made her whole body sing with joy, taking her places she'd never dreamed existed outside of God's own heaven. A little flush of pleasure surged through her again at the memory alone.

When she came to Crescent Hill, all she'd seen was how handsome he was, every inch the charming rogue the gossips described. She hadn't known him the way she did now, how he could be thoughtful, and maddening, and tender, and passionate, and furiously angry, and kinder, when he let himself, than a pack of softhearted old spinsters. She couldn't have known at Crescent Hill because she hadn't loved him then, but God help her, how she loved him now!

She pulled back from his mouth, propping herself up on his chest to study him. Fondly he smiled at her, his teeth white against his dark, unshaven jaw, and she felt the ache of love and desire deep within her. But beneath her fingers she could feel the uneven ridge of the long scar across Gabriel's body, and she thought of the young man she'd watched die. How much longer could Gabriel's luck keep him from the same fate?

"I *wanted* you to know, Gabriel," she said softly, "so you'd understand. All I had with Daniel was that one night. I needed to have at least that much with you."

"I understand, sweetheart." And understand he did, with a painful empathy she'd never know. He'd never had even that single night with Catherine. Mariah wasn't asking for more than this, but to his confusion he realized he was. He looked at her, her lips red and inviting from his kisses, her tangled, dark hair barely covering her breasts, her round young body lying so intimately across his own, and he tried to tell himself what he felt for her was lust alone. A week or two, he argued, and he would be done with her, the way he was with all the others. He'd see that she and her sister were both sent safely back to Newport, he'd kiss her farewell on the wharf and that would be the end of it.

But somehow he knew already that wouldn't be enough. He couldn't tell what would. He wanted her with him not just in bed but at his side. He liked how she spoke her mind, even at the most inconvenient times, and how she could make him laugh and how he could tease her. He liked her quick wit, how she listened so he didn't have to explain things twice to her, and he liked her courage and her loyalty, fine, rare things in a woman. He didn't want to send her back to Newport. He wanted her here.

The same way he'd wanted Catherine with him on board the old *Rose*. Recklessly, selfishly he'd let her come with him, and look what had happened.

He closed his eyes against the memory, his arm tightening protectively around Mariah's narrow waist. He wouldn't take that risk again, not with his pretty poppet. Today had been warning enough. He would leave her safe in Bridgetown, with his parents, until the old score with Deveaux was settled. Then, only then, when he'd cut the last of the old pain from his heart, would he be free to begin again with Mariah.

She curled closer into his body, guessing that he'd fallen asleep, and pulled the coverlet over them both. "I love you, Gabriel Sparhawk," she whispered softly, knowing he wouldn't hear her. "You won't leave me."

But already he was thinking of Bridgetown.

"Wake up, Jen!" whispered Elisha urgently. "Something's wrong, I swear it. Listen!"

Disoriented, Jenny rolled over in the narrow bunk and tried to focus on Elisha's anxious face, the lantern he held too bright for her sleepy eyes. "It's the middle of the night, Elisha," she grumbled, and pulled the coverlet higher over her shoulders.

"Nay, Jen, you must get dressed!" He tore the coverlet back as she squealed with protest. "The *Felicity*'s hove to, stopped dead, and I swear I heard men speaking French on deck. Hurry, lamb, hurry!"

"French!" Frightened into action, Jenny tumbled from the bunk and began to pull on her gown over her shift. Remembering Mariah's plans for the *Revenge*, she'd once tentatively asked Captain Richardson if the *Felicity* was in any danger from French privateers, but he'd only laughed and patted her cheek indulgently, promising that the war was still too new for the French to have outfitted any vessels. She would have done better listening to her sister. "Here, Elisha, help lace me up! Oh, please God we haven't been captured!"

He hooked the lantern on the edge of the bunk as she turned her back to him, lifting her hair clear with both hands. "Quit your wiggling, Jen, or I'll never get—"

The door to the tiny cabin exploded inward, followed by the bearded man whose shoulder had forced the hinges. He wore brass hoop earrings and canvas trousers and a rough calimanco waistcoat with no shirt beneath it, and in his hand was a cutlass, the steel guard battered but the blade polished and gleaming. Jenny shrieked, and Elisha shoved her behind him, cursing himself for being caught without a weapon.

"Do whatever they say, lad," stammered Captain Richardson from the companionway. Another unfamiliar seaman kept the captain's arms pinned behind his back and held a long-bladed knife across his throat as he shoved him forward to the cabin's doorway. His wig was knocked askew, and Richardson's throat quivered against the blade, his round face gleaming with perspiration. "There's no help for it that I can see. They have the ship."

Jenny whimpered, clutching at Elisha's waist.

"What a wellspring of information you are tonight, Richardson!" said a third man, bemused, as he smiled from the shadows at Elisha and

Jenny. He was different from the other two, slightly built but a gentleman, from his three-cornered hat to the cut steel buckles on his shoes, and his English bore only a hint of an accent. He, too, carried a sword, but on his the hilt was bright with wrapped gold wire, the guard enamelled in red and blue. He tapped the blade twice on the shattered door. "So this is the young lady in question, eh?"

"Miss West's none of your affair, you thieving French pirate!" said Elisha furiously. Deep down he knew he didn't have a chance against three armed men, but he couldn't bear to let them harm his Jenny. "You all just clear off and let her be, the lot of you!"

"*Écoutez-moi,* boy, I intend her no harm," said the gentleman, clucking his tongue. "Though your gallantry is quite touching, considering how you've absconded with her."

"I mean to marry her, damn you!" Elisha began to step forward, and the bearded man raised his sword.

"No, Elisha, don't!" Frantically Jenny grabbed at Elisha's sleeve and tried to hold him back. She'd rather die herself than have anything happen to him. "Don't let them kill you!"

"Listen to her, boy," said the gentleman. "She's right, we will kill you if we must. There's four Englishmen dead topsides who'd I'd fancy rather wished they'd had such a warning. Now, *mademoiselle,* if I might ask you to show yourself, eh?''

Elisha shook his head, lifting his arms to shield her. "Nay, Jen, keep back, stay where you are."

But Jenny slipped beneath his arm to stand before him in the lantern's light, clutching the open back of her bodice with one hand. She'd comply even if Elisha wouldn't. Her modesty wasn't worth his life.

Richardson coughed nervously. "I told you she was a beauty, captain, didn't I? Think what the sister must be like if Sparhawk left this one behind!"

The gentleman clicked his tongue again, frowning. "You talk too much, Richardson." He stepped closer to Jenny, into the light himself, and Jenny gasped. He should have been a handsome man, with high cheekbones and pale blue eyes, but the left side of his face was horribly scarred by a long, ragged seam that ran from beneath his powdered wig to the edge of his jaw and pulled the lid of his left eye half-closed. With the flat of his sword he lightly touched Jenny's arm. "What's your name, *mademoiselle?*"

Jenny recoiled from the cold blade on her skin. "Jenny West." She tried to swallow her fear, thinking how her sister would handle a man like this. Mariah always knew what to say. "And it doesn't matter what Captain Richardson's told you about Mariah. She's all the way back in Newport, safe where you'll never find her.''

"Indeed." The scar twisted his smile downward, robbing it of any warmth.

Eagerly Richardson inched forward again. "I told you where you'll find the other girl, captain. I told you how Sparhawk took—"

"Captain Richardson, I grow weary of you and your faithlessness," said the French gentleman. "Consider what sorrow your chattering will bring to this young lady!"

Confused, Richardson tried to shake his head. "But you—you wanted to know!" he stammered. "You said you'd let me pass unharmed if I told you about the girl!"

"You'd part with your mortal soul to save your cargo, wouldn't you, Richardson?" The Frenchman sighed with resignation. Without taking his gaze from Jenny, he raised his left hand in a slight, dismissive gesture, the cabachon ruby he wore on his little finger glinting red.

Behind him the man holding Richardson pulled the knife smoothly across the English captain's throat. With a spurt of blood and a surprised gurgle, Richardson's knees buckled and he fell to the deck, his wig tipping off his bald head as the life drained from his body. Too shocked to scream, Jenny could only stare in horror at the dead captain's startled, empty eyes, and at the blood that seemed to have no end as it spread across his shirt, his coat, his wig.

"You murdered him, plain as day!" cried Elisha hoarsely. He'd never felt as helpless, or as fearful as he did for Jenny's sake. "Any judge in the colonies would see you hung for that!"

But the French captain ignored him. "Jenny and Mariah, Mariah and Jenny," he said in a musing singsong. "Charming names, charming ladies. But then Gabriel Sparhawk has always had the best of taste. It's a pity your *maman* will lose you both."

Still smiling, he turned away. Swiftly the bearded man lunged forward and struck Elisha on the side of the head with his fist. As Elisha crumpled to the deck beside her, the man seized Jenny and tossed her effortlessly over his shoulder.

"Elisha!" she screamed in terror, clawing at the man's broad back as he carried her from the cabin. Behind her Elisha lay lifeless beside Richardson's body, his yellow hair fanned out on the deck and into the puddled blood from the corpse. "Oh, God, *Elisha!*"

Chapter Ten

"Oh Gabriel, the *Felicity*'s not here!" cried Mariah with disappointment as the Bridgetown pilot brought the *Revenge* safely into Carlisle Bay. She leaned farther over the rail, straining to see if perhaps she'd missed the other Newport ship among the crowd of vessels in the harbor. "I thought after we'd lost so much time with the *Marie-Claire,* they'd surely be here first."

"Not with Richardson for master," said Gabriel, slipping one arm around her waist to guard her from falling overboard. After four weeks at sea she seemed steady enough, but he didn't want to take any chances with her this close to the safety of the town. Besides, with the pilot at the helm, there wasn't much else for him to do, and he welcomed the excuse to feel her in his arms again. Why, at least a full quarter hour must have passed since he'd last kissed her. "We could come limping in with all our sticks jury-rigged and I'd warrant we'd still do better than Richardson. He doesn't like blue water, and creeps and clings his way along the coast like an old lady."

Unconvinced, Mariah turned to face him. "They might have been caught in storms or been taken by another privateer."

"Aye, they might, but most likely they're just slow." He chucked her beneath the chin. "Your sister and her swain will be well enough, and glad enough of the extra days together before they face your wrath."

"I can't very well sit in righteous judgment now, can I?" She grinned ruefully, though she hadn't a single regret for what she'd done. These last days and nights with Gabriel had been the best of her life, and no amount of moral lecturing would convince her otherwise. "I'll see them marry, if they're not already, and bring them back as man and wife. Elisha's been begging to marry her for months, and Jenny could do far worse. That wasn't what Mama wanted, I know, but I can't see any other way. No other decent man would have her now, anyway."

Suddenly distant, Gabriel didn't answer, looking instead over her head at the other ships, and miserably she wished her words unspoken. As much as Gabriel seemed to like her, as much as he desired her, not once had he mentioned love, or any sort of arrangement between them that might continue beyond this voyage. She knew it would be that way from the moment she'd met him, and she'd accepted it. All Newport gossiped about how women never lingered in Gabriel Sparhawk's life. Bachelors as old as he didn't suddenly up and marry, especially not with girls nearly half their age, and if she weren't more careful of what she said, he'd probably leave her now. *Leave her.* Just the thought made her begin to panic.

Staring at the town and seeing nothing, Gabriel told himself he shouldn't have been surprised, but still, somehow, he'd hoped she'd be different. Chattering on about how her sister must marry. Did she really think that was a subtle way to make him propose? Young as she was, he'd come to expect more from her. It wasn't that he had tired of her. Oh, he still *wanted* Mariah, and often, but he didn't want a wife, not her, not any other woman. He wouldn't make that mistake again. Regardless of what his sister Sarah had warned, no outraged mama with an eye toward his fortune was going to change his mind. With unhappy cynicism, he wondered if Mariah had planned this from the first time she had come to Crescent Hill.

"And what of you, Miss Mariah?" he asked lightly, letting his hand wander intimately from her waist to the underside of her breast. "What will your mother say to you?"

"To me?"

He saw the panic widen her eyes, startled, no doubt, at having her game uncovered. "Aye, you. About me."

"What my mother says won't matter." She lifted her chin higher as she forced herself to meet his eyes, easing herself away from his caress. "Unlike Jenny, I am of age. I can decide my future for myself. And I already have. I swore to Daniel I'd never marry another, and I won't."

For an instant he thought of Catherine, if she would have made a similar vow to him. "All women want husbands."

"If that were true, then why have you found so many of them willing to throw over those self-same husbands to dawdle with you?"

"You wouldn't be content without a husband."

"I'm content enough at present."

Skeptical, he raised one brow. If she *was* content, then he was the reason.

For Mariah, that single raised brow was like spark to dry tinder. "Please remember you weren't the one to 'ruin' me, Captain Sparhawk," she said tartly. "I've no intention of placing that burden on your name. Whatever else you may accuse me of, I am honest."

A sight more honest than he'd been with her, and if she'd slapped him outright she couldn't have shamed him more. Grudgingly he once again admired her courage. He wanted very much to believe her, especially with that intemperate fire in her eyes that he'd come to know so well. "I haven't once doubted your honesty, Mariah."

"No, I suppose you haven't." She sighed deeply, wondering what he'd make of her honesty if she told him truthfully how she felt toward him. She hadn't meant to sound so shrewish.

Self-consciously she took the trailing end of his neckcloth and tucked it through the second buttonhole of his coat, the way she'd seen it done in the fashion pictures of London gentlemen at Madame Lambert's shop. Not that Gabriel—dressed for shore in a dark blue broadcloth suit edged with gold braid, the polished buttons flashing in the sun—couldn't already put every London gentleman to shame. Here on his own quarterdeck he was indisputably confident and undeniably master, his sheer masculinity more potent to her senses than any liquor. Beside him she felt tiny and insignificant, and painfully aware of how slight her claim to him was. She let her hand rest lightly against his chest, the felted cloth velvety beneath her fingers. God in heaven, why did she have to love him so?

"I don't want to quarrel with you, Gabriel," she said sadly. "Not about husbands or wives or anything."

"Neither do I, sweet. But the best part of any quarrel is the patching up that comes afterward." Her regret was so genuine that his suspicions were fading. No woman bent on matrimony could ever be this guileless, this disarming. As for her mother—her mother was more than three thousand miles away. "And I've always found quarreling with you, poppet, to be vastly enjoyable."

He lifted Mariah's fingers to his lips, watching how prettily she blushed. "I have business on shore here, but I'll return tonight, and I expect to be able to show you the full measure of my contrition."

But she didn't smile in return the way he'd expected. "Can't I come with you? Please, Gabriel."

She was asking, not begging, but again he saw panic flicker across her face, and now he wondered why. "Nay, I've too much dry, dull business to amuse you. You'll be better off here."

"It was never dull with you in Newport," she said wistfully.

"In Newport everyone knew who you were," he said lightly. "Here you'd be treated as no more than some impudent little baggage who'd coaxed her way onto my arm. If I'm to sail again in less than a week—and I should, if I've any hope at all of making you the rich woman I promised—then I'm going to have to beg, bribe and threaten my way into the stores King George keeps for his navy. I'd rather you didn't see how low I must sink in your name."

The truth was he'd rather she didn't witness his reunion with his parents. More than four years had passed since he'd last walked out on his father, both of them so angry that only his mother had kept them from swords in the back garden. He had no notion what kind of reception he'd find, but he was sure that arriving with Mariah on his arm would not improve it.

Mariah twisted a button on the front of her bodice. Less than a week before Gabriel once again would face French guns, and in her name, too. She couldn't hope to have a claim on his heart, but at least she could try to keep him alive. "How much will the *Marie-Claire* bring?"

In the breeze the ribbons from her wide-brimmed hat floated across her face, and he brushed them back. "I can't say for certain until the vice admiralty courts make their judgment."

"Enough to clear my father's debts? Enough to pay you back for what you lent me and for outfitting?"

"Aye, with a bit left over to buy yourself new garters and stockings. I'm quite partial to pale rose silk, if you're of a mind to please me."

But she was in no mood for playfulness. "Then I've done what I've had to, Gabriel. I'll sell the *Revenge* and her commission here in Bridgetown," she said, urgency rushing her words. "You said yourself you're rich enough. You don't need to risk your life again. You can return to Crescent Hill and forget I ever asked you to leave.''

For a long moment he didn't answer, studying her upturned face for a clue. Even for Mariah, this was abrupt. "If you put the *Revenge* up for sale, Mariah," he said evenly, "then I'll buy her myself."

She gasped, shaking her head. "But you can't!"

"Why not? As you say, I'm rich enough." He still couldn't figure out what she really wanted, or why her expression seemed so pinched. Perhaps it was only the memory of what she'd seen in the surgery and the fear of another engagement with the French. He'd put an end to her worries soon enough, once he spoke to his mother about letting Mariah stay with them at Westgate. But whatever was making Mariah threaten to sell the *Revenge*, it wasn't going to dissuade him from finding Deveaux.

"By my reckoning, you owe me close to five thousand pounds, sweet," he continued. "'Twill be months, maybe even a year, before you're able to collect on the *Marie-Claire*. Until then you won't be able to pay me back or sell her out from under me, and I'll continue to follow the orders in my commission from you and the governor."

With a great splash, the *Revenge*'s anchor plunged into the bright blue water. Already the bos'n was giving the orders to lower the boat to carry Gabriel to town and the pilot back to his own boat. From the corner of his eye Gabriel could see the pilot coming toward him, looking for his fee, and he knew he didn't have much time left with Mariah.

"I promise I'll be back by nightfall, poppet, and I'll want you waiting for me, mind?" He swept off his hat and ducked his head beneath the wide straw brim of her hat to kiss her, his arm curled around her waist, and her lips parted with the melting sweetness he'd come to cherish. But when he released her to join the others, her eyes stayed tightly shut, so tightly that he almost didn't notice the glitter of the tears that beaded her lashes.

"Would you please call the boat for me, Ethan?" asked Mariah as Ethan cleared away the dinner she'd left uneaten. "I should like to go into Bridgetown now."

Surprised by her request, Ethan squinted at her over his shoulder. "Into Bridgetown, miss?"

"Yes, into Bridgetown," she answered firmly. "I know we shipped two boats, so don't tell me Captain Sparhawk's taken the only one."

"Bridgetown, ye say." Ethan thumped the tray down on the table. "Th' cap'n didn't say nothing to me about ye going to Bridgetown."

If either one of them said the town's name again Mariah was sure she'd burst into nervous giggles at the ridiculousness of it. "I'm to meet him there, by his invitation. I suppose he was too busy to mention it."

Ethan wiped his sleeve across his mouth. "An' where do ye be meetin' him?"

"At an inn called the Lady Anne," she answered promptly, having read the name from her father's water-stained paper only minutes before. "I believe it's near the water."

"Aye, it is, but th' only lady that's ever seen there is the one on th' signboard." His forehead wrinkled with concerned suspicion. "I can't fancy th' cap'n takin' ye there. Are ye certain of th' name?"

"Quite certain." She rose and twitched at her skirts, trying to look imperious before Ethan. "Now if you please, I shall be ready to leave in five minutes."

"Aye, Miss Mariah, whatever ye please," he said with a lack of respect she couldn't miss. But just before he kicked the cabin door shut after him, he turned, thrusting his bald-topped head through the doorway.

"Ye sure it's the Lady Anne, now? I can't fathom the cap'n takin' ye to such a place." He shook his head unhappily. "Ye mind yerself in that wicked ken, hear?"

Mariah nodded, and still muttering to himself he left her alone. Ethan was being protective, that was all. Unhappy though he might be, Mariah didn't doubt that he'd relay her order and that the boat would be waiting. He couldn't know that she'd seen her share of rum shops and pothouses in Newport from the times she'd had to go claim her father, and she doubted the ones in Bridgetown could be much worse. Not that Ethan hadn't learned plenty else about her already. The man had been the first to see that she and Gabriel had become lovers, and made it clear enough, too, that he thought Gabriel had wronged her. No wonder he kept fussing around her like an old mother tabby, almost as much as Gabriel did himself.

Swiftly she flung her cloak over her shoulders, more to shield her skirts from the spray in the open boat than for warmth, for the summer sun here in the Caribbean was hotter than she'd dreamed possible. She frowned with dismay at her reflection in the mirror as she tied on her hat. That same summer sun had played havoc with her complexion, burning her cheeks as ruddy as a farmer's daughter's, and dusting freckles—*freckles!*—across the bridge of her nose.

One last time she took the paper from her pocket and read the faded ink again. Five thousand guineas the man had owed her father. To find the man would be a wonder in itself, and to coax the money from him an out-and-out miracle, but she had to try. With five thousand guineas to her name, she might be able to convince Gabriel to stop privateering and return to Crescent Hill.

Seated in the stern sheets of the *Revenge*'s second boat, Mariah looked between the twin rows of men at the oars toward the wharf and the town they were quickly approaching. From the harbor, Newport's waterfront was many colors, weather-silvered shingles or whitewashed clapboarding, rosy red bricks and shutters that were blue and green and yellow. But Bridgetown was only white, a blinding, unrelieved white that sparkled in the sun, with every house and building, even the streets, fashioned from the same white coral rock. Beyond the town the land undulated in gentle hills, all green from the cane plantations that were the island's only crop.

Blue water, white houses, green land and people the color of ebony. Mariah had never seen so many Africans in one place. In Newport there were thirty, maybe forty slaves at most, and that many again as freemen. But here the English were outnumbered, their fair hair and ruddy skin standing out among the men who toiled along the docks.

"Careful now, Miss Mariah," said Allen Welsh, beaming as he helped her from the boat. He had let his beard, white blond and curling, grow on the voyage from Rhode Island, and with his broad, flat face he looked like a good-natured sheep. "Don't want the cap'n sayin' I didn't treat you fine, nor old Ethan nippin' at my heels, neither."

"They won't hear otherwise from me, Allen." Mariah shook out her skirts and looked past him to the crowded, busy streets. Off the water, the day seemed even hotter, the sun glittering relentlessly from the white buildings and streets, the air more oppressive, and beneath her stays her shift was already plastered damply to her back and arms. "Now if you'll direct me toward the inn—"

"Nay, miss, Ethan says I'm to go wit' you an' keep you safe until th' cap'n claims you," declared Allen stubbornly, his legs spread and his arms folded across his wide chest to block her path if she tried to leave without him. "A fair little lass like you would be gobbled up in a place like this."

Mariah sighed impatiently. Lord, did they all think she needed protecting? "Very well, then, but let's stop dawdling in this sun. The inn is called the Lady—"

"Th' Lady Anne," said Allen proudly as he shouldered a path for her through the crowd. "Ethan told me. We all knows the Lady Anne."

One look at the inn and Mariah knew too well why her father had known the Lady Anne, too, just as she knew why Gabriel never would. On a once fine town house closed in on either side by other, meaner buildings, the faded signboard with the lady herself hung crookedly from its post, and on either side of the well-worn doorstep the white walls were stained with the leavings of past customers. Exactly the kind of third-rate tavern where

Mariah's father had felt most comfortable drinking and gaming, away from the disapproving eyes of the better sort that included her mother.

"Wait for me outside," said Mariah, fingering the gambling chit in her pocket. The Lady Anne looked like a most unpromising place to find five thousand guineas, and she'd rather the *Revenge*'s entire company didn't learn of her fool's errand. As it was, she still hadn't quite figured out how she was going to explain it to Gabriel. "I'll go look for Captain Sparhawk."

Welsh shook his woolly head. "Nay, miss, my orders was to stay wit' you."

Mariah smiled winningly. "You stay here and watch for him. If he's not within, I'll come back directly." She lowered her eyes demurely. "Besides, Allen, I need to visit their necessary."

Speechless with embarrassment, the sailor flushed beneath his tan and nodded stiffly, and Mariah hurried through the open door before he changed his mind. Inside she paused, letting her eyes adjust to the murky shadows of the taproom.

"In or out, ye hussy," whined a man's nasal voice from deep in the room. "Like th' bawd said to th' drunken vestryman, you're no good at all to me when you're stuck twixt and between."

Quickly Mariah stepped inside. The room was empty except for two mulatto women in tawdry gowns on the bench along the fire wall, their faces relaxed in sleep, and both as worn as the table and chairs around them. Years of candle and tobacco smoke had darkened the walls and beams overhead, and although the shuttered windows were thrown open, the air within was stale with last night's ale and rum and the stench of the unwashed customers. It *was* worse than those Mariah had seen in Newport, but she'd come this far and she wouldn't run now. Besides, with Allen Welsh outside, how much trouble could find her?

"Away with ye, chick-a-biddy," ordered the whining man, "if yer only business be in gawking."

This time Mariah could see that the voice belonged to the keep, a slack-faced man barely visible behind the grillwork of his bar. At midday, he was his own best customer, and cradled in his hand on the counter was a half-empty bottle of rum.

"But I do have business with you," she said, inching toward him. "I'm looking for a man who was here throwing dice last winter."

The keep snorted derisively. "Last winter! There's been a precious lot of water out wit' th' tide since then!"

"You would remember this game, I think. He lost five thousand guineas to my father."

His whistle through the gap in his teeth was low and appreciative. "I might be recalling something o' that, though me memory turns more faulty ev'ry day."

Mariah was expecting that, and slid two silver coins across the counter. Immediately they disappeared into the keep's grimy birdet waistcoat.

"What come o' yer daddy that he be sendin' a chit like ye be on his errands?"

"He's dead," said Mariah, "and I mean to collect what's owed him. The man's name, if you please, and where I might find him."

"Hey ho, Bob, what pretty have ye found for me today?" The sunlight from the open door was blotted out by the newcomer, but Mariah didn't turn.

"The man's name, sir," she repeated urgently, "and where he lodges!"

Two hands grasped her waist and pulled her back. With a shriek Mariah seized the rods of the bar's grill and held tight. "Let me go, whoever you are!"

The man who held her guffawed, and Mariah nearly gagged as his breath flooded over her. "Who *she* be, Bob? By th' black spy, but she be a plump little piece, an' fresh as country cream!"

The keep shrugged, drinking deeply from the bottle. "Ah, some little ladybird, lookin' for th' cove what cheated her daddy. Mind, if ye take her, th' silver in her pocket's mine by rights, for findin' her for ye."

"You've no rights to anything, you fat thief!" yelled Mariah. "Allen! Allen, help me!"

Still hanging tightly to the rods, she twisted around to look for Welsh. But the place across the street where she'd left him was empty, and as she turned the man who held her grasped her jaw and tried to turn her mouth to meet his. He was unshaven and stank of onions and stale sweat, and as angry and frightened as she was, Mariah was sure she'd rather die than let those lips touch her own. She jerked her head free and kicked him in the knee as hard as she could. *"Allen!"*

"Fight me, will ye, ye little bitch?" The man swore, and roughly tore her fingers from the bar. She lunged forward, desperate to regain her hold, but effortlessly the man slammed her against his body. Still plunging and twisting to free herself, she felt the man's fingers against her skin as he ripped her gown off her shoulder, felt his wet lips, his yellow teeth against her bare skin.

"Let her go or you die."

Abruptly the man turned around, dragging Mariah with him. In the doorway stood Gabriel, his arm raised and steady, the sunlight behind him glinting off the silver inlays on his pistol's long barrel.

"I found her first," blustered the man, his arm tightening around Mariah. "No flash buck's goin' to take what's mine!"

"My name's Captain Gabriel Sparhawk, and I'm no flash buck."

"Sparhawk!" Mariah felt the fear that shivered through the man, and wondered that Gabriel's name alone could do that. But then she'd never seen Gabriel like this before, his eyes hard as green ice, the lines carved deep around his mouth, all of him calm and cold and very, very deadly.

"If ye kill me, ye shall kill the chit, too!"

"Oh, you'll find my aim's better than that. But I'd rather not soil the lady's gown with the spattering of your brains." Gabriel cocked his head slightly to the left, appraising. "And she *is* a lady. *My* lady."

"Take her, then, an' th' devil claim ye both!" The man shoved Mariah before him and swiftly reached into his coat for his knife. Off-balance, she stumbled forward, and all she saw was the spark and the acrid white smoke, rising up from the flintlock that followed the gunshot. The two mulatto women were instantly awake, screaming and clutching each other, and the man who'd held her was swearing and gasping from the floor where he'd fallen as he cradled his shattered, bloody right hand with his left.

Stunned, Mariah stared at Gabriel, his expression unchanged as the gunpowder smoke drifted about him. Slowly he lowered the pistol to his side, and now she saw Allen Welsh, his face equally grim, behind him in the doorway.

"Come along, Mariah." Gabriel didn't look at her, his eyes instead intent on the writhing, wounded man. "You've caused trouble enough."

"*I've* caused trouble!" she exclaimed indignantly, settling her hands on her hips as her torn bodice slipped off her shoulder. With the danger seemingly gone, anger quickly overcame her fear. "*You* might have killed me, Gabriel! Since when do gentlemen go into town with pistols on their belts?"

"Since you, Miss West, keep giving me reasons." He hooked the gun at his waist and pulled off his coat. "Here. Cover yourself."

While Mariah tugged the torn sleeve higher over her shoulder, she only glared at the offered coat. "Stop giving orders, Gabriel. I'm not one of your crew."

"Very well." He tossed the coat over her bare shoulders, barely able to contain his fury. What the devil was wrong with her? Didn't she realize how close she'd been to real harm? When he'd seen that bastard's hands on her, he could have killed the man in an instant, without any remorse, merely for touching her. So why wasn't she soft and trembling in his arms, grateful for her deliverance like any normal woman would be, instead of yowling at him like a fishmonger's wife?

With no more gentleness than the other man had shown, he seized her by the arm and yanked her toward the door. He tossed a coin to the boy who held his horse, and before Mariah could argue more he lifted her up and across the saddle and then climbed behind her. He nodded curtly to Allen Welsh, who looked as wretched as a man his size could. Well, let him, thought Gabriel grimly. What had he and Ethan and the rest of them been thinking, letting Mariah go off by herself like that?

"Could you please possibly tell me where we're going?" asked Mariah with icy politeness as he turned the horse's head away from the waterfront and toward the hills.

"I'm taking you to my father's house, where I trust my mother will do a better job of keeping you from mischief than my men did on the *Revenge*. She, at least, won't have her head turned by a pretty face."

"No, Gabriel, I won't! I don't know your parents. I want to stay on the sloop. That's where I belong, not—"

"No more, Mariah." Angry as he was, all he heard was her defiant refusal, and none of the panic that colored it. "And not another word until we reach the house."

It was another order, but one Mariah felt she had little choice but to obey. How could she have any sort of reasonable conversation when she was being jostled and bounced against the horse's neck, clutching at a fistful of its mane with one hand and Gabriel's coat over her torn bodice with the other? Not that she feared she'd fail. Gabriel's arm around her waist was like an iron band, not protective because he cherished her and wanted her safe, but because he'd fought for her and won, as if she were no more than the bone contested by two mongrels. By now she knew the difference and it only fueled her anger and anxiety.

He couldn't make her stay, she told herself. She didn't belong to him. If anything, he should be listening to *her* orders because he was sailing her sloop. He couldn't possibly leave her behind.

The road to his parents' plantation curved along the hillside overlooking the bay, the crushed white coral crunching like broken ice beneath the horse's hooves. She knew he was driving the horse too hard in the heat, with flecks of foam from the animal's mouth flying onto her skirts. When they reached the house, a black man trotted forward to catch the reins Gabriel threw to him. Mariah had only the briefest impression of the house—long and low and white, with porches along the front that faced the sea—before Gabriel was pulling her off the horse and up the steps.

"Wait, Gabriel, stop," she said breathlessly, trying to stop. She'd lost her hat at the Lady Anne, her hair was half unpinned, her clothes torn and stained. What would Mrs. Sparhawk make of her like this? "I can't meet your mother like this!"

"You won't. She's visiting and won't be back until next week." His eyes narrowed, inspecting her critically. "By then you should have had time to make yourself decent enough for her."

With his fingers tight on her arm he led her through the front door, past two black housemaids in the hallway who watched them with interest but not with much surprise, and into the drawing room. He released her then, so he could close the double mahogany doors against the servants, and Mariah darted across the room. Although the tall windows that lined the walls were thrown open to catch whatever breeze came from the water, the air in the room was nearly as hot as it was outside—nearly as hot as Mariah's temper as she rubbed her arm where he'd held her too tightly.

He'd had no right to do that. As much as she loved him, he'd no right to do any of this. Her heart pounding, she threw Gabriel's coat onto a chair and shoved back her hair, prepared to face him, whatever came next.

And please God, please, please don't let it end like this. . . .

Chapter Eleven

"So what shall it be, Gabriel?" asked Mariah, her voice shaking. "Will you tie me to a chair to keep me here, or perhaps your father has chains to manacle me to the cellar wall like a slave?"

"My father doesn't own slaves, Mariah, any more than he owns chains." He had never seen a woman who could look so bedraggled and forlorn and yet be so infuriating at the same time, and he was torn between wanting to punish her and wishing to tell her how much he'd feared for her, to kiss her and reassure her, and himself too, that she was all right.

She swallowed hard, her mouth dry. "Then what next?"

"You might begin, Mariah," he said, struggling to stay calm, "by telling me what you were doing in that filthy place."

She shook her head. She was certain the Lady Anne's keep had known the man she sought, and somehow, she still intended to find him. "I can't."

"Can't, or won't?" Where her sleeve had been torn away from her bodice was a small, ragged triangle that framed the shadowed curve of the side of her breast and it caught his eye, a little patch of secret skin that he heartily wished he could ignore.

"I had business there. My father's business. You need know no more than that."

"The hell I don't! Mariah, if Ethan hadn't sent one of the men from the boat to come find me, you could already be locked up in the garret of some brothel, waiting to become the evening's prime entertainment!"

She frowned, feeling betrayed by Ethan though she knew she should be grateful. "I don't believe it would have come to that."

"Five minutes later and I would have found you on your back with your skirts rucked up, and that bastard between your thighs!"

"I was there for your sake, Gabriel!"

"For *my* sake! My God, Mariah, what could you have possibly been doing there that would have been for my sake?"

"Because I wanted to help you!" She hadn't intended to say even that much, but now that she'd begun, she couldn't stop. "There's a man who owed my father money and I thought if I could get it from him and then pay you back, you'd agree to go back to Crescent Hill.''

He stared at her, incredulous. He remembered the magpie's nest of papers her father had left behind. How could she trust anything that came from that?

"Mariah, listen to me. I wouldn't take that money from you even if by some divine miracle you'd found it. I'm here to help fight a war, not just settle your accounts. I can't go back until this cruise is done, even if I wanted to.''

"Can't, or won't?'' she said, repeating his words. Why couldn't he understand that the money didn't count anymore? "You're the one who makes all the decisions, aren't you? You think I'm your poppet, your pet, your little doll, who can't be trusted enough to choose the proper color for her stockings!''

"It's your life that concerns me, Mariah, not your damned stockings!''

Wild-eyed, she paused, her breath coming in short gasps that were dangerously close to sobs. "If you're so blessed concerned for me, then why have you dragged me clear up here? Why didn't you let me go back to the *Revenge* where I belong?''

She was rubbing her wrist again, and for the first time he noticed the angry red blotches on her pale skin. God, had he done that to her? He'd never meant to hurt her. Appalled, he remembered how he'd almost killed the man at the Lady Anne. How had he let that same violence—that cold, detached, easy violence that made him so good at privateering—spill over onto the one person he cared for the most?

And he did love her. He realized that now, suddenly, just as he was so close to losing her. Maybe he already had. He'd never before seen the haunted, weary look that was in her eyes now, nor heard in her voice the bittersweet acceptance of things she believed would not change. He longed to reach out and take her in his arms, to hold her and tell her how he felt, but he was afraid it was too late.

"All I've wanted, Mariah," he said hoarsely, "is to keep you safe."

"How, Gabriel? Locked away in an ironbound strongbox while you're free to do whatever you please?"

She lifted her hands in unspoken supplication, the fingers spread, then with a sigh brought them together in a tight, clenched knot at her waist. "You can't change the world by wishing. I know, because I've tried. I've wished for a world where we weren't at war with France and Spain and everyone else who's so eager for a chance to kill you. I've wished that my father hadn't died and my mother didn't need Geneva and limewater before her tea at breakfast. I've wished that Daniel still lived and I was his wife, with his baby dawdling on my knee while I waited for him to come home for supper. And most of all, Gabriel Sparhawk, I wish to God I'd never let myself fall in love with you."

Swiftly she turned toward the windows, away from him. She didn't want to see the contempt, or worse, the pity, she knew would be all over his handsome face, any more than she wished him to see the tears that filled her eyes. Surely she wasn't the first woman to tell him she loved him. He'd never denied his experiences. Just as he'd known how to make her body sing with pleasure beneath his touch, she thought bitterly, he would know exactly which words would lessen the pain of caring too much.

"Mariah, no." She stiffened as he lay his hands on her shoulders, but she couldn't make herself pull away. "No."

No was not what she expected. *No* could never be a word of practiced comfort, even whispered so close to her ear. His hands eased down her arms, pulling her against him. Why did they have to fit together this well?

"Don't wish me from your life, Mariah." His hands were so large, so sure as they traveled down her body, his fingers tightening on the softness of her hips. "Because, God help me, I can't ever wish you from mine."

"No," she said softly, her eyes squeezed shut as if that alone could shut out the now-familiar sensations only he could bring. "No, Gabriel, please." She shook her head in denial, of him, of herself, and gently he caught her face and turned her around and into his arms. His mouth was hot on hers, her legs melting beneath her, beneath the heat that centered low in her belly, low where she felt it most, where Gabriel belonged.

"No," she whispered, a syllable sighed against his lips as they sank together, her upturned skirts an island of crumpled white linen around them against the dark, polished floor.

"No," she moaned feverishly as he slid his arms beneath her knees and thrust deep within her, the heat between them white-hot, pulsing, so close to release and redemption as she roiled beneath him, meeting him, loving him as if this was the final time.

"*Yes,*" he gasped, his head arched, the word forced from him as he thrust into her for the last time, her shuddering cry an echo of his own. His heart still pounding, his senses drugged with the lush sweetness of her still holding him, he raised himself up on his arms to kiss her, and instead found himself staring through the half-open door into the stunned blue eyes of his mother.

"Thee must call me Damaris, child, not Mistress Sparhawk," chided Gabriel's mother gently for the third time. "Such titles are creaturely, and I have no place to set myself above thee through such empty words. Now turn, so I may see how my Sarah's old gown does for thee.''

Bewildered, Mariah turned as she was told. Gabriel's mother had brought her upstairs to her bedchamber, had herself helped Mariah from her torn and soiled clothing and washed her and braided her hair and let her weep, and not once had she mentioned either her son or the shameful circumstances in which they'd been caught.

Although Mariah had known Gabriel's mother was a Friend, this tall, soft-spoken woman wasn't at all what she'd expected. The severity of her slate blue dress and green apron suited her, and Mariah was certain that she'd been considered a beauty once, with her clear blue eyes and fair hair beneath her white cap. From her had come Gabriel's gift for listening to what another said, and the kindness he often tried so hard to hide. Wistfully Mariah wondered how different life would have been with a mother like this, one who would offer comfort instead of demand it.

''There, Mariah, that shall do quite well until thy own clothing is fetched,'' said Damaris, giving Mariah's borrowed skirt a little twitch of approval. '''Tis not the fashion thee is accustomed to, being a good ten years old, I know, but at least thee is decent.''

''Why haven't you said anything?'' blurted Mariah. ''You've been so good to me, when I know you're thinking I'm a wicked little trollop that should be swept from your doorstep and out of your son's life!''

"Oh, no, Mariah, thee is quite wrong." With a sigh, Damaris leaned back against the red cushions in the walnut armchair and studied Mariah. "I've no wish to see thee gone. Thee can't leave, for thee must wed Gabriel."

"No!" cried Mariah, shocked. "Marry Gabriel—no, no, I can't!"

"But thee loves him. The way thee looks at him speaks that more clearly than words," said Damaris gently. "Has thee not considered that thee might already be carrying Gabriel's child?"

"But I can't marry Gabriel." Mariah's voice broke beneath her anguish. She couldn't marry Gabriel, and she knew he wouldn't marry her. "I swore to someone else who—who was lost at sea that I'd never marry another."

Damaris smiled wryly. "Thee honors his memory by lying with my son?"

"I knew you thought I was wicked!" wailed Mariah.

"Not wicked, lass, just young. Come, thee must not cry." She held her hand out to Mariah, and slowly Mariah went to her, slipping to her knees before the older woman's chair as she buried her sobs in Damaris's apron.

Gently Damaris stroked her hair. "None of it is thy fault, Mariah. Gabriel is an easy man to love, and always has been. Mothers aren't supposed to have favorites among their children, but Gabriel was my last, my baby. Though now thee would never believe it, he was a tiny little mite when he was born, nigh a month before his time. I was on board the old *Leopard* with Jonathan then, and he was forced to be my midwife, and, oh, how he despaired of us both! Because of how close I came to losing him as a babe, I've always been more forgiving with my Gabriel, while for the same reason Jonathan has been harder on him than all the others combined. It is strange, isn't it, how men will always try to huff and bluster when they fear they'll lose what they care for most?''

With a loud snuffle Mariah raised her head. ''Not Gabriel,'' she said vehemently. ''Gabriel cares for nothing beyond himself and his own pleasure.''

''Brave words, lass, but thee doesn't believe them any more than I do.'' She fished in her pocket for her handkerchief and handed it to Mariah. ''He hasn't been home, here to us at Westgate, in more than four years, but still I cannot fault him for it—though I will credit thee for bringing him back.''

Mariah wiped the handkerchief across her eyes. ''Credit the French, not me. Once the word had come from London, he insisted on being the first privateer out of Newport.''

Damaris's smile grew tight. ''So Gabriel has turned to the bloodshed again, as Jonathan said he must. I wanted so for it to be otherwise! It grieves me sadly, but Gabriel has more demons than most men, and I can do no more than pray for him to find his way." She sighed deeply, and touched Mariah's tear-streaked cheek. "Has he ever told thee how much thee favors another girl he knew long ago?"

Mariah shook her head and blew her nose. "He's known so many women he's likely forgotten her."

"He has not forgotten Catherine, any more than thee has forgotten thy love lost at sea," said Damaris sadly. "Catherine was special. She was from this island, from a plantation in St. Bartholomew's Parish, and as pretty as thee is. Gabriel would have done anything for her. Though Catherine hadn't joined my meeting, her mother had, and I'd hoped that if she'd wed Gabriel they would together have come into the meeting. She would, I think, have made him happy, and spared him from much of the suffering he has brought to himself."

She smoothed Mariah's hair from her forehead. "Catherine couldn't do that for him, but perhaps thee can. Thee loves him already with thy heart and thy body. Thy head will follow soon enough."

Sarah had warned him that their father was growing frail, but to Gabriel the old man hadn't

changed at all. His tall, broad-shouldered frame
bent only slightly with age, the long white hair he
still wore untied in the old fashion, the thick black
brows that somehow hadn't grayed pulled down
low over green eyes that missed nothing—with
eerie certainty Gabriel could study his father and
know how he'd look himself in forty years. Perhaps Captain Jonathan Sparhawk leaned more
heavily on his walking stick than before, for even
in Barbados's warmth the old wounds to his leg
plagued him, but that, decided Gabriel, must be
the only difference.

Certainly his father's temper hadn't lessened a
whit with age. To listen how he railed at him now,
here in the same room where only a quarter hour
past he'd been loving Mariah, made Gabriel feel
like he was six again instead of thirty-three.

"What's your poor mother done to deserve such
disrespect from you, eh, boy?" thundered Jonathan, his voice raised loud enough for a quarterdeck. Both men stood, neither willing to give the
other the advantage of height. "To find you here,
without warning and after four years, on the floor
of her drawing room rutting away at some weeping *child* with her clothes torn apart!"

"Mariah's not a child, Father," said Gabriel as
calmly as he could, determined, this once, to keep
his temper. "She's eighteen, of age by anyone's
reckoning."

"And young enough to be your own daughter, if what your brother's said of your precocious appetites is true." Twice he thumped the walking stick on the floor for emphasis. "You must have paid handsomely for a piece that young."

"Damn it, Father, she's not some five-shilling strumpet!"

"True enough," agreed Jonathan shrewdly, clearly pleased to have gotten that much from Gabriel. "Your women tend to be more costly. So what poor husband were you cuckolding today?"

"She has no husband. She came with me freely from Newport on board the *Revenge.*"

"The armed sloop new to the harbor this day." Jonathan smiled with grim satisfaction. "You're going after the French now, aren't you? All the Spaniards you slaughtered for their gold weren't enough. I should have known a new war would draw you out."

With a deep sigh he lowered himself heavily into the armchair, and for the first time he looked like an old man. "You know full well that this will break your mother's heart all over again."

Gabriel winced, knowing his father was right, but he didn't try to defend himself. There wasn't any point. To his father, privateering was no better than pirating, and because long ago Jonathan had lost a ship and nearly his life to pirates, he had little interest or sympathy in Gabriel's reasons for leaving the family's own shipping business to become a privateer. Not that Gabriel had wanted to explain to anyone why he'd gone out to fight the Spanish. Then the pain had been too new and raw, and now it was too late.

"It's only one cruise, Father," he said. "The sloop belonged to Mariah's father and now to her, and I—"

"The girl's father was a Newport man, a shipmaster?" Jonathan interrupted impatiently. "Did I know him?"

"Edward West?" Gabriel shrugged carelessly. "You wouldn't have known him, Father. A low, drunken man, a miserable excuse for a captain, unworthy of his daughters."

"Captain West of Water Street. Oh, aye, I knew him well enough, and his father, Ezra, before him. Wed Letitia Martin, didn't he? Traded mostly in sugar and rum. And now my son has debauched his daughter, ruined her good name with his whole crew and his own mother as witness."

The undeniable sadness in his father's voice caught Gabriel off-balance. Most men would be proud of a son who'd made his fortune in the king's service and had half the women in the colonies swooning over him. But his father, he knew, wasn't one of them. His father expected more, and always had. Impulsively Gabriel reached out to put his hand on his father's arm, as if by touch he could make up for all the disappointments he'd brought him over the years.

"You've gone to the devil this time, boy." Ignoring the hand on his sleeve, Jonathan shook his head wearily without looking at his son. "You'll marry this lass, Gabriel. If you don't, I'll see that the governor tosses you in his prison and keeps you there until your damned French war is done."

Mariah sat stiffly on the bench, her back straight as Hepzibah first brushed her hair with long, even strokes, then rubbed it carefully with a scrap of silk to make it shine, and finally began to roll and pin each piece of hair in place into a glossy crown of curls. Mariah wore only her stays and shift and stockings—pale rose stockings—for though she could see the sun sinking lower through the open window, a red ball that stained the blue Caribbean crimson, the evening air was still stifling. She would wait until the last possible moment to dress, or rather, to be dressed, so she wouldn't wilt the delicate patterned silk of the gown lying on the bed, and the flowers she'd carry wouldn't be picked from the garden until after she was dressed. Everything spoiled in this miserable climate, thought Mariah. *Everything.*

For two weeks she'd only seen Gabriel at dinner, and then his father and his friends had kept him so busy with talk of the French war that he'd scarcely found the time to nod at her across the room. He had much to do, that was all, and she told herself it was such business that kept him away from her. Business, not neglect. But what did she expect with this preposterous marriage his parents were forcing on them both? Before, when he told her she had a place in his life, she let herself hope that maybe he had come to love her as she did him. But what kind of love could grow when forced like this?

"You shouldn't set yourself to worryin', miss," said Hepzibah critically as she paused to pat at Mariah's bare throat and chest with a cool, damp cloth before she dusted more powder on her skin. Hepzibah had been borrowed from the next plantation, since Damaris kept no lady's maid herself, and though Mariah had always wondered what such a luxury would be like, tonight she found the girl's attentions only one more gift she didn't want. "In Bridgetown, worryin' makes ladies melt away like th' dew before th' sun. And why should you be a-worryin' at all, miss? Tonight you'll have most ev'ry woman on this island sighing wit' envy, wishin' they was in your place an' marryin' Captain Sparhawk!"

Mariah didn't want the envy of women she didn't know. She wanted to be back home on her own island with her sister and mother. She gazed out the window to the harbor, forlornly searching again for Jenny's ship. No one else seemed concerned by the *Felicity*'s delay—winds and weather, an overcautious captain—but Mariah hadn't stopped wishing that her sister would arrive safely, and in time to be here when she stood with Gabriel before the red-faced Anglican minister. Jenny could have wed Elisha at the same time, so there would have been at least one happy couple for the guests to raise their glasses to.

"Do you like the gown, Mariah?"

Mariah closed her eyes for a moment at the sound of Gabriel's voice, trying to control the wild beating of her heart before she turned on the bench to face him. He'd opened the door without her realizing it, without asking her permission or knocking, and as he stood there with his hand resting on the polished knob he was so breathtakingly handsome that she almost wept. He was wearing the same green velvet suit she remembered from the windmill, and foolishly she wondered if he'd remembered, too, and selected it for that reason. "Is the gown of your choosing?"

"Aye. Though she won't admit it, there are some things best not left to my mother." Pointedly his gaze swept to her legs. "I sent you three pair stockings. I'm glad you picked the rose ones, though I'd scarcely flatter myself that 'twas to please me."

Though he'd seen every inch of her naked, she still felt unbelievably wanton sitting before him half-undressed with Hepzibah arranging her hair. Strange to think that in an hour, when she and Gabriel were husband and wife, such conversations would be considered wholly respectable—or at least as respectable as anything involving Gabriel could be.

"I chose the rose ones because they best suited the gown," she said stiffly.

"A more diplomatic answer than I'd expected from you, Mariah." He smiled so slightly that Mariah couldn't tell if he was truly amused. "Although you still haven't said whether you like my selection or not."

"This gown is even more beautiful than the one from Madame Lambert's shop." Lord, how did he manage to stand there wearing so much clothing and not show the heat? She felt sure she'd melt the way Hepzibah warned, just from the way he was looking at her. "But you knew that already, or you wouldn't have asked my opinion."

"Another neat reply, though this time more astute than politic. Perhaps I *shall* have to abandon calling you poppet, as you wish."

He glanced at Hepzibah. "Leave us. Miss West will call you."

"Oh, but Captain Sparhawk, sir, it don't be proper for you to be here now with Miss West before you're wed! Mistress Sparhawk told me not—"

"Hush now, hush." Smiling at the maid, he briefly touched his forefinger across his lips. "Mistress Sparhawk won't know unless you tell her."

The maid turned scarlet with pleasure at his attention, dipped a quick curtsy and left the room, making sure her skirts swept against Gabriel's legs as she squeezed past him. Unwilling to watch, Mariah looked into her lap. To see him flirt so unthinkingly with another woman hurt.

"You could always marry *her*," she said defensively once they were alone. "She told me every woman on Barbados envies me tonight."

"You don't agree?" he asked softly. He doubted she knew how much she tempted him, her breasts raised invitingly by the tight lacing, her bare shoulders glistening with the same soft sheen that her skin always took when passion or anger warmed her blood. But now he wanted more from her than desire alone could satisfy.

Hidden by her skirts, her hands gripped the sides of the bench. "Don't try to sweeten the truth, Gabriel. I no more want this wedding than you do."

He hadn't come here expecting that sharpness from her, and it surprised him. "Then why did you agree to it?"

"Why did *you?*" she asked in return, her small chin lifting belligerently.

He didn't answer because he wasn't sure himself, any more than he knew why he'd come to see her now, before this sorry, trumped-up excuse for a wedding. These days he didn't seem to know much of anything.

If he'd really wanted to, he could have found a way to buck his father's threat. He'd done it often enough before, but this time he hadn't even tried. Fighting his father could mean losing Mariah and he couldn't risk it. She'd become a part of his world, and a part of him, and he couldn't bear to lose her, even if it meant marrying her with his father's pistol jabbing him in the back.

So why was he having such a hell of a time telling her how he felt? He wanted to give her more than the easy, pat endearments he'd whispered to all the other women, and ruefully he knew that now, when it mattered so much, he'd become as tongue-tied as any mooncalf cabin boy. Once he'd finished with Deveaux, he would make all this up to her. He'd begin again, woo her the way she deserved.

But for Mariah, each moment he stood there in silence before her stretched like an endless, painful hour as he didn't even bother to explain to her. The last time he'd told her she had a place in his life, if not his heart, but now he didn't even seem to want to offer that.

"You don't have to pretend for my sake, Gabriel," she said, struggling to protect herself against his silence. "I never wanted to be your wife, and I still don't."

He stood very still, studying her against the fading light of the setting sun. What had his parents told her to make her like this? Not even his father would have threatened her with prison.

"Once you loved me," he said carefully, "and I think you still do. You don't have to go through with this, Mariah, not unless you wish it."

She shook her head and looked into her lap. She wondered that her eyes were dry. If ever there was a time for tears, this was it.

"I have no choice, Gabriel," she said in a voice scarcely more than a whisper. He was feeling trapped enough without her adding her sad little reason, and she wouldn't do that to him. "None at all."

"I don't believe that of you, Mariah," he said firmly. "No one—not your mother, not mine—can make you do anything against your will."

"But *you* can, Gabriel, and you already have."

"Mariah—"

Swiftly she turned away from him. "It's bad luck for you to be here now. Go, please, before your mother finds us together again."

"I'll leave if you wish it, Mariah," he said at last, "but I won't give you up."

This time she heard the door as it closed softly behind him, and she didn't say the words that might have made him stop. It was too late for any words to help either of them now.

As stiff as a wooden doll, Mariah let Hepzibah dress her, tying and pinning the elaborate gown in place, easing on her slippers, clasping on the twin pearl bracelets that were the gift from her new father-in-law. One last time Hepzibah dusted her shoulders with rice powder. "There now, miss," she declared, pleased with her handiwork, "you are perfection itself!"

Mariah stared at the elegant young woman in the mirror and saw nothing of herself. "I should like to walk in the garden alone for a few moments, Hepzibah," she said, her voice hollow. "Please tell the others I shall join them shortly."

"But Mistress Sparhawk said you was to go down with the old captain, that he'd come for you when all the guests was here!"

"Mistress Sparhawk will understand," called Mariah as she escaped down the narrow back stairs, her full skirts over panniers brushing against the whitewashed walls. Three minutes later she stood in the darkened garden alone, Hepzibah's last careful dusting of powder already sacrificed to the moist evening air. Before her the windows of the house were gold with candlelight, and women's laughter and men's voices drifted out through the open sashes. Behind her lay the murky shadows of the tropical garden, the white blossoms of the begonias ghostly pale against the dense foliage, alive with the shrieks and calls of a hundred strange birds and animals Mariah couldn't name.

She sank down on a teakwood bench and pressed her palms to her cheeks. In Newport this late in August, there was already a chill to the air after sunset, a hint of autumn and winter to come, but here there was no respite from the heat, no evening breeze rising from the water.

The twenty-third of August, her wedding day. She would always remember it now. She wondered where the summer had gone, how the days had slipped by so effortlessly since the June night when she'd met Gabriel. Beneath his spell on board the *Revenge* she'd had no sense of time passing at all, not until Jonathan had mentioned the date at breakfast yesterday. The twenty-third of August meant her courses were sixteen days late, and because she was never late, she didn't doubt that the fervent prayer she'd made for Daniel had instead been answered with Gabriel.

She closed her eyes and tentatively lay her hands across her belly. She felt no different, looked no different, yet her life was irrevocably changed. She had wanted so much to tell Gabriel tonight, but this way was better. This way he couldn't say she'd trapped him into the marriage that neither of them wanted. She tried to imagine what their child would look like and couldn't. Dear God, how could she bear the child of a man who'd never once said he'd loved her?

She gasped with surprise when the sweet-smelling cloth was pressed tightly over her nose and mouth. She tried to cry out and only inhaled more of the odd fumes, and when she struggled to push aside the hand that held the cloth her fingers were clumsy and weak. Fleetingly she thought again of Gabriel, and then without a fight she slipped headlong into the waiting darkness.

Chapter Twelve

Jenny sat on the narrow cot with her feet curled up beneath her to keep clear of the centipedes and large black beetles that crawled from the damp walls and scurried across the stone floor. The grid of sunlight that filtered through the single high window had shifted far enough across the opposite wall so that she knew it was late afternoon. By the time she counted to one thousand, the crippled woman would come with her dinner and fresh water for the bucket in the corner. Only four days had Jenny been here, and already she'd learned to pass the hours with such small diversions, to try to keep her mind as blank as the walls before her so the horror of remembering wouldn't swallow up what remained of her sanity.

Dear God, there was so much she wanted to forget! There had been more bodies tumbled across the *Felicity*'s deck, the bodies of Newport men she'd talked and laughed with on the voyage now silent forever with their throats slit like their captain's. Below the deck the horses that were the brig's cargo had neighed and kicked wildly against the bulkheads, panicked by the scent of the fresh blood that soaked the decks. It seemed to Jenny that she and the horses were the only things the Frenchmen had left living on board, and as the longboat had pulled away from the *Felicity*'s side she had felt the same terror that had made the animals scream and plunge.

Jenny curled herself more tightly on the straw-filled mattress, fighting the remembered panic all over again. At least the horses had had each other for company. None of the Frenchmen spoke English except for their leader, the gentleman with the scarred face, and once he'd seen Jenny seated securely between two burly oarsmen, he'd turned his face toward his own ship and ignored her completely, just as he had since they'd brought her to his plantation and locked her in this cellar. The other men, often clearly drunk, came to peer at her through the grated window and make gestures and suggestions that were unmistakable in any language, and each time Jenny caught herself thinking indignantly what Elisha would say to them for treating her like this. But then she'd remember that Elisha was dead, and the pain of her loss was so sharp that she wished they'd killed her, too.

Jenny looked up as she heard the footsteps in the hallway outside. It was too soon for the woman with her supper, and besides, she never wore shoes or boots. This sounded like a man, no, two men, maybe more, and fear rose in her throat. All they'd taken from the *Felicity* had been poor Captain Richardson's strongbox and her. Maybe now she'd learn why she'd been valued as much as the gold, but as the key scraped in the lock, she wasn't sure she wanted to know, after all.

"Bonjour, mademoiselle," said the man with the scarred face, bowing from the waist with his cocked hat tucked under his arm. He smiled cheerfully at Jenny, as if they were old friends meeting on the street, as if the two other huge, bearded men with pistols and swords on their belts weren't lurking in the hallway behind him, staring coldly, hungrily at Jenny.

"Forgive me for being an inattentive host, *ma cher,"* he continued. "My time, alas, has not been my own these last days. But we shall talk now, shall we not?"

He flicked his hand with the cabachon ring, and a servant scurried into the room with a carved armchair. Without bothering to make sure the chair was anywhere but behind him, the man flipped up the skirts of his coat and sat, his legs crossed with careless elegance. Gently he waved his hat back and forth before his face like a fan, the silk eyelash trimming along the brim fluttering with the motion.

"I have nothing to say to you," said Jenny, her wavering voice betraying her as she tried hard to sound scornful and aloof. "I don't speak to pirates."

"And I don't, as a rule, speak to filthy, ill-bred English chits." He was careful to keep the scarred side of his face turned away from her. "But since I'm not a *pirate*, I'm willing to overlook your lack of breeding."

"If you're not a pirate, I don't know who is!" She twisted her fingers in the edges of her skirt and willed herself not to cry. "By English law you'd be strung up and rotting at the mouth of a harbor for what you did to Captain Richardson alone! And for the others...the others..." She faltered when she remembered Elisha.

The Frenchman sighed impatiently. "I sail for my own king, *mademoiselle,* not that I owe you any explanations. I don't bow my head to any Englishman's law. And I'd advise you to remember such things before I tire of your whining and listen instead to my men. I am your only protector, you know." He lifted his hand with the same airy, dismissive gesture that had ended Richardson's life. "My men wouldn't be as particular. I doubt they'd even grant you choice of which one took you first—though after the tenth man or so you'd likely be beyond caring."

Sickened, Jenny knew he was telling the truth. "What do you want from me?" she whispered. "Why didn't you kill me at once like the rest?"

"What I want, *mademoiselle,* is to hear all you know about an old friend of mine." He leaned back in the chair and set his hat in his lap, making a little tent of his fingers on the black beaver crown. "A privateer like myself, but from your town of Newport, sailing for your fat Hanover king. Gabriel Sparhawk, *oui?* Captain Richardson assured me that you know him most intimately."

"I don't know him at all," said Jenny anxiously. How could her fate depend on Captain Sparhawk? "I've never met him—never even seen him! It's my sister he fancies, not me. I swear to you I don't know anything!"

"You know more than you realize, *ma cher,* " he said easily, bouncing his fingertips together. "The name of his ship, perhaps?"

"Oh, of course I know that, because the ship belongs to my mother and Mariah and me," said Jenny with relief. "It's the sloop *Revenge,* bound for Barbados and then to cruise the Caribbean. Eighty-two men, twelve guns. She's the first privateer out of Newport against the French, and Mariah and Captain Sparhawk just outfitted her so everything's new and fresh."

"So Richardson said, too. Between the two of you, you must be telling the truth." Watching her closely, he forgot to keep his head turned, and the sunlight from the grate fell harshly across the scar. "But I would have you tell me more, little Jenny. Tell me of your sister. Is she in love with Sparhawk, or better yet, is he in love with her?"

Confused, Jenny shook her head. "I don't know. I believe Mariah is fond of him and he of her, but I cannot say if they love one another."

"Of course she is in love with him. Every woman he meets falls under his spell," he said harshly, all pretense of good humor gone. "They're all panting, eager slatterns for the brave, handsome Captain Sparhawk, like the cock in the barnyard with his choice of willing companions!"

"Not Mariah!" exclaimed Jenny, too indignant to be afraid.

"Why should your sister be any different, eh? He smiles at her, he calls her pretty love names, and she will spread her legs for him like every other little English whore."

"You've no right to say such things about Mariah! I know my sister, and she'd never lie with a man who wasn't her husband, especially not one so old as Captain Sparhawk." She raised her head, wounded for her sister's sake. "It's most impertinent of you to say such things of any lady, particularly when she's my sister!"

He stared at her, his pale eyes cold and his mouth set, until with a conscious effort he forced his features to relax and once again turned his profile toward her. "You are right, *mademoiselle*," he said. "Pray forgive me. You have been most cooperative, and deserving of better from me."

Gracefully he rose to his feet, and the servant hurried forward to take the chair. He glanced around the bare cellar room as he settled his hat on his flawlessly powdered wig, and when he smiled at Jenny, she shrank back, suddenly more frightened than she'd been since he'd appeared at her door.

"You're lonely, aren't you, *ma cher?*" he asked with false, suggestive concern. "You need companionship. You are too young to relish this solitude, *non?*"

"No—I mean, yes." Panicking, Jenny remembered the company he'd suggested before, and swiftly shook her head. "I'm happy enough. Truly."

"Happy, are you? Then you're as false as every other of your sex, Jenny, shedding empty tears for your dead lover."

"That's not true! I loved Elisha, and you *killed* him!"

He smiled again, pleased. "So, perhaps, I did."

"I hate you," said Jenny vehemently through the tears, real tears she couldn't contain. "I don't even know your name, but you killed my Elisha, and for that I'll always hate you!"

"My name is Capitaine Christian Saint-Juste Deveaux," he said softly. "And as for hating me—ah, *ma petite*, I've scarce begun to give you reasons for that."

"Mariah?" Gabriel's heels crushed the ground white stones of the path as he walked swiftly through his mother's garden. Damn that simpering servant girl for letting Mariah escape! He didn't really expect to find her in the garden where she'd said she'd be. In the strange mood she'd been in, she'd probably struck out for Bridgetown and the *Revenge* by now, determined to leave him standing like a solitary idiot before the minister.

But she wouldn't get far. He'd seen to that. First he'd checked the stables to make sure she hadn't taken a horse, then he'd sent servants with lanterns down the road to town. With luck they'd haul her back before any of his parents' guests were the wiser.

"Mariah? Mariah, damn your foolishness!" Barbados wasn't Aquidneck, and Bridgetown wasn't Newport. He thought she'd learned as much after the scene at the Lady Anne. She'd no business wandering around this island unattended, especially not in pearl bracelets and a silk gown. Desperate thieves and rogue sailors, runaway slaves and brothel procuresses—didn't she realize the danger she'd be courting wandering about on her own? Likely she'd risk it all, he told himself grimly, and gladly, too, if it meant she didn't have to marry him. Had she really come to hate him that much? "Mariah!"

"Thee hasn't found her yet, Gabriel?" asked Damaris. The lantern she carried illuminated the concern on her face. "Thee has been searching for nearly an hour."

"Oh, aye, and doubtless Father's had to make excuses to his friends, hasn't he?" Wearily Gabriel raked his fingers through his hair. Four years he'd been gone, and it might have been yesterday, the way he'd slipped into exactly the same old patterns with his family. "I can hear him now. 'Blast it all, the bride's cut and run, but who can blame her, with the prospect of my wastrel, blaggard son for her groom?'"

"Hush, Gabriel, thee is being unjust. Thy father would never speak thus of thee, not on this night. He's as worried as I am." She sat on the teakwood bench and hooked the lantern on her arm, the neat efficiency of her movements peculiarly comforting to Gabriel. Among the things that hadn't changed in his family was his mother, the only constant peace in the Sparhawk storm, and for that alone he'd always be grateful. "Thee mustn't concern thyself with the others. If they've noticed the delay at all, they've decided it's no more than maidenly reluctance on Mariah's part, quite proper."

"Reluctance! Damnation, Mother, Mariah would rather run off among the snakes and sugarcane than marry me!" He struck his fist against the trunk of the cedar beside the path, wondering how he'd make her understand. "A fortnight ago she said she loved me, and now she can't bear to be in the same room with me! I know it's Father's fault, I know he's gotten to her and told her—"

"Gabriel, sweet, thee has lost thy senses," said Damaris firmly. "Listen to me. Thy father has said nothing to Mariah. Not a word, mind thee? Besides, the poor child loves thee too much to believe anything ill said of thee."

"Then why did she leave?"

"Perhaps it's thy own doing, Gabriel. For a man who is so fond of women's company, thee is still quite ignorant of their feelings. Has thee ever told Mariah that thee loves her in return?"

"For God's sake, Mother, surely she must know that!"

"She won't unless thee has told her. She's very young, Gabriel, and frightened, too, of what thee has made her feel. She'll be back, and she'll wed thee, but she needs to be told that thee cares for her, that thee loves her above all others." She smiled sadly and held her hand out to him. "As thee does, my sweet lad, doesn't thee?"

She shifted sideways on the bench, her plain silk skirts rustling, and patted the seat beside her to encourage him to join her. With a sigh, he dropped down on the bench.

"Mariah's different, Mother, though I can't—" He stopped abruptly, his eye caught by a flutter of white in the grass at his mother's feet. Frowning, he plucked up the paper and unfolded it beside the lantern.

"What is it, Gabriel?" asked Damaris curiously as she looked over his arm at the smudged black fleur-de-lis.

Without answering he seized the lantern and held it up to the shrubbery behind the bench. The glossy leaves had been bent, the branches carelessly broken by whoever had pushed through them. He swung the lantern lower, and saw the crushed and muddied grass and the deep footprints in the white stones of the path. Drifting from a twig was a torn strip of silver lace and pale blue silk, ripped from the flounced hem of the wedding gown he'd had made for Mariah, the gown she was meant to wear when he made her his wife.

She was going to be his second chance at happiness. Redemption, that's what Ethan had called her, and instead he felt his whole life crashing in beneath the awful irony. His second chance at happiness was no more than one more time to be beaten by the man who'd stolen his first love.

Dazed, Gabriel was suddenly surrounded by people, his father's face foremost. His mother had been right. For once the old man did look worried, his bristling black brows drawn together, his mouth grim. "Gabriel, this boy says what he's got to tell you won't keep."

At first he didn't recognize the young man with the untied yellow hair that kept falling in his red-rimmed eyes. "Cap'n Sparhawk, sir, I'm sorry to come to you this way but I've grievous news, and you be the one man can help me."

"Then spit it out, Elisha," he said tersely, crumpling the paper that told his own misery in his fingers. Elisha Watson, Jenny West's sweetheart. God in heaven, why did they have to arrive now, with Mariah gone?

"Everything was fine, Cap'n," began Elisha manfully, "with me and Jen bound together here to wed, and her not suspecting it was your money what done it, just the way you swore it would be."

Elisha gulped and stared at his feet, and Gabriel waited, giving him the time he needed to recover. Beside him Jonathan swore beneath his breath, and without looking Gabriel knew he'd shamed his father again, without the old man knowing the half of what he'd done to bring Mariah with him on the *Revenge*. Couldn't he see that none of that mattered any longer?

"It was pirates, Cap'n, French pirates, the devil take them! They boarded us at night and murdered all the watch and Cap'n Richardson, too. Slit their throats like they was dumb animals, fit only for slaughter! Why they didn't kill me, I don't know, but I would've died content if it would've saved my darling Jen.'' Elisha's voice broke, and Gabriel felt himself tense with the certainty of what would come next. ''When I think of Jen with that French bastard, him with the face marked like Satan's own curse—''

''Christian Deveaux,'' said Jonathan, his voice flat.

Finally Gabriel raised his gaze to meet his father's, and held out the paper with the black fleur-de-lis. ''He has Mariah, too.''

''Dear Lord, not again!'' Damaris clutched desperately at Gabriel's sleeve, her eyes wide with fear for him. ''Thee must not go, Gabriel, thee must not even consider it! Let the others go, the navy men who can destroy this madman. But not thee!''

Gently Gabriel pulled her hand free of his sleeve, squeezing her fingers to reassure her. ''I must go, Mother. You know I must.''

''But can't thee see that this is what he wants? This time he will kill thee, Gabriel!'' Frantically she turned to her husband, beseeching. ''Thee must stop him, Jonathan. Thee must not let him go!''

Over his mother's head, Gabriel's eyes held Jonathan's, bracing himself for the condemnation that was sure to follow. It was *his* fault that Deveaux had had the opportunity to capture

Mariah and her sister. He'd known it even before they'd cleared Newport, and now his father did, too. Selfishly he'd put his own wishes before the safety of the West girls, and this had happened. If ever he'd deserved the old man's rebuke, this was it. Damnation, why didn't he speak?

Slowly Jonathan reached out to lay his hand on Gabriel's shoulder. "Your mother's right, lad. I won't let you go alone," he said gruffly. "Together we'll find your Mariah."

Fish rotting in the hot sun, long days past being caught, a stench so powerful it could turn the stomach of any but a fisherman. That was what finally woke Mariah. Her eyes had barely opened before she felt her stomach rebel, and she scarcely managed to reach the side of the open boat before she retched. Clinging weakly to the side, she stared at the turquoise water and tried to remember how she'd come to be in a tiny fishing sloop.

"You 'wake now, lady?" asked a man behind her, his accent thick. "You sleep two days, two nights, with Gigot's help. Nice an' quiet, like lady." He laughed heartily, pleased with himself.

Her head still spinning, Mariah turned and tried to focus, squinting up at the man squatting against the too-bright sky. He was short but powerfully built, his bare chest and arms thick with muscles beneath a tattered red waistcoat. He wore a tricorn hat woven from straw, and large brass earrings, and his long sailor's queue flopped over his shoulder in the wind.

"Who are you?" she rasped, her mouth dry as sand. "And where are we? I was on Barbados, at Westgate Hall."

The man handed her a wicker-wrapped bottle of water, and she drank eagerly, washing away the sour taste in her mouth.

"No Barbados now, lady. No more English! Now you go to French. You go to Martinique with Gigot." He struck his chest proudly with his fist. "I am Gigot."

"But I don't want to go to Martinique," she said plaintively as she returned the water bottle. "I'm an Englishwoman, and I want to go back to Barbados."

Using a line for support, she pulled herself unsteadily to her feet, breathing deeply of the fresh Caribbean air. She could just remember being pulled off the bench in Damaris's garden, her slippers dragging across the dewy grass before someone—apparently Gigot—had finally hauled her up into his arms to carry her as the last bit of her consciousness slipped away before the drug.

Two days, two nights, Gigot had said. What would Gabriel have thought in all that time? Because she had sent him away, he'd be sure to believe that she'd disappeared on her own, the way she had when she'd walked to the Lady Anne. Was he searching somewhere for her now, worrying for her, or was he relieved to find her gone?

Lord, why did she have to love him so much? She looked down at her pale blue gown meant for the wedding, the fragile silk irreparably torn and stained by dirt and salt spray fluttering around her in the breeze, and she forced herself not to think of everything she might have lost. She had survived eighteen years without any assistance from Gabriel Sparhawk, she reminded herself sternly, and there was no reason she should suddenly turn helpless and mewling without him. What mattered now was finding a way to Barbados.

Aft, nearly hidden by the sail, she could see another man at the tiller, dressed much the same as Gigot and listening closely to what the Frenchman said. She'd find no help from him, nor would she have much chance if she jumped over the side. Although like everyone else in Newport she'd learned to keep afloat as a child, she doubted now she was swimmer enough to make it to either of the islands before them, and she'd no notion of how to sail a boat, even a small boat like this one. She'd simply have to convince these two men to turn about and take her back to Bridgetown.

"No more Englishmen, lady," repeated Gigot, shaking his head as he, too, rose, his bare feet widespread against the little boat's roll. "No more Barbados. Martinique."

"And I say no more of this Martinique nonsense, Gigot," said Mariah as firmly as she could in the voice she reserved for recalcitrant bill collectors. "Do you understand that? I don't know why you've carried me off this way or what you hope to gain by it, but if you take me back to Captain Jonathan Sparhawk's plantation outside of Bridgetown, I'll see that you're paid well for your trouble, and no questions asked."

"No questions? No trouble? Ha, lady, *you* are trouble! If you don't go to Martinique with Gigot, Gigot die. No questions!"

"Oh, and I'm the queen of England—or maybe France." Mariah clicked her tongue with disgusted disbelief. "Why would anyone want to kill you over me?"

Gigot's round face lost its merriment. "No anyone. Capitaine Deveaux."

Mariah shrugged. "Deveaux? The name means nothing to me, and I can't imagine why he'd have any interest in me."

They were steering toward the larger island, toward a cove with a cluster of makeshift buildings near the beach. Beyond Gigot's shoulder Mariah spotted another fishing boat much like theirs, and quickly she darted across to the lee side, hanging on to the line with one hand while she waved wildly with the other, yelling as loudly as she could.

With a growl Gigot grabbed her by the waist and jerked her down to the deck. In an instant he was astride her, his broad thighs on either side of her hips, her wrists yanked over her head in his grasp and the blade of his knife pressed close against her throat. She tried to inch back, and the blade relentlessly followed, so tight she could feel her heartbeat throbbing against the cool steel.

"I no die for you, lady," said the man, his mouth twisted with grim determination. "Capitaine Deveaux wants you, and you go. Mind?"

She was too afraid to speak, too afraid to nod with the blade at her throat and her body pinned beneath his. She thought of the tiny new life she carried within her, Gabriel's child, and she knew she did not want to die.

When she didn't answer he jerked her wrists higher and she yelped with the pain. "Mind me, lady?"

"I'll mind," she whispered, and he climbed off her, sheathing his knife.

"Be good," he warned, "and nobody die."

Slowly Mariah sat upright, hugging her bent knees to her chest as she fought back the tears of frustration. Why would any French captain care enough about her to have her kidnapped and threaten his men with death if she escaped? It made no sense, no sense at all, and she didn't like not knowing.

And she *would* get free. She would simply have to be more careful and not act on impulse. She remembered her father's map of the Windward Islands. Martinique was not so very far from Barbados, perhaps the same distance as Newport was from Providence at home. She had no money, but to her surprise Gigot hadn't robbed her of her pearl bracelets. Surely they were worth enough to buy her passage. If this Deveaux had found Gigot to steal her away, then she could find someone else to steal her back.

She studied the cove as they drew closer to land, noting the arrangement of the buildings near the water, the boats pulled up onto the white sand beneath the coconut palms and the path that disappeared into the heavier vegetation—things she might need to know when she fled.

But the closer they came to the beach, the less the little cluster of buildings looked like the homes of decent fisher folk. The nets that were hung to dry had been stretched out so long in the sun that they'd rotted on their lines, and red-flowered vines curled up through the edges closest to the ground. In the center of the clearing stood a tall pole strung with signal flags, fluttering halfheartedly in the breeze. There were no children or old people, and the only women were three unkempt slatterns sprawled in the shade of a palm tree, laughing and talking, each with an earthenware jug in her lap.

As Gigot jumped from the boat and guided it the last few feet through the surf to the beach, two men with battered cutlasses and pistols hanging from their belts came from one of the houses to meet them. Lightly Gigot caught her by the waist and lifted her out of the boat, over the water to the dry sand. But Mariah hung back, her apprehension growing. Though she couldn't understand their conversation, she knew from the way the other men openly appraised her that she was their subject, and she knew, too, that she'd have little chance of fair dealing with any of them.

One of the women sauntered forward, her skirts looped up over her bare legs and her shift pulled low over her breasts. Her amber-colored eyes narrowed with contempt as she looked at Mariah, then she spat at her feet. Mariah gasped and tried to step back, but the woman reached out and curled her long fingers into one of Mariah's pearl bracelets to wrench it from her wrist. Instantly Gigot stepped between them and cuffed the woman so hard that she tumbled backward into the sand with a shriek.

"*Allez-y,* Cici. This one's Deveaux's lady." Unceremoniously he grabbed Mariah by the arm and pulled her after him as he headed toward the path leading into the trees. "We go now."

The path was steep and overgrown, and though Gigot went first the long sharp leaves lashed at Mariah's arms and face and shredded her skirts. With no food in her stomach, she felt light-headed from the climb and the heavy, damp heat, and by the time they finally reached the clearing her skin was flushed and clammy and she was weaving unsteadily on her feet, dependent on Gigot's grasp for support.

Before them was the back of a large plantation house, the whitewashed walls rosy in the late-afternoon sun. Obviously familiar with the house and its grounds, Gigot steered Mariah through the outbuildings and gardens toward a bright metallic sound, scraping and clashing. At the door of a walled garden, Gigot paused long enough to take off his hat and smooth his hair before, with a deep breath, he threw open the door and led Mariah inside.

The clashing and scraping rose from two men fighting with cutlasses, the curved blades ringing each time they met each other. Though the fight was clearly only practice, Mariah, exhausted as she was, watched, fascinated by the intensity and skill the younger man showed, each thrust and parry calculated and perfect. Equally perfect was the man's classic profile beneath his snowy wig, and the natural grace of his lean body in the soft ruffled shirt and plum-colored silk breeches.

With a final lunge, the younger man managed to disarm his opponent, catching the other's cutlass with his blade and tossing it harmlessly onto the grass. He laughed, triumphant, and wiped his face with a lace-trimmed handkerchief while the other man bowed curtly and went to retrieve his weapon.

"Monsieur le Capitaine," Gigot said loudly as he shoved Mariah forward. *"Regardez, la femme de Sparhawk."*

The man turned eagerly, and Mariah gasped at the scar that so severely deformed his face. For an instant in his eyes she saw the pain her thoughtless reaction caused, followed swiftly by a kind of wondering recognition and then the same triumph he'd shown when he'd won.

"One look at you, *mademoiselle,*" he said softly, "and everything becomes clear. And this time I shall not lose."

Chapter Thirteen

After the bright sun, Mariah stumbled as Deveaux's turnkey led her into the dark cellar hallway beneath the house. Impatiently the man swore in Spanish, dragging her roughly after him until he reached the last door. Quickly he unlocked it and with another oath shoved her inside, the door slamming behind her with grim finality.

"Mariah!" gasped Jenny as she rushed to help her sister up from where she'd sprawled across the stone floor. "Oh, God, help us both! How could they have gotten you?"

"Jenny, for all love!" Mariah hugged her sister fiercely. They sat side by side on the bedstead with their hands clasped together, reluctant to part. "Mama meant for me to find you, and I came after you to Barbados on the *Revenge*. Then that awful Frenchman had me kidnapped and brought me here because of Gabriel, but you—why ever would they want you? Where's Elisha? If that boy has deserted you now—''

"They killed him, 'Riah." Jenny stared into her lap, knowing she wouldn't be able to stop the tears. "They killed Elisha and Captain Richardson and everyone else on the *Felicity*. I saw them do it. I'm the only one they took alive, and I still don't know why."

"Elisha's *dead*? Oh, Jenny, love." Mariah pulled her sister close, letting Jenny bury her sobs against her shoulder. It was so hard to imagine Elisha's good-natured grin gone forever, but Mariah knew Jenny had no reason to lie. In the few minutes she'd spent before this Capitaine Deveaux, she'd seen enough to believe any sort of cruelty from him. But why poor Elisha Watson? And why Jenny?

Jenny raised her head, smudging the tears with her fingers. "Everything was going so well, 'Riah, like it all was fated to be. Everything was going to be so *right* for Elisha and me! First came the gold pieces from Elisha's aunt so we could run off together, then Captain Richardson up and offers us passage on the *Felicity* when he's never taken passengers before and then finally you going off to dine with Captain Sparhawk on the very night we sailed, when you never go out at all!"

Mariah listened uneasily, resisting the conclusions her mind was forming. Her sister might believe in fate, but to Mariah, so many happy coincidences seemed more the work of man—one man in particular, who had the money and the connections to bring about any manner of coincidences.

"Gold from his aunt?" she asked. "Jenny, you know as well as I do Elisha and his brother Timothy have no one else in the world besides themselves, certainly no one with gold to give away. 'Twas one of the things about him that rankled Mama most."

"I saw the coins myself, 'Riah, milled Spanish gold pieces. Where else would Elisha get them if not as a gift?" She closed her eyes and shook her head, her face twisting with renewed grief. "But none of it matters now, now that my sweet Elisha's dead."

But to Mariah it did matter, and as she held her sister she cursed Gabriel Sparhawk for the sorrow his lust had brought to her family. If he had loved her, he would simply have asked her to sail with him. That would have been enough, and most likely she would have agreed. But instead he'd gone and made a game of her seduction for his own amusement, arranging all of this knowing she'd insist on following Jenny. Mariah remembered how he'd shown no surprise at all when she'd come to board the *Revenge*. He must have paid off both Elisha and Captain Richardson, and with Spanish gold, too, which no one else in Newport would have. How much trouble Gabriel had gone through merely to bed her, and how easily, really, she'd succumbed. Lord, how he must have laughed at her lovesick predictability!

And now the elaborate ruse was over, at least as far as Gabriel was concerned. He'd been careful never to say he loved her. Not once had he promised her any sort of future together beyond this cruise. When he looked at her, he saw some long-dead woman. His own mother had told her that. She should probably count herself fortunate that when they'd lain together, Gabriel had never called her Catherine instead of Mariah. Even when he'd sworn he wouldn't let her go, she had felt more like a prized possession than a cherished woman, one more bit of privateering plunder.

She was quite certain now he wouldn't have wed her, despite his parents' insistence. If she hadn't been kidnapped by Gigot, Gabriel would still somehow have escaped, or been called away, or produced some sort of eleventh-hour reason he couldn't marry, and she would have been left standing before his parents and the minister and the crowd of witnesses she didn't know. She could have walked away from their pity, just as she could have taken off the silk gown and the pearl bracelets, but the child she'd conceived, his child, she'd have as a constant reminder long after he'd forgotten her. How many other bastards had he left in his wake, how many other foolish, smitten women who'd believed in his kindness?

She was sick and exhausted and frightened, and she longed to weep like her sister and sink beneath the weight of her betrayed, broken heart. But for Jenny's sake, she couldn't. Despite what Gabriel had planned, *her* reason for sailing south was to set her sister's life to rights, and that she still intended to do.

"Listen to me, Jenny, please," she said softly, turning her sister's tear-swollen face toward hers. "We don't have anyone else here to trust but each other."

"What about your Captain Sparhawk? Won't he come try to rescue you?"

"Nay, Jen, I wouldn't dare wager a farthing that he'd risk his handsome neck to help me." She sighed, rubbing her temples with her fingers. "I don't know what this French captain wants of either one of us, but whatever it is, I don't mean to give it to him."

Jenny sniffed loudly. "He said if I didn't tell him what he wanted to know about Captain Sparhawk, he'd give me to the other pirates to—to use. Oh, 'Riah, I wouldn't even let Elisha do that, not until we were married!"

"Hush, Jen, no more weeping. Elisha wouldn't have wanted you crying all the time, would he?" Mariah sighed and leaned against the damp wall, trying to think. "I'll have to try to convince this Frenchman to let us go. I'll tell him all he wants to know of Gabriel, if that's what it will take to get us back to Newport."

"Do you know what he said about you, 'Riah? He said you, *you*, were Captain Sparhawk's whore!"

Mariah's smile was bitter. "Perhaps the man knows Gabriel better than I do."

The door opened and a crippled woman crept into their cell with a basket of fruit and bread for their dinner. Whatever else Deveaux meant for them, the meals he sent were generous enough. When Mariah reached out to take the basket, the woman started, shrinking from the contact.

"I don't mean to hurt you, mistress," said Mariah quietly. "I only want you to tell your master that I wish to speak with him. Can you do that for me, please?"

The woman shook her head, her eyes wide with fear. She seized the empty basket from Jenny's breakfast, and with her eyes downcast, she hurried to the door, her twisted leg dragging unevenly.

"Please, mistress, I beg you with all my heart." Gently Mariah caught the woman's arm, surprised by the knots of scars she felt beneath her sleeve. She thought the woman had been born crippled, but perhaps her handicap had resulted from some accident instead. When she moved into the grated square of light from the window, Mariah saw that the woman wasn't as old as she'd first guessed, either, not so very much older than Mariah or Jenny. "Please help us and tell the French captain!"

Again the woman shook her head, not daring to meet Mariah's eyes as she tried to pull her arm free.

"She won't talk, 'Riah," said Jenny. "I've tried every day and she hasn't said a word."

"Maybe it's our language she doesn't understand." Mariah frowned, trying to remember the bits of Spanish she'd overheard on the *Revenge*. With her sharp cheekbones and silky black hair, the woman could be one of the island Indians who'd mingled their blood with the Spaniards. *"Por favor, señora,* Capitaine Deveaux—"

But at the mention of the Frenchman's name, the woman jerked free from Mariah as if she'd been struck, her eyes wild with panic. Without thinking she opened her mouth to speak, but only awful, guttural sounds came out, and as soon as she realized what she'd done she clapped her hand over her mouth and fled, leaving the laughing turnkey to slam and lock the door after her.

Jenny clutched fearfully at her sister's arm. "'Riah, did you see—?"

"Yes." The few teeth that remained in the woman's mouth had been broken off, jagged yellow stumps, and she could not speak because her tongue had been cut from her mouth. Mariah closed her eyes, but the awful image remained,

and she tightened her arm protectively around her sister's shoulders. "Oh, Jenny, we must leave this place. And God help us, we must leave soon."

Early the next morning, Mariah and Jenny stood in the drawing room of the grand house above their cell, watching while Christian Deveaux finished his breakfast. Mute though the crippled woman was, Mariah's request had somehow reached him, and to the sisters' surprise and trepidation, he had agreed to see them.

They waited in silence, the way the guards had ordered, and near the open window, so their unwashed bodies and clothing wouldn't offend the Frenchman as he ate. Dressed for morning like a Parisian gentleman in a bright silk banyon and an embroidered cap over his shaved, wigless head, Deveaux dined alone, ignoring the two Englishwomen in favor of La Fontaine's *Fables*, propped up against the sugar bowl before him.

Her temper fraying, Mariah watched as he neatly pared away the skin of a tamarind orange with a porcelain-handled knife. If she'd any sense at all, she knew she should be terrified of this man. What he'd done to Elisha and the crew of the *Felicity* and to the mutilated serving woman should have left her as shaken as Jenny was, who trembled beside her. But instead of intimidating her, his arrogance and plain rudeness angered Mariah as much as they did in any bully, whether a Newport dressmaker who looked down her nose at the Wests or a French pirate without the manners to match his silk dressing gown.

"Exactly how long, Captain, do you intend to keep my sister and me waiting on your pleasure?" she asked, her voice crackling with irritation. "As miserable as our quarters are, I prefer them to standing here while you paddle marmalade on your toast."

Deveaux wiped his mouth with his napkin and slipped a silk ribbon into the book to mark his place as he closed it before, at last, he raised his eyes to Mariah. Or rather one eye. Mariah noticed again how he kept his face in profile to them, hiding the scarred side that had made her gasp before. She doubted his care was for her consideration alone. There were no looking glasses in the elegant room, none of the polished silver hollowware that would be expected on his table, not even silver teaspoons that might reflect his ravaged face.

"*Bonjour, mademoiselle,*" he said pleasantly. "Might I assume then that you find my hospitality lacking?"

"Hospitality is a word most use to guests, not prisoners." Beside her Mariah heard Jenny's small noise of alarm, and to reassure her she slipped her hand around her sister's fingers. "Guests are free to come and go when they please. We, I'll wager, cannot."

Deveaux waved his hand wearily, reaching for the porcelain coffeepot. "The hour is far too early for such brilliant repartee, Mademoiselle West, and so I shall concede. You *are* my prisoners, and I'll take no more pains to pretend otherwise."

As he poured the coffee into his cup, a small black goat trotted into the room, her little hooves clicking on the parquet floor as she came to stand tamely beside Deveaux's chair. With a fond pat to the animal's neck, he lowered his cup and squeezed her milk directly into his coffee.

"Pray, *mademoiselle,* don't be so scornful of my little Miou-miou's presence in my *salon,*" he said as the goat butted gently against his knee, begging to be scratched behind her ears. "In these islands, no milk will keep above an hour, and *ma petite* answers quite nicely. If you visit more widely here, you'll find that even your English ladies keep goats to make their wretched tea more acceptable. Though none so fine, so accommodating as my Miou-miou."

Mariah thought bitterly of the serving woman as she watched Deveaux smile and pop a bit of sweetened biscuit into the goat's mouth. "You treat that animal with more kindness than you show people."

"Indeed, and unlike people she returns that kindness." His voice sharpened, the world-weariness gone. "*She* comes to me willingly when

I call. *She* doesn't recoil before me as if I were the devil himself.''

"It's your actions, not your face, that mark you as the devil's own son!''

"If you weren't more useful to me alive than dead, *mademoiselle,* that remark would have earned you your grave." He pushed his chair back from the table, the little goat forgotten, and came to stand to one side of Mariah. He was taller than she had realized, and it took all Mariah's will not to back away from him. "You've made this all so easy for me, you know. I didn't even have to seek you out. Announcing yourself instead of asking for me at the Lady Anne as if I were some low, scraping gamester!''

"You?" Mariah struggled to reconcile the smeared signature on the gambling chit with the man before her. In her mind she'd always thought of the name as Dah-vee-a-ucks, but she should have remembered that the French were notorious for their strange pronunciations. "*You* lost at dice to my father?''

He shrugged elaborately. "I wanted his sloop, and at the time he was in Bridgetown I hadn't the resources there to take it by force. It was the whim of a moment, no more. You don't truly believe I'd pay off a mean little wretch like your father?''

"My father was no mean little wretch, and believe me, if you'd won, he would have paid his debt honorably, like a gentleman!'' Outraged,

Mariah's gaze swept around the room's exquisite furnishings, at the paintings and porcelain and the ormolu clock on the mantel. Beyond the tall windows, green lawns swept down to the waterfront, where a ship far finer than the *Revenge* sat at her moorings. The wager would be an effortless one for Deveaux to honor, while her poor father would rather have ruined himself and his family than default. "You, sir, owe my mother and my sister and me five thousand guineas!"

Deveaux frowned. "*Mon Dieu,* but you're a vulgar creature! I can't begin to fathom why Sparhawk could have fallen in love with a harridan like you."

"You're wrong," she said quickly, her heart beating too fast at the mention of Gabriel. "He doesn't love me."

Deveaux tipped his head quizzically. "*Non?* Then why has he bought you this gown, these pearls? Not even he is so generous with his mistresses. No, he loves you well enough to have married you. All the islands have been aflutter over your wedding. It must be your resemblance to his long-lamented Catherine, for to my eye you have little else to recommend you."

His criticism stung Mariah as keenly as he'd intended. "I ordered the gown made myself," she lied defensively. "The pearls were a gift from another gentleman. Gabriel—I mean Captain Sparhawk—doesn't love me, and he never meant to marry me." That much at least was true enough.

"He loves you," said Deveaux firmly, "and he will come for you."

"No!" Regardless of whether Gabriel loved her, she still loved him. If Gabriel followed her here, this man would kill him, and it would be her fault. "No, Captain, you are most mistaken. He took me to his bed, that is true, but he never *loved* me, not in the way that you mean!"

Beside her Jenny gasped at the truth, but Mariah barely heard her. "You must believe me, Captain. I mean nothing to him. You might as well let me and my sister go, now, so that we can return home to Rhode Island, and—"

"Sparhawk loves you, and he will come."

The note of sadness to his repetition unsettled Mariah even more. "I swear to you he won't! The wedding was his father's notion, not his, and he never would have married me! What we shared was idle pleasure, the same as with all his women. I mean nothing more to him, and he means nothing to me!"

She was panicking, babbling, the desperation palpable in her voice, and she knew with it she was losing any chance of the man releasing her and Jenny unharmed. Thank God at least he knew nothing of the child she carried, and she fought the impulse to shelter her belly with her hand in a gesture that would give away that last secret.

But still there was none of the triumph she'd expected to find in Deveaux's eyes. "Ah, *mademoiselle,* every word of denial betrays your true feelings. You love him, and he loves you. So simple, so right. You would do anything for him, wouldn't you? *C'est bon.* I'd want you worthy of the man who will give his life in the empty hope of saving yours."

Deveaux brushed the back of his hand gently across her cheek, and this time Mariah couldn't help herself from pulling away, bumping into Jenny beside her. For a long moment the Frenchman left his hand suspended in the air, the red stone in his ring bright in the morning light, before finally, slowly, lowering it to his side.

He turned and walked to the table, the banyon drifting behind him. Carefully he began to peel another of the tamarinds, the blade of the porcelain fruit knife slipping deftly under the bright pebbled skin, never piercing the flesh beneath it.

"Oh, he will come, *mademoiselle,*" he continued, almost talking to himself instead of her. "And when he does, he will die not only for you, but also for how he left me unable to know the sweetness of a woman's love, the sweetness that he so carelessly squanders. Once I was like that, too, you know. Though you will not believe it, once women were eager for my company. Now they all cringe with horror, and even those whose favors I buy look away from me, just as you yourself have done. And it is all Gabriel Sparhawk's fault."

He let the knife slip, and the blade thrust deep into the tamarind's pulpy flesh, the golden red juice trickling down his wrist. He looked up at Mariah and smiled, not bothering now to hide his scar, and in spite of herself she shivered.

"But it's nearly done, *ma cher*. Our score is nearly equal. Just as he has lived, *mademoiselle*, so shall your Sparhawk die for love. And so, alas, must you."

From the quarterdeck of the *Revenge,* Gabriel stared hungrily at the bright green island on the horizon, knowing that somewhere on it was his Mariah. Only three days he'd been without her, and it felt like three lifetimes. He told himself that Deveaux wouldn't dare harm her, at least not yet. He knew well enough that she was merely the bait to draw him into his old enemy's range. As a trap, it was more obvious than Gabriel expected from a man like Deveaux, but it had worked. He'd go to hell itself if Mariah were a prisoner there, and Martinique was a good deal closer.

"There's not much use in hanging back, not when the bastard's expecting you," grumbled Jonathan as Gabriel handed him the spyglass. "Most likely his people have spotted us already. He owns half the damned island."

"How many men on the plantation?"

"One hundred, maybe more. No one gets close enough to know for certain. Deveaux's got long guns mounted on either side of the cove, there, that take care of anyone getting a mite too curious. The navy men in Nassau looked the other way on account of Deveaux claiming to be chasing the Spanish, but you know as well as I that he takes whatever he wants, no matter what flag it's under. This new war with France only gives him another excuse." Jonathan spat over the rail. "He's a pirate, pure and simple."

Gabriel's face hardened. "You should know by now that you can't count on the English navy to settle New Englanders' affairs. We'll take care of this ourselves, same as always."

Jonathan grunted in agreement. "We'll be waiting for you here tonight, giving Deveaux an eyeful out near his harbor. But once we set you down on the north side, you and young Watson go straight to the house now, fetch the lasses, and back you come. Nothing more, mind, or your mother will have my head." He thumped at the railing with his stick, his thick black brows drawn together. "You should've killed Deveaux last time, boy, when you had the chance."

Gabriel smiled wryly. "I thought I had, Father. He looked dead enough when they carried him off, though I'll wager he thought the same of me."

"Sweet Lord, your poor mother won't let me forget it! She'd faint clear away if she ever saw the fancy piecework your Dr. Macauly made of your chest. I thank the Lord you've got lives enough for a cat, Gabriel, and I hope there's a few left to spare." His weather-worn face softened, and self-consciously he patted Gabriel's shoulder. "Once I had to do my share of swordplay and tomfoolery to get your mother out of trouble, and your Mariah's just the same. She's worth it, too, same as your mother was, and they're both better than our rascally hides deserve, eh?"

Gabriel looked at Martinique, unwilling to let his father see the raw emotion he knew was plain as day on his face. Even as a boy, he'd never heard his father speak this way to him, never shared this kind of camaraderie, and he didn't trust it. How could his father know what he felt for Mariah? Any minute now the old man would call him a sentimental mama's boy and try to knock him with that stick of his. Nay, it was best not to let his guard down around his father.

"I can't answer that," said Gabriel at last. "When I bring her back tonight, you can ask Mariah herself."

"You're certain you can do this, Jenny?" whispered Mariah fiercely that night through the darkness of their cell. "Not that we have any other choice. No weeping or whimpering, mind?"

"I know it's our only chance, 'Riah." Jenny's quavering reply mingled resentment with fear. "I don't want to stay here any more than you do. I swear I'll moan and toss on the floor like a proper bedlamite until the turnkey's in the door.''

"Your bodice is unlaced?" Mariah gave an extra tug to lower her sister's neckline further. "Kick your skirts up to your knees, too. You'll have to give him a proper eyeful so he doesn't notice me. At this hour he should be alone.''

In the inky shadows, Jenny's blond head bobbed nervously, and Mariah gave her a final hug. "Well enough, Jen. We'd best be at it, eh?"

She took one final deep breath to steady her nerves and closed her eyes long enough to murmur a brief prayer for success. True, she'd rather die now than at Deveaux's hands later, but given another possibility, she'd much rather live. She flexed her fingers around the handle of the heavy bucket and yelled for the turnkey.

"Oh, sir, sir, you must come at once! It's my sister, sir, taken with some sort of fits, tearing all the clothes off her very body! Oh, sir, pray, come and help me tend to her before she's naked as Eve in the garden!''

The turnkey had never admitted to speaking English, but Mariah was gambling that he'd understand well enough that the young woman he'd been forbidden to harm was now quite open to ogling. From the way he rushed panting down the hallway, keys jingling, Mariah knew she'd guessed right.

He threw the door open and lifted his lantern high, rewarded by the sight of the blond girl writhing lasciviously on the floor. He licked his lips eagerly and stepped toward her just as Mariah swung the oak bucket down onto the back of his head.

Jenny scrambled across the floor, snatching the lantern from where the turnkey had let it fall before the candle guttered out. "Lud, 'Riah, did you kill him?"

"Nay, the fat pig's still breathing, more's the pity." Swiftly Mariah dragged the unconscious man into the center of the cell and rolled him onto his stomach. Together she and Jenny tied his wrists and ankles with strips of ticking they'd torn from the mattress cover, then gagged him with ticking stuffed with straw.

"Now douse the candle quick," said Mariah breathlessly as she slung the iron ring of keys onto her wrist like another bracelet among the pearls. The man wore a small leather purse with a few coins in it, and she took that, too, looping the strap around her waist. "Hurry, Jen!"

Yet Jenny hesitated, the lantern in her hand. "Can't we take the lantern with us? The night's so dark."

"And every guard in this place will see it bold as the beacon on Aquidneck Point! Use your wits, Jenny!" Mariah snuffed the candle's wick herself, plunging them both into darkness once again.

She took Jenny's hand and pulled her along
through the doorway, pausing to lock the door
with their gaoler inside. "The moon's three-
quarters full and we'll see well enough once we get
outside. Here, feel along the wall until we reach
the outer door. 'Tis not so far, thirty paces at
most.''

Outside the moonlight was as bright as Mariah
had promised, and though the hour was past mid-
night, candlelight from the tall windows in the
house streamed across the lawn, and male laughter, raucous with drink, rumbled out through the
open casements. Ahead of them lay the harbor
with the large ship and a handful of smaller vessels, but Mariah was certain all of these would be
heavily guarded by men loyal to Deveaux, rough
French and Spanish pirates who'd be especially
unwilling to risk their lives to help two Englishwomen escape.

Instead she and Jenny skirted the shadows to the
back of the house, the grass wet and slick with dew
beneath their feet as they searched for the path
that Gigot had used from the smaller beach.
Though she didn't exactly relish the thought of
meeting Gigot's friends again, they'd probably be
more willing to trade passage to an English island
in exchange for the pearl bracelets—if they didn't
simply steal the pearls outright. She'd have to
promise more of a reward when they reached their

destination unharmed, and borrow the gold from the Sparhawks against the *Revenge*'s prizes.

Finally she found the opening in the trees to the path, and with a quick grin she beckoned to Jenny to follow. "Be careful of the roots," she whispered, shoving aside a hanging vine. "I must have tripped a score of times before, and that was in daylight."

But as soon as they began down the path, Mariah realized that half-buried roots were the least of their hazards. Bright though it had been on the open lawn, the moonlight barely filtered through the dense growth of trees and vines overhead, and it took all of Mariah's concentration to keep them on the path at all. Twice she wandered off onto dead ends, forcing them to carefully feel their way back. She could have wept from frustration at how slow their progress was. By now the turnkey might have awakened to give the alarm, and Deveaux's men might already be scouring the island for them.

Mariah swatted away the insects that dropped onto her shoulders, while countless others bit and stung her unprotected face and arms. Though she knew it was foolish, she wished now they'd brought the lantern. The branches and bushes around them were alive with all kinds of shrieks and whirrings and squawks that she couldn't place, and she tried not to imagine the animals that could make such sounds. And lizards and snakes. Dear Lord, she hated snakes, and they wouldn't make any sound at all. Something skittered across her foot, a long, flat tail swishing against her ankles, and she shrieked and jumped back against Jenny, who shrieked too.

Ashamed of her own response, Mariah grabbed her sister's arm and shook her. "Jenny, hush, it was nothing, I swear!"

"But 'Riah, I'm scared, and I don't want to be here!"

"Then think of what Captain Deveaux had planned for us if we'd stayed back in that cell instead!" Mariah snapped. "Think of everything he promised he'd do to us, and that was before we ran away! If he catches us now—"

"He'll skewer and roast you alive," said a man's voice with a heavy accent behind them. Mariah whipped around, and her heart sank when she saw the size of the man who stood behind them, in one hand, a large cleaverlike knife he'd used to cut away the vegetation and in the other, a pistol pointed directly at them. "*Buenas noches, señoritas.* We can discuss Captain Deveaux's preferences all you wish, but for now, *muchachas,* consider yourselves my prisoners."

Chapter Fourteen

The man lit the floating wick in the crude lamp on the table in the middle of the tiny house's single room, then dropped onto the bench along the wall, the long-barreled pistol resting across his thigh. "You're the two Englishwomen Deveaux's been keeping, aren't you? *Madre de Dios,* what I'd give to see his face when he learns you're gone!"

Mariah didn't answer. With no other place to sit except the man's bed, she preferred to stand, Jenny beside her. Exhausted and discouraged, she had little fight left. She'd already offered him the bracelets and money in exchange for his help, and he'd laughed outright. By the flickering lamplight, the man's bearded face was too crafty to offer her any hope, and she knew it was only a matter of time before he returned them to Deveaux.

"Sisters, aren't you? Night and day, *noche y dia* —like the moon and the sun." He smiled wolfishly, stopping just short of licking his lips. "No wonder Deveaux's so certain Sparhawk will come for a pair like you!"

"If you're going to take us back to him, than pray do it swiftly," said Mariah wearily. Because the man hadn't bothered to unbar the shutters to the two windows, the room was stifling and close.

"You're eager to return to Deveaux?" Frowning, the man leaned forward, fingering the pistol. "You are Sparhawk's woman, aren't you?"

"How many other Englishwomen does that madman have prisoner?" Mariah put her palm to her damp forehead. "I'm Mariah West, and this is my sister Jenny and yes, I'm the woman who was to wed Gabriel Sparhawk!"

"The one man in these seas who can kill Deveaux!" crowed the man happily. "You have seen what your man has done to Deveaux's handsome face, *Jesús,* how with but one cut of his sword he made him as ugly as his soul! What he will do now in the holy name of vengeance, now that Deveaux has dared touch his woman!"

Sickened, Mariah closed her eyes to stop the words she didn't want to hear, stop the spinning of the little room around her. Since that night long ago in Newport when Gabriel had killed the two thieves, she'd known he was capable of killing swiftly and efficiently. She didn't doubt that Gabriel had been the one to disfigure Deveaux, and when she remembered the long, jagged scar that seamed Gabriel's body, she now knew it was Deveaux's work. When they met again, one of them would die.

"He has lied to me and cheated me for the last time, the *bastardo*," the man was saying. "For years I had been my own master, until Deveaux's treachery left me the choice of hanging or joining him. I chose life, but what slavery it is under him! A lieutenant on his precious ship, eh, under him it means nothing, pays nothing! But now I will see him ruined, I will see the skin flayed from his breathing carcass, and I will dance on his devil's grave!"

In her mind's eye Mariah saw Deveaux's deadly sword practice, the polished blade flashing in the hot sun, but now she saw Gabriel there, as well, heard the clash of steel as their swords met, the final gasp and cry as one of them fell, one of them died. No matter which one it was, she would be the reason. It would be all her doing if Gabriel died....

"Mariah, it's Jenny. Your sister, Jen." Mariah tried to focus on Jenny's face peering down at her, trying to make her have two blue eyes full of concern instead of four. "You fainted, but you'll be well enough now. I had Diego open the windows before he left."

"Diego?" Weakly Mariah tried to rise, but when Jenny pushed her against the pillow she didn't try again. She was lying on a bed, the lime-washed walls around her belonging to a room she didn't recognize. "Who's Diego, Jen?"

Jenny couldn't hide her relief. "He's the man who found us in the jungle. Diego Figaroa. He's gone to find some food for you. You frightened him when you fell over like that, plopping right down at his feet."

Mariah sighed and sipped water from the battered cup that Jenny offered her. "Likely he just saw his chance to dance on Deveaux's grave slipping away, laid out on the floor."

"Don't be so harsh, 'Riah." Jenny settled back on her heels on the floor, working her fingers through the tangles in her hair. "Whatever his reasons, he's going to help us get home. He says they sighted the *Revenge* to the southeast this afternoon, so your captain's come after you, just like everyone said he would. Everyone, that is, but you."

"The *Revenge* here!" Mariah struggled to rise, her legs tangling in her skirts, her head still swimming. "Dear God, Jenny, we must go to them now! I have to warn Gabriel before Deveaux finds him!"

"Not until tonight," said Jenny, again gently pushing Mariah onto the bed. "Diego says Deveaux has the whole island out looking for us. He says we'll be safe here because Deveaux doesn't know about this place, and anyway, he still trusts Diego. Look, it's almost dawn now. If we try to leave by daylight, they're sure to catch us. Besides, 'Riah, you couldn't walk ten feet without tumbling over onto your face again. You rest, and tonight we'll go with Diego."

"But if I don't see Gabriel—"

"If you don't wait until tonight, you won't see him at all, and let that be an end to it." Jenny looked at her sideways, her face still bent over her hair. "I thought you didn't love Captain Sparhawk, 'Riah. I thought neither one of you cared a whit, yet here you're both practically tripping over each other's feet trying to save the other from Captain Deveaux."

Mariah groaned, feeling trapped. "I told you before I don't at present wish to discuss Gabriel with you."

"Oh, la, then I'll tell you what I think. I think that you're scarce eating more than a bird, and then being sick to your stomach yesterday, and now fainting when you've never fainted before in your life—I think all that reminds me of my friend Abbie Connor's sister Patience the month after she wed James Cartwright."

"Abbie and Patience and James have nothing to do with anything!" Mariah hated it when her sister tried to lecture her like this. "Jenny, in the last three days I've been drugged and kidnapped by a mad French pirate who wants to kill me, and if my constitution has been unsettled—"

"And *I* think you did lie with Captain Sparhawk, the way you told Captain Deveaux," interrupted Jenny, tossing her hair over her shoulder. "I'm not a fool, 'Riah. You can't even say the man's name without your face going all soft and dreamy. You never were that way with Daniel. And I think that, just like Patience, you're with child. Excepting that Patience Cartwright is married, and you're not."

"Jenny!"

"Mama sent you after me and Elisha to save my reputation, didn't she? Only she didn't know that I wouldn't get the chance to be Elisha's wife or even his widow, and that you, my perfect, trustworthy, spinster sister Mariah, you would be the one who was ruined instead!"

Jenny broke off with a sound halfway between a sob and a laugh, an anguished sound that wrenched at Mariah's heart. "Jenny, love, please, you don't have to—"

"No, this once hear me out!" She leaned close to Mariah, her blue eyes luminous with unshed tears as she touched the little garnet ring that Elisha had given her the night they'd sailed from Newport. "You love your old Captain Sparhawk, and clear as day he must love you. So marry him, 'Riah, you marry him, for his sake and yours and your baby's, and for me and Elisha that didn't have your chance. You marry Gabriel Sparhawk, and when we get back home to Newport, for the first time one of us will make Mama the happiest woman in the entire colony."

And for once there was nothing Mariah could say in return.

Years had passed since Gabriel had last climbed up this damp, overgrown Martinique hillside and felt the oleander leaves slash at his face and his boots sink into the black, moist soil. Seven years, but still he knew the way to Deveaux's house. Strange to think of how much in his life had changed since then, and yet at the same time how little, that he'd be here again, in a dark linen shirt with a sword in his hand.

Damnation, the moon would have to be full and bright as day! He gazed across the lawns to the grand house before him, the royal palms around it swaying gently in the evening air. When he'd been here before, the limestone walls had barely been in place, swathed by scaffolding, while Deveaux still lived on his ship. It couldn't compare to Crescent Hill, of course, but Gabriel would grudgingly grant the place was handsome enough for any gentleman. It was a pity he meant to burn it to the ground this night.

He frowned, searching for the guards that Deveaux would never be without. The house seemed too quiet, all the windows dark. He'd seen the *Chasseur* in the cove himself, so he knew the Frenchman was home, but Gabriel refused to be-

lieve that Deveaux would be peaceably in his bed
with the candles snuffed. Like the devil, the man
he remembered had never seemed to sleep.

"There be th' door to th' prison place, Cap'n,"
whispered Rawlin, one of the five men from the
Revenge Gabriel had brought with him. All vol-
unteers, all had fought Deveaux and his men before, except for Elisha Watson. Inexperienced
though Elisha was, Gabriel hadn't the heart to
leave him behind, not when he was as desperate to
save Jenny as Gabriel was for Mariah. "Th' bloke
in Ste-Luce was real particular about how it looks
like a cellar door, nothin' special. There be one
guard, th' turnkey hisself, an' that be it. Don't
need more. Ye know how Deveaux be, Cap'n,
never takin' prisoners less'n he can help it. 'Cep-
tin' with th' women—"

"Thank you, Rawlin," said Gabriel curtly. He
didn't need to be reminded of what Deveaux did
to the women unfortunate enough to be on the
ships he captured. Catherine's fate was reminder
enough. Even in a society of ruthless men, Deveaux's penchant for cruelty was legendary, and
despite his wealth he was no longer welcome at
gentlemen's brothels from Kingston to Tortuga.
From the beginning, Gabriel had prayed that Deveaux would judge Mariah and Jenny too valu-
able to harm, but with the Frenchman there was
no way of being certain. Mariah would have
fought like a wild animal, just as she'd fought

Gabriel, but with Deveaux—God in heaven, Gabriel didn't want to imagine how the Frenchman might have made her suffer.

His fingers tightened on the hilt of his sword. He'd waited long enough. Swiftly he eased out from under the oleander trees, and with three of his men ran for the door. Two with pistols were left behind in the trees to cover them.

Every nerve on edge, Gabriel waited while Rawlin picked the lock on the door rather than risk the noise of forcing it. Slowly he shoved the door open, hanging back in the shadows with his sword ready until the turnkey appeared. But again there was nothing, no sounds, no people, nothing but the flame in the hanging lantern dancing unevenly in the draft. If anything felt like a trap, this was it. All his experience and every instinct told him that the two women were gone, if they'd ever been here in the first place. He should turn on his heel and leave now while he had the chance.

But still Mariah could be waiting for him at the end of this hall....

"I'll go the rest of the way myself," he said softly to the others. "You wait here, or better yet, outside. I'll be as fast as I can. If I don't return in a quarter hour, come after me and the women."

"But Cap'n Sparhawk, sir, I have to come!" whispered Elisha urgently. "Beggin' pardon, sir, but you can't go alone! If Jenny's in there—"

"You'll follow orders, Watson," said Gabriel curtly, "and you'll stay with the others."

Elisha shook his head dejectedly as Rawlin pulled him back. "Come along, lad, ye don't want t'go crossin' th' cap'n. We'll wait here like he says. They'll be plenty o' chance for glory."

Glory. The word rang emptily in Gabriel's ears as he cautiously began inching along the half-lit hallway. He'd never done any of this for glory. For money, he'd admit if he were cynical, for revenge, for a way to fill the emptiness that had yawned too widely in his soul, if he were feeling more honest. But no longer. Now every step he took was for love, and for Mariah.

He crept around a corner. Little of the lantern's light filtered through the darkness here, and he paused as his eyes adjusted. The long hallway was empty, with only three barred doors along the wall. High in each door was a grated window, faintly lit by moonlight from the facing window. Three doors, three windows, three chances to find his Mariah.

The first door guarded no more than a storeroom, filled with the ghostly shapes of barrels and chests. The second had clearly held prisoners, and Gabriel's fury and fear grew when he saw the empty leg irons and manacles attached to the two mean bedsteads. Could Deveaux really have put Mariah in irons, heavy rings around her little ankles and wrists that would chain her spread-eagle across the dirty mattress?

Grimly he pushed on to the last window in the last door. This room was dark, the facing window in the wall blocked. Expecting no answer, he still said her name softly into the blackness. With a sigh, he turned to rejoin the others, then heard a rustling from within the room. Rats or lizards, he told himself, but still he said her name again, more loudly. More rustling, a faint sound that could have been a moan, and Gabriel was yanking the heavy bar from the door, not stopping to consider that the padlock that should have held the bar was gone, that the heavy oak bar itself lifted too easily from the catches.

"Mariah, poppet, it's Gabriel," he called as he swung open the door. "Mariah, love, where are you?"

"I was rather hoping you'd be able to answer that question for me yourself," said Deveaux dryly from where he sat on the bed. He flipped open the shutter on the lantern at his feet, and the light gleamed off the pistol he held aimed at Gabriel's heart. "Now drop that, *mon ami,* if you please. And don't give a thought to your friends behind. By now my men have dealt with them. This time, I believe, love has made you careless."

Heavy footsteps in the hall behind him told Gabriel that Deveaux spoke the truth. He didn't bother to turn and count their number. Only briefly did he consider his chances of disarming Deveaux before the pistol could fire, then tossed his sword at the other man's feet. Wounded or dead, he'd be of little help to Mariah. "Where is she, Deveaux? You have me now. That's what you wanted. Where are the two women?"

"I told you I don't know." Without taking his eyes from Gabriel, Deveaux picked up the sword and stood. "Your little *bonne femme* and her sister have flown away without any assistance from either one of us."

Gabriel watched the other man closely. He'd heard how badly he'd wounded Deveaux in their last fight, but this was the first time he saw the scars for himself. No wonder there was more than a touch of madness to the man now, and no wonder, too, his own reputation had survived so well the years in Newport with an advertisement like Deveaux's twisted face still in the Caribbean. "Why should I believe you?"

"Why indeed?" Deveaux shrugged his velvet-covered shoulders. "At first I didn't believe Rivera, either, when he claimed they'd escaped from his keeping. Such little girls, to defeat a man like Rivera! But he kept to his story with his dying breath, so I suppose we must give credence to it. *Certainement,* with your ship as brazen as a sign-board on the horizon, I was sure that you'd come for them—until now, of course."

"Damn you, Deveaux," said Gabriel quietly, almost conversationally, as if a gun in the hands of a man who hated him weren't pointed at his heart, as if he weren't furious over what could have happened to Mariah and Jenny. It was, he knew, his only recourse for dealing with Deveaux. "Two young women, wandering unguided in the jungle."

"Oh, it's a terrible waste, I'll agree." Deveaux sighed dramatically as his pale eyes glinted with pleasure. "Pretty little creatures, your two. I'd rather anticipated displaying their newly learned . . . *accomplishments* for you. But at this time of year the fer-de-lance—a serpent, you know, found nowhere else but my little island—is at its most poisonous, and that's only if the two-legged snakes of Martinique don't find the ladies first. In my distress over Rivera's failure, I fear I may have offered a bounty on their recapture, with no stipulations as to condition upon return."

Gabriel fought the impulse to lunge at Deveaux and throttle him outright for what he'd done to Mariah and her sister. He remembered the chains on the bed in the other cell and the stories of how Deveaux, his handsome face destroyed, could no longer bear to leave any other's beauty unmarked. Desperately he tried not to think of Mariah in his hands. Not his sweet poppet, her creamy, flawless skin as fine as China silk, as soft as cut velvet, and the way her round, high breasts quivered when she lay naked on his pillows and laughed at some silly jest.

With enormous effort he kept all emotion from his voice. "If you have harmed her, Deveaux," he said slowly, "I'll make you beg for death before I'm done with you."

But Deveaux only laughed, the sound echoing with eerie distortion down the hallway. "Brave words from a man in your situation, Sparhawk. What would you do to me, eh? Carve the other side of my face like a feast-day pheasant? Maim me, dismember me, by way of a prettier punishment?"

"Return my sword," said Gabriel evenly, "and I'll see what ideas present themselves."

"*Non, mon ami,* you have already done your worst to me. But you, ah, you still have so much to lose. If she still lives, if you survive, would your little girl love you as much without your handsome face? If your body were broken and bent, would she still seek your bed? Would she want a husband who was less than a man? What I mean to offer you, Sparhawk, is a chance to test your love."

Abruptly he turned and thrust Gabriel's sword into the straw-filled mattress behind him, leaving the blade swaying gently back and forth beneath the weight of the hilt. Deveaux stared at it, his eyes focused on the heart-shaped guard of the hilt.

With a twist of his hand, his men stepped forward to roughly bind Gabriel's wrists.

If she still lives, if you survive. Deveaux's words mocked Gabriel as the tarred cords cut into his skin. From the moment he'd met Mariah, he'd longed for the second chance at love and happiness that only she could give him. Had it really all come down to this?

A chance to test his love....

It was nearly dawn when the little boat that Diego Figaroa had hired finally bumped against the steep side of the *Revenge,* but Mariah was the first to climb up the swaying rope ladder and clamber onto the deck, the tattered remnants of her silk gown fluttering around her.

"Ethan!" She threw her arms around his shoulders with a joyful whoop, ignoring his embarrassment. "Oh, Ethan, I can scarcely believe I'm back!"

"And happy we are to see ye, miss," declared Ethan as belatedly he pulled off his knitted cap, "delivered back to us all sound an' safe."

She laughed, feeling like a true prodigal who'd finally returned, and beneath her feet the *Revenge*'s swaying deck did feel like home, in a way more than Newport itself. Crowding all around her were familiar faces, surprised and wondering in the lantern light to see her back, and she hadn't realized how very much she'd missed them all. But

the face she wanted most to see wasn't among
them.

Her smile fading, she disentangled herself from
Ethan. "Where's Captain Sparhawk, Ethan?"

"Captain Sparhawk?" Ethan's discomfort was
unmistakable. "Eh, he's below, miss. But
miss—"

"I'll surprise him myself," Mariah said quickly.
Whatever that "but" had begun could wait until
she was alone with Gabriel. She turned to help
Jenny, climbing uncertainly over the rail with the
assistance of two admiring sailors and followed by
Figaroa. "This is my sister, Ethan, Miss Jenny
West. You know she's as much the *Revenge*'s
owner as I am, if you can bear two of us on board.
And this is Mr. Figaroa, who saved our lives and
brought us here tonight."

"Eh, Miss Jenny!" Grateful for a distraction,
Ethan beamed and touched his forehead. "The
one what Elisha's always a-sighin' and a-moonin'
after! At least to see ye now, I'll grant the boy's
got reason enough for bein' addled!"

Jenny's smile seemed so shaky that Mariah was
certain she'd cry. "You knew Elisha?"

Ethan nodded fondly. "Knew him, know him,
aye, how couldn't I, miss, when the poor moon-
struck whelp's been underfoot every minute since
the cap'n brung him aboard?"

"Aboard here? Now?" Slowly Jenny shook her head, not daring to believe what she was hearing. "But I saw him struck dead on the *Felicity*."

"Struck he was, miss, an' still got the knot to prove it," said Ethan. "But dead he ain't, not by half. He's the one what came to the cap'n an' told him Deveaux had you for prisoners. 'Course he ain't here right now, but he's alive, no mistake."

"Elisha's alive? Alive, you say? Oh, thank you, thank you!" Weeping now with happiness, Jenny flung her arms around Ethan, and for the second time that night he found himself awkwardly supporting one of his owners. "Praise God, Elisha's alive!"

Stunned, Mariah knew that somehow, some way, Gabriel had done this, had brought Elisha back from the dead and onto this ship for Jenny. No, he had done it for *her*, Mariah, the same as he'd come after her to rescue her. No matter what he'd done in the past, he'd always come back, just as he'd promised. Now that she was finally here, she couldn't bear another moment apart from him.

Quickly she slipped away from the others and ran down the steps of the companionway to the cabin. Remembering all the things that she and Gabriel had done in that cabin made her breathless with anticipation, and without knocking she threw open the door and rushed into the arms of Gabriel's father.

"Ah, lass, so you're safe after all," said Jonathan, trying to smile as he politely overlooked her stammering apology. He was leaning heavily for support on Gabriel's desk where he'd been sitting when she'd surprised him, his shirt rumpled and his jaw grizzled from a long, sleepless night. "But then you're looking to hear that from my son, not me. I'd hoped it was his boat when I heard your hail."

He didn't have to explain to Mariah. Already she knew what had happened. "I'm too late, aren't I?"

With an exhausted groan Jonathan dropped back into Gabriel's chair, running his fingers through his long white hair. "The thought of you in Deveaux's hands drove Gabriel nigh mad, and he had to go after you. He never dreamed you'd find a way to free yourself. Damnation, why couldn't you trust him long enough to stay put?"

"I wasn't sure he'd come," she whispered miserably. "Not after the night of the wedding. Not after I'd sent him away."

"You sent him away? For God's sake, Mariah, the boy loves you more than his own life!" said Jonathan harshly, striking the desk with his fist.

"He never told me!" she cried defensively. "Not once has he ever said he loved me!"

He stared as her coldly. "Maybe you weren't listening."

Too numb to speak, Mariah looked down at the deck. Strangely she could hear the same words in her mother's voice and the disappointment behind them.

Jonathan sighed and slumped back in the chair. "Ah, it's no matter now. Gabriel's clever enough. Likely he had to lay low for a spell on the island when he found you'd flown, and he's on his way back to us now."

"Nay, *señor*," said Figaroa from the open doorway. "If he's not back by now, then Deveaux's got him. No use pretending otherwise."

Jonathan glared at him. "Who the hell are you?"

Figaroa drew his shoulders back, appraising Jonathan. "A friend of Sparhawk's, *señor*. That's enough for you to know."

"No friend of my son would be calling me *señor*," declared Jonathan. "You're one of those damned *guardacostas*, those Spanish thieves sailing out of Cartagena, aren't you? Pirates, that's what you are, more of the same lot my son's been trying for the last five years to clear out of these waters."

"And a pretty profit he's made doing it, hasn't he, *señor*?" Figaroa's sly grin flashed white against his black beard. "Spanish *dólars* in his pockets, English guineas in mine. *Guardacosta*, privateer or pirate, only our flags mark the differences among us."

"Damn your insolence, you rascally don!" To Mariah's surprise Jonathan swiftly pulled a pistol from the desk drawer. "Off this ship, I say, or I'll have you thrown over the side!"

"But he means to help Jonathan!" Mariah rushed to the Spaniard's side. "He's served as Deveaux's lieutenant, but he's ready to abandon him for Gabriel. He's the one who found Jenny and me and brought us here, and never expected a farthing in return. Look, I still have the bracelets you gave me!"

Jonathan muttered, but slowly lowered the gun.

Figaroa leaned across the desk. "Sparhawk's the only man with the ship and the cunning to destroy Deveaux, *señor*," he said, "and I mean to see him do it."

"The devil take Deveaux!" thundered Jonathan as his fist struck the desk again. "I want my son! If you can do that, I don't care if you've sailed for the man in the moon. You can have whatever you need, guns or men."

"And I'm coming with you, Mr. Figaroa," said Mariah quickly, before her resolve could falter. "Because I was there, I know the prison beneath Deveaux's house, and I know the way out."

"Your place is here, Mariah," said Jonathan sternly. "You've done more than enough to confound Gabriel as it is."

She raised her eyes to meet Jonathan's, steadfastly accepting all the guilt his cold green eyes offered. "I know Gabriel wouldn't be there if it weren't for me," she said softly. "I have to help bring him back. Whatever it takes."

Chapter Fifteen

That night, Mariah sat in the stern of a small boat as Figaroa deftly guided them over the foaming wavelets toward the shore. She tugged the rough hounscot shawl over her bare shoulders against the spray. As part of their plan, she was dressed in cheap, common clothing he'd provided for her—a coarse linen shift with a sleeveless bodice laced tightly over it, and short, bright petticoats that barely reached her bare ankles—and with her hair loose and brass rings in her ears, she felt as brazen as the women she'd seen on the beach with Gigot. At least that had been her goal, and from the way Figaroa was leering at her, she guessed she'd succeeded well enough.

"They'll believe you're who I say, *no problema*," he said, grinning as if he'd read her mind. "But then men always believe a pretty face, eh? You keep quiet, and do like I said, and everythin' will go fine."

"I'm sure it will." Mariah nodded, a quick, nervous twitch of her head that betrayed her anxiety, and pulled the shawl even higher as she stared out at the dark mass of the island before them. Only for Gabriel would she have agreed to anything so reckless, going off alone with a Spaniard she scarcely knew.

And for Jenny. She'd never forget her sister's face when she'd learned Elisha had disappeared with Gabriel. As foolhardy as Figaroa's plan seemed, she felt she had little choice but to join him. Yet when they'd pushed off from the *Revenge,* Jonathan's face at the rail, and Ethan's beside it, had been very long, indeed.

"Don't lie, *señora.*" Figaroa laughed, his thick, tattooed arms effortlessly drawing the oars through the dark water. "You're worried plenty. *I* worry you! But I swear by all the saints you're safe with me. I only want women who want me, and you only want Sparhawk. Ha, that old man can't see it, maybe, but you're Sparhawk's woman. Your heart is on your face. But we'll find him for you, *señora.* We'll steal your man back from under Deveaux's long French nose, eh?"

This time Mariah didn't answer. All the Spaniard's bravado wouldn't change the odds, two of them against the scores of men Deveaux kept on his island. Nor were Gabriel's odds any better. Each hour that had slipped by without him returning to the *Revenge* meant another hour he was in Deveaux's hands, another hour in which he could die. Continuing to live in a world without him was unthinkable. Unconsciously her hand slid low over her belly, and yet again she prayed their child would know its father.

Well into the cove, they crossed beneath the bow of Deveaux's ship, Figaroa answering the hail from the lookout in French. Though Mariah couldn't understand his response, she was certain from the ribald laughter that followed them across the water that he'd explained her presence in the boat with crude directness. Automatically she stiffened, trying to look indignant and aloof.

"I told you, *señora,* you've nothing to fear from me," Figaroa whispered sharply in English. "Remember why we're here, and what you're supposed to be, eh?"

He jumped into the shallows to pull the boat up onto the white sand, and Mariah climbed out over the prow, carefully cradling a large crockery jug of rum, rum the Spaniard swore now carried enough laudanum to fell a horse. Figaroa slung his arm across her shoulders, his steps weaving a bit as if he'd already tasted more than his share of the rum, and he led her up the winding path to Deveaux's house.

She had only seen the house from the back, and here overlooking the water the formal facade was far grander than anything she'd ever seen in New England, with carved stone flourishes over each tall window and a sweep of stone steps leading to the double front doors. But waiting in the shadows of the palms were the guards that Deveaux was never without, the moonlight picking out the barrels of their pistols. Elegant but cold, the house was just like the owner, decided Mariah grimly, and with an ugly side to hide, as well.

Her mouth grew dry as they came around to the back of the house and the familiar door to the prison. Unlike the night when she and Jenny had escaped, there were now three men standing guard at the doorway, and her hopes rose a fraction higher. Deveaux wouldn't bother guarding a dead man. Figaroa called out to the guards, his steps growing more erratic as he leaned against her, and with a start Mariah realized her role in rescuing Gabriel was about to begin.

"You're cup-shot, Figaroa, I can smell th' stink o' rum from here," answered one of the men. To Mariah's surprise he spoke not only in English, but Connecticut English, at that. "You'd best get yourself back t'the ship afore Cap'n Deveaux sees ye here wit' a wench. You know his orders about women."

"Eh, but the little sweetheart wants to see the English cap'n you're watching, Thompson." Figaroa ran his hand possessively down Mariah's arm to rest on her hip, and she forced herself not to flinch. Instead she shook her hair from her face the way the tavern women near the docks did, her brass earrings swinging, and rubbed her hip against Figaroa's side. "The *famoso* Gabriel Sparhawk with his wings clipped!"

"Not much left t'see," said Thompson with a careless shrug. "Deveaux's been none too gentle. Takin' a special interest in breakin' this one, he is."

Sickened, Mariah remembered the crippled, mutilated woman who'd brought their food, and the obvious pleasure Deveaux took in his cruelty. Dear God, what had he done to Gabriel?

Thompson smoothed his hair, smiling at her. "If'n you want t'gaze at a lion o' a man, lovey, there be far better ones about than that poor bastard in there."

"*Si, si,* but you know how women are," said Figaroa impatiently. "A man who'd trade his neck for love! Makes them sick with delight, just considering it. Here, *muchacha,* if you want Señor Thompson to let you in to gawk, you might have to share your rum, eh?"

Figaroa prodded Mariah, who belatedly offered the jug to the other man. Thompson took it and drank in long, greedy gulps. He smacked his lips with satisfaction, holding the jug just out of Mariah's reach, and the second man grabbed it from Thompson to drink his share, too.

"This rum be fine enough for beginnings, lass," he said suggestively, squinting to get a better look at her in the dark, "but there's other, better ways t'coax my favor."

His mouth still wet with rum, he leaned close to kiss Mariah, and without thinking she slapped him so hard he staggered backward into the shrubbery. At once she gasped, wondering if she'd just cost them the chance to free Gabriel, but instead the other men were merely guffawing at Thompson's expense. He tried to pull himself out of the bushes, but fell wobbling backward while the others roared with laughter.

Her heart pounding, Mariah darted forward to rescue the jug from the second man and try to offer it to the third, still standing in the darkest shadow of the doorway. If he didn't drink it soon, he'd be the only one left standing when the drug in the liquor claimed the other two, and they couldn't risk that.

"'Ere ye go, Thompson, back on yer pins!" The second guard held his hand out to help Thompson until he, too, began to sway precariously and toppled over into the bushes.

With a drunken whoop, Figaroa slapped his thigh. "Eh, *muchacha,* your drink's too strong for English heads! But this other one, he'll do better, I swear by the saints he is no such weakling!"

Taking her cue, Mariah walked toward the last guard, swinging her looped-up skirts around her hips as she held the jug with both hands and willed him to take it from her. He had to drink and fall down insensible like the others so she could take the ring of new keys he wore at his waist and free Gabriel.

Relief washed over her as the man finally reached for the jug, relief that disappeared as soon as he spoke, his familiar face beneath the straw tricorn now clear to her in the moonlight.

"So, lady, you wish to serve poor Gigot the same way I served you? Make me sleep and sleep, while you do how you please?" With genuine sorrow Gigot pushed the jug away with the back of his hand. "*Non,* lady, I will not drink. Diego, how you not know her? An *anglaise?* Truly her rum took your wits. Come, we take her to Capitaine Deveaux, and I will split with you the gold for her capture."

"Deveaux would not give us his gold now, Gigot, any more than he has before," said Figaroa, his feigned drunkenness vanished. He spat in the dirt beside the Frenchman's feet, and in a single swift motion his knife was in his hand. "Deveaux can go to hell, eh? The girl stays with me."

"*Traître!*" Gigot crouched down low and flung off his hat, the blade of his knife flashing in the moonlight. Mariah backed away, her hand pressed across her mouth with horror as she watched the two men slowly circle each other. She remembered the night when the thieves had attacked her and Gabriel in Newport, and she'd seen then what damage a long sailor's knife could do.

Figaroa attacked first, lunging as Gigot darted sideways, his long braid swinging across his back. Then, so quickly that Mariah couldn't tell who moved first, the two men closed in on each other, falling to the ground in a wild tangle of flailing arms and legs. Over and over they rolled in the dust until with a loud grunt Gigot arched stiffly backward and then suddenly fell still.

Unsteadily Figaroa rose to his feet, his blood-stained knife clutched in his fingers. Breathing hard, he looked at Mariah and slowly shook his head twice. He opened his mouth to speak, but instead of words only a gurgle of blood trickled over his lips, and the last expression in his eyes was confused surprise before he crumpled dead across Gigot's body.

For a long moment, Mariah stared at them and the spreading dark stain of their blood in the dirt. God in heaven, what would become of her now? Without Figaroa, she was on her own again to find Gabriel and to somehow get them both to the *Revenge*. But she couldn't let herself panic, not for Gabriel's sake or her own. She raised her head, straining her ears to listen for any sound that could be another guard coming to investigate, but all she could hear was the thumping of her own heart. How much longer would her luck hold?

She kneeled down beside the two bodies, and fighting her revulsion, she forced herself to roll Gigot onto his back. His tattered waistcoat slipped back, and she gagged when she saw the long, ragged knife wound beneath his ribs that had killed him. Swiftly she pulled her gaze away, and with shaking fingers pulled the ring of keys from the belt around his waist, wiping them clean on the dead man's waistcoat. Dear Lord, she'd never seen so much blood.

She unhooked the lantern from the wall and with it in her hand hurried down the long hallway to the three cells. When she and Jenny had been here, they'd been the only prisoners, but from the scufflings and snores behind two of the doors she guessed to her dismay that Deveaux now had a fuller complement of "guests." Too short to look through the grated window, she'd have to open each door in turn and hope she'd chosen the right one. She fitted and turned the key into the first padlock and with both hands lifted the heavy bar from the door, praying she'd made the right choice.

"Gabriel, are you there?" she called breathlessly as she pulled the door open. "Gabriel, I— oh, God in heaven!"

Though she'd thought she'd been prepared for what she might find, how she found him still shocked her and cut straight to her heart. Heavy iron manacles bound his wrists, and the chains were fastened to the wall high enough to keep him dangling by his arms, his bare feet tantalizingly grazing the stone floor. He was naked except for his breeches, his body covered with angry purple bruises, and his head hung limply forward, his long, untied hair shadowing his face. He didn't move when she called his name, and as she rushed across the narrow room to him she feared again she'd come too late.

"Oh, love, what they've done to you!" She couldn't keep from crying, and she didn't try. Crushing down on her was the awful certainty that he'd suffered all this for her. "I wasn't worth this, Gabriel. Dear God, I loved you so much!"

His voice was thick and so hoarse she barely heard it. "You're not real. The devil take you for trying to trick me! You're not real, damn you!"

"But I *am* real, Gabriel! It's Mariah, and I'm really here. Look at me, love." Standing on her toes she reached up and touched his face as gently as she could. "I'm here for you."

"Mariah." He breathed her name almost like a prayer, daring to hope that she really had come. How or why didn't matter. In the long nightmare of this day, her memory had been the only thing that had let him keep his sanity. Too many times had he thought he'd heard her voice call to him to believe it now, but her touch, her fingers on his cheek, he couldn't dream that. Slowly, painfully, he lifted his head to look at her from the eye that wasn't blackened and swollen shut. "My pretty poppet."

Through her tears her smile was so tight that it hurt. "Come, I must get you down. We don't have much time."

On the ring of keys was one she knew must fit the manacles, but she'd need something to stand upon to reach the lock. Swiftly her gaze swept over the room's scant furnishings, past the crude bedstead and the bucket in the corner to stop at the carved, gilded armchair with the red brocade coverings in one corner. Too easily she could imagine Deveaux sitting there, his wrist elegantly cocked and a half smile of pleasure on his face as he directed the men who tortured Gabriel.

Mariah shoved the chair across the floor and climbed on the seat, finding a small joy in putting her bare, dirty feet on the silk brocade. If she balanced on the narrow arm and stretched up tall, she could just reach the padlock. With a rusty scrape the key turned, the chains dropped through the ring in a rush and Gabriel collapsed to the floor with an anguished groan.

Immediately she was beside him, pulling the iron rings from his wrists as he struggled to sit. Hell, he was so weak. He didn't want her to see him like this. She needed him to be strong, and he had nothing left, not even for her. His eyes were squeezed shut and his breathing ragged and shallow from the pain of the blood returning to his arms. Wordlessly he let his head fall against Mariah's shoulder.

"Oh, Gabriel, love, I'm so sorry." As gently as she could she took his hands and began rubbing them in her own, forcing the life into them, and he stifled another groan of agony. "Do you think you can walk?"

"No choice," he croaked.

"Not really. We have to go now."

"Where are the others?" He tried to look past her for his men, Rawlin and the rest of them. They should be here to help Mariah, no matter what she'd told them to do. He'd counted on them to escape and rescue him, though he damn well wished they'd been a bit quicker about it. "Rawlin and Watson and—"

She sighed, thinking sadly of Figaroa. "There aren't any others. Just me."

Gabriel frowned, for it made no sense. No woman, not even Mariah, could have come here on her own. Using her for support, he clumsily pulled himself upright, his legs threatening to buckle beneath him. The simple effort left him pale and sweating, and he clung to her shoulders with real desperation. There was not much left that they could do to him, but if they found her again it would be different. Deveaux wouldn't let her slip away twice. "The guards—"

"The ones outside won't bother us, but I can't swear how long before the rest come." She slid her arm around his waist and felt him wince from the contact. For the first time she could see his back and the bloody, dirty latticework a lash had made, digging deep into his flesh and muscle, and again she gasped.

"'Tis nothing, lass, I've survived worse." He took a deep breath and tried a few tentative, limping steps. "Come. I can't risk Deveaux doing the same to you."

"To *me!*" She stared at him, aghast. "Gabriel, you great fool, he's nearly killed you because of me already!"

His hand trembling, he pressed his thumb to her lips. "Did you mean it when you said you loved me?"

She nodded, loving him more then than she ever had before. "But Gabriel, we must—"

"I love you too, Mariah. And I'll wager that's the truest answer I can give." He lifted his thumb away from her lips and touched his own before he smiled as tenderly as his battered face would allow. As a declaration, he knew it wasn't much, not nearly what she deserved. When this was done, he'd tell her again and again, and show her, too, how much he loved her. "Now on with you, Mariah, while this feeble old man can still hobble after."

She bowed her head, her wonder and joy for once stealing away all her desire to argue with him. He loved her, small, serious Mariah West. *He loved her.*

In the distance she heard a man's laughter, and her head jerked up. No amount of love would help if Deveaux caught them again. She steadied him as best she could, and haltingly they made their way toward the door.

Gabriel stopped at the sight of the two dead men and the two others tumbled in the shrubbery and whistled hoarsely under his breath. Yet again there was no sign of Rawlin or the others. Had Deveaux's beatings addled his wits?

Mariah saw the question on his face. "It's too much to explain now. The two over there, the Englishmen, are only asleep, and I don't want to be here when they wake."

Gabriel grunted. She'd explain, all right. "Deveaux runs his guards on land on watches, same as at sea." He glanced at the moon, slipping in and out of the clouds as it dropped lower in the sky. "Likely we have another hour before this lot's relieved. Fetch me two of their pistols, a knife and a sword. We'll need them more than they will. Go on, lass, they're all past caring now!"

Unwilling as she was to touch the corpses again, Mariah did as he asked, helping Gabriel fasten the buckle on Figaroa's bloodstained sword belt around his waist. He checked the pistols critically and hooked them onto the rings on the belt himself, determined to show her he wasn't as helpless as he seemed, but Mariah saw how badly his hands shook and the way he swayed on his legs as if a strong breeze could topple him over. Even after this small exertion he was forced to lean against the wall and rest. There was no way he'd ever hold his own in a fight, nor would he be able to row Figaroa's boat to the *Revenge*.

"At least the blasted cove is at the bottom of the hill," he finally said when he could speak without gasping. "In this heat, I'd never reach it otherwise."

Her face taut with concern, Mariah smoothed Gabriel's hair from his forehead, doubting that he'd reach the cove uphill or down. His skin was clammy and feverish, his eyes too bright.

"Where the devil are Rawlin and Welsh and the others, anyway?" he was saying. "Can't they heed orders any simpleton could follow? If we want to be away in the boats before dawn, they should have already begun to set the fires. And to leave you here on your own, poppet—they'll answer for that, the lazy dogs."

Mariah stared at him, wondering if he'd turned delirious. "What are you talking about, Gabriel? I told you, I'm alone. The man I came with, Mr. Figaroa, is over there, dead. I haven't seen Mr. Rawlin or Elisha or—"

She stopped abruptly, suddenly realizing what had happened. The men she'd heard in the other cells had been from the *Revenge*, and in her concern over Gabriel she'd left them behind. She grabbed the ring of keys and kissed Gabriel quickly on the forehead.

"Wait for me here, love," she said quickly, not wanting to take the time to confess what she'd done. If she didn't go back for the others, Deveaux would take out all his anger on them, and she'd never be able to face her sister knowing she'd abandoned Elisha to that. She hated leaving Gabriel again, but with the two guns he'd be as safe here as anywhere on the island, and with the help from the others maybe she'd be able to get him to the boat. "I'll be back in a few moments."

"Mariah, what the hell are you up to?" He grabbed for her, but she'd already run out of his reach. "Mariah, come back here!"

"I will, I swear!" she promised. Instead of the anger she'd expected to find on his face there was only a Gabriel she'd never thought she'd see—sick and lost and despairing, and she very nearly returned to his side. She turned and ran as fast as she could to the other cells, her short skirts flying around her bare legs.

She pounded on the second locked door. "Mr. Rawlin! It's Mariah West! Are you in there?"

She heard the scuffling of men hurrying to their feet and murmurs of disbelief, then Rawlin's unmistakable voice. "Aye, miss, we all be 'ere, save th' cap'n."

"He's already outside, cursing you all for lazy dogs." She quickly unlocked the door and Rawlin was the first out, beaming with joy as the others swarmed around them.

"Bless ye, Miss West, for bein' a very angel!" he said warmly. "I won't even ask how ye come t'be here, I'm that happy t'see ye. Three days that devil-faced bastard gave us to turn coats against our king an' cap'n an' sign wit' him, else he'd make us dance from th' yardarm, an' tomorrow would be our last day."

"Mariah!" Elisha sized her in a wild, sudden hug that almost knocked her off her feet. "Where's Jenny? Is she with you? Is she well? I swear if that Frenchman touched her—"

"She's fine, Elisha, and waiting for you on the *Revenge.*" She squeezed his hand affectionately, glad she'd have him soon for a brother-in-law. "But we must go now. Hurry!"

Though none of them dared say so, Mariah knew as soon as she led them to Gabriel that his men were as shocked by his appearance as she'd been. But before them he'd managed to pull himself upright, his hoarse voice somehow as commanding as ever, and stern with disapproval, at that.

"I haven't the time to read you shiftless culls the sermon you deserve," he said, his unblackened eye studying them each in turn. "But rest assured you'll hear it soon as we get back on board. Did they let you keep your flints?"

"Aye, aye, Cap'n, they did at that," answered Rawlin promptly. "Wit' th' tobacco an' pipes, too."

Gabriel grunted. "Very well. Then try and redeem your worthless hides by following some part of my orders. We'll meet at the boats." In spite of himself, his expression softened. Displeased though he was, he still liked his men, and there'd been times this day when he wondered if he'd ever stand before them again. "Watch your tails, and may God preserve your souls."

At once they scattered, running off into the night, and Gabriel allowed himself to slump wearily against Mariah. "Come, poppet, it's time we fled our own selves. I don't want you near when the flames find Deveaux's powder."

"Flames?"

"Aye, flames, love," said Gabriel with satisfaction as they walked slowly. "Before they're done, I hope they'll burn every last wall of this place to the ground, and teach *monsieur le Capitaine* the folly of meddling with Englishmen."

Looking over her shoulder, Mariah could just make out the shadow of one of the men clambering up one of the tall palm trees beside the house. As the tree swayed beneath his weight, the man tugged away a handful of the dried, dead fronds from the underside and bound them loosely together. There was a brief flash as he drew a spark from his flint, then a brighter one as the dried fronds ignited. Gently he waved the bundle to fan the spark to flame, and when he was sure it had taken, he tossed it across to the roof of the house.

For a long moment the little fire sat there like some misplaced illumination until suddenly the shingles beneath it caught, the yellow flames spreading along the roof as the man shimmied down the palm's trunk. In two other places Mariah could see fires on the roof, one already licking at a gabled dormer, and farther away, near the gardens, one of the outbuildings burst into flame. At last came a cry of alarm in French, too late to save the roof, and Mariah turned toward the forest before them.

Even on the dark, overgrown path to the beach, the fire glowed bright enough to light their way. The roar of the flames was audible now, the brittle little pops as the growing heat burst each window and the frantic, garbled shouts of the men trying vainly to combat the fire. Finally came the explosion that Gabriel had predicted when the fire found the powder magazine, a thick, rolling, percussive blast that Mariah felt as well as heard, and a flash that lit the sky bright as day. She was certain by dawn there'd be little left of the plantation but charred timbers and smoking shadows of stone walls.

But Gabriel didn't notice any of it. His last reserve of energy had been spent before the crew and leaving the house, and now as he tried to keep walking his feet seemed to belong to someone else, stumbling and faltering beyond his control. His lungs felt so tight in his chest that the effort to breathe made him dizzy, and he felt oddly hot and cold at the same time.

Only a little farther, he told himself. The beach and the boat and then his own bunk on the *Revenge* were only a little farther. The pillows would be soft, so soft, and Mariah would be there beside him for him to hold in his arms, warm and sweet as meadow grass. His pretty poppet. She loved him, and he loved her, oh, so much. He'd never let her go again, even while he slept. *Sleep.* Lord, he wanted to sleep for a fortnight.

Mariah struggled to support Gabriel, her strength nearly gone. They would never reach the boat, but they were nearly to Figaroa's little house. They'd be safe there for tonight, and tomorrow, and when they'd both rested, they'd find their way to the beach.

By the time she helped Gabriel to Figaroa's bed, he was nearly unconscious, and the sleep that overcame him was so deep she had to tug his long limbs onto the mattress. Exhausted though she was, she still took the time to clean the swollen, angry wounds across his back as best she could. She had no dressings, no bandages, only a half-empty jug of rum and one of Figaroa's old shirts. It was Gabriel's fever that terrified her most. If the infection took hold when he was this weak, he would die.

The sky had paled with dawn by the time she was done, the morning air thick with the smell of smoke and tiny, drifting bits of ash from the fire they'd left behind. Carefully Mariah climbed on the bed beside Gabriel, pulling the worn coverlet over them both. He stirred slightly in his sleep, murmuring her name. Although she longed to put her arms around him, she didn't want to hurt him more, and she contented herself with threading her fingers through his, lying as near to him as she dared.

It wasn't supposed to have ended like this. She had done everything she could for him, but it wasn't going to be enough. She was going to lose him again, this time forever, before she'd really gotten him back. Even though he'd told her he loved her, she hadn't had the chance to tell him about their child, and now it was too late.

Too late. With a dry, smothered sob she closed her eyes. She was too tired to cry again, but her heart still felt the pain of her love and her fear.

She had never before in her life felt so completely helpless.

Chapter Sixteen

When Gabriel woke, the sunlight from the window was warm on his face, but at last his skin was cool. From the angle of the sun he guessed it was late morning, and the trees outside the window were alive with tiny yellow birds darting among red flowers. He let himself wake slowly, relishing the drowsy sense of well-being. Though his body still ached enough that he was reluctant to move, the intense pain and the fever were finally gone, and he realized that the swelling over his eye had diminished enough that he was able to see again with both eyes.

How long had he been lying here? From the growth of beard on his face, he must have been sick at least a week. He remembered the fire, and coming through the trees to this place, and then the memories broke into fragments, Mariah bending over him to lay a cool cloth on his forehead, Mariah leaning wearily at the open win-

dow, Mariah propping him up with her arm to tip
water into his lips, Mariah kneeling on the floor
beside his pillow, her face so close to his that her
tears had fallen on his cheek. So where was Mariah now?

With a groan he pushed himself up on his elbows and called her name. He didn't recognize this
one-room house at all. Why hadn't he seen its
owner as well as Mariah? The cold fireplace, a few
crockery dishes, a musket leaning in the corner, a
clumsily carved crucifix on the wall—none of
these offered any clues, but he caught his breath
when he saw the bright blue coat with the brass
buttons that hung from the peg near the door, the
bright blue that Deveaux preferred for himself and
for his officers on the *Chasseur*. He called Mariah's name again, this time more urgently.

And then she sighed and stirred in her sleep beside him on the bed, and he felt like the greatest
fool in the world. He rolled over carefully, trying
not to wake her. His Mariah, his pretty poppet. He
smiled, and felt his love for her warm him more
than the sunshine. She slept deeply, like a child,
curled on her side with one hand folded beneath
her chin and her dark hair tumbled on the pillows. But he was disturbed by how exhausted she
looked, how the translucent skin beneath her eyes
was shadowed with weariness. His smile faded.
She must have tended him by herself, just as alone

she'd nearly had to drag him here from Deveaux's house. Or was this Deveaux's house, too?

Slowly he swung his legs over the side of the bed and sat upright, pausing to gauge his strength. Beside the bed was a small bucket of water with a dipper, and he drank gratefully. He was light-headed from hunger and the healing skin on his back felt tight, but otherwise he was well enough, and he needed to know who that blue coat and musket belonged to.

"Gabriel?" Her voice was thick with sleep, rapidly sharpening as soon as she realized he'd left the bed. "Gabriel, come back, you shouldn't be up just yet!"

Grimly he held the coat and the musket out to her. "This belongs to one of Deveaux's men, and I'd wager this is his house. Where is he, Mariah? Damnation, did they take us again?"

"We're free, Gabriel, as safe as we can be on a French island." She sat up, shoving her hair from her face. "If they haven't found us in all this time, they never will. The man who owned this house is the one who helped me find you, and he's dead. I told you, we're free."

She began to laugh, oddly giddy, and pressed her spread fingers over her mouth as if to stifle the sound. "You're well, Gabriel. You're standing there glowering at me with a gun in your hand and not a stitch to cover your nakedness. You're going to live, aren't you?"

"You'd best damned well believe I will," he growled. With her head tipped back to laugh, the sunlight streaming around her, she was the most beautiful sight he'd ever seen. Life with her in it seemed very fine, indeed. He smiled, then chuckled, then laughed outright with her. He dropped the musket and the coat and climbed onto the bed beside her.

"I may be naked, but at least it's a gentleman's nakedness." He hooked his finger into the front of her calico bodice and tugged it lower. "What's this foolishness you're wearing? I've never seen any Newport lady fitted out like this!"

Still laughing, she rapped his hand with feigned primness. "It's all I have, Gabriel. I wanted to look common."

"You succeeded famously." He lifted her hand to his lips and kissed it. "It's well enough for some Thames Street tavern wench, but I won't have my wife gotten up in calico and hounscot."

She pulled her hand away from him, her laughter gone and her face pinched. "I'm not your wife."

"Nay, not yet, but I hope you will be, as soon as we can get back to Barbados. I love you too much for it to be otherwise." Gently he took her hand back. "I'm asking you properly this time, Mariah. My father's not standing with a pistol to my back, and my mother's not preaching to you about your mending your lost virtue. It's just be-

tween us now, the way it should have been from
the first. Mariah West, will you do me the inesti-
mable honor of marrying me?''

Mariah held her breath, afraid the moment
might vanish. She'd fallen asleep still worrying
over the fever that wouldn't leave him, and now
this morning his skin was cool and his green eyes
were as clear as the sea in the cove, and he was
laughing and teasing and touching her in the way
that always made her heart beat faster. And he
wanted to marry her.

His dark brows drew together as he searched her
face for her answer, his face severe with the black
beard. ''What is it, poppet? Did I confess to too
many sins while I was ill?'' He tried to keep his
tone light, teasing, but too much depended on her
answer. ''Or perhaps you've a mind to take a
younger man as your husband, one who won't
need as much coddling and cosseting as this an-
cient rogue?''

''Oh, hush, Gabriel, I won't hear you fault
yourself.'' She tried to smile and couldn't. ''And
yes. Yes, yes, yes, I will marry you!''

He closed the distance between them in an instant. ''You're a trial and a torment to me, Mariah,'' he said as he gently pushed her down on the
pillow. ''I don't know why a man with anything
more than straw for wits would let himself fall so
completely in love with you.''

"Maybe because I feel the same about you." She linked her arms around his neck, pulling him closer. The bruises on his handsome face were nearly gone now, faded to faint yellow patches, but she'd never forget how he'd looked the night she'd found him in the cell, how close he'd come to death these last awful days. "I missed you so much, Gabriel, and when I thought I'd lose you forever—"

"Nay, no more of that, poppet," he whispered. "I'm here, and I mean to stay close for the rest of my days."

He lowered his mouth to hers, tracing the bow of her lips with his tongue, teasing and testing the plump cushion of her lower lip before her lips parted willingly with an eager sigh for him. He tasted her deeply then, relishing the sweetness that was hers alone, already feeling the fire that only she brought to his blood. He had thought of this moment so many times when he'd felt the worst of Deveaux's cudgel and lash, used the dream of Mariah's love to stave off the pain, that now, when at last her kiss was reality, he meant to savor it, to make it last.

Yet as Mariah gave herself to him, responding to him with all the warmth and passion of her nature, there was still a poignancy to their loving that frightened her. She ran her fingers across his arms and chest with a feather-light touch, haunted by the sight of the fading welts and bruises layered over the lattice of older scars. She thought of how many men she'd seen die—from her father to George Clarke in the *Revenge*'s surgery to Figaroa and Gigot—and how they'd all been privateers like Gabriel. He might promise her a life together, but she could not forget how fragile that life could be. All she could know for sure was that he was the only man she'd ever truly love, and that he was hers now, for this moment.

Gabriel slid his hand around her waist, lifting her into his kiss. He wanted the rough calico of her bodice gone. He wanted nothing between him and her soft, warm skin. Impatiently he slid his hands beneath the cloth, tugging the bodice and shift from her body.

"Careful," she murmured as she helped him, her fingers as clumsy with urgency as his. "Mind, this is all I have."

"And you are all I want, Mariah." He tossed the last of her clothes onto the floor, settling down beside her with a contented groan. "I need to touch you."

She gasped with pleasure as his hand covered her breast, her sensations intensified by the new life within her. She arched into his caress, the soft peak hardening beneath his fingers, and she felt the pull of desire low in her body. Restlessly she moved beneath him, luxuriating in the feel of his long, hard body beside hers. Her eyes closed, and she shivered as his lips burned a path along her neck, nipping at the pulsing, sensitive hollow at the base of her throat.

When his mouth moved lower to suckle the hard crest his fingers had teased, her breathing grew ragged and she moaned his name, the only word she could form as she tangled her fingers into his dark hair. The combination of his tongue, warm and insistent as it swept across her swollen breasts, and the rough bristle of his beard was almost more than she could bear. Her whole body was aching with need, throbbing with the pulse of her desire for him. Only he could fill the emptiness that lay waiting deep within her, only he could bring release from the tension that coiled every muscle taut and left her gasping for breath. She clung to him desperately, her fingers digging deep into his shoulders.

How Gabriel loved her like this, her skin sheened with her passion in the slanting sunlight, her throat and breasts flushed with anticipation! He stroked the length of her small, rounded body, delighting in how she rose to meet his touch, fitting herself against his hand. He swept away the damp cloud of her hair from her face and kissed her again, hungrily demanding more of her sweetness as his fingers sought and found the velvety secret place between her thighs.

She tore her mouth away from his, and he answered her broken, animal cries with dark, whispered promises of what he'd do with her, how he'd love her, the erotic images only more tinder to the flame they shared. The honeyed fragrance of her filled the air, and recklessly her hands explored his body, pulling his hips closer. Wantonly she rubbed the hardened tips of her breasts against the coarse hair of his chest. His breath caught when she touched the hot flesh of his arousal, and he shuddered as his careful control began to fragment. Sweet Jesus, but he'd been too long without her!

"Please love me, Gabriel," she whispered fiercely, easing her legs around him in welcome. She could feel him tremble with the force of his need above her, his face strained and harsh. "Make me yours again, love. Oh, please, Gabriel, now!"

She cried his name when at last he entered her, the sweet ripples of pleasure drawing him deeper into her. She could never forget how well they fit together, how easily she matched the rhythm he set. Her whole body was tightening around him, for him, and she drew her legs high over his back to hold him closer. With each stroke, each caress, he took her higher and higher, to a peak that was almost unbearable, until at last with a cry torn from deep within her soul she found her release in an ecstasy so brilliant her eyes were wet with tears of joy and love.

Afterward he held her, just held her, sharing together the peace that came from having her in his arms. She'd saved him once by coming to Deveaux's prison for him, but even that paled beside the salvation she'd given him with her love.

He drew back to look at her, tracing his fingers along the curves of her body so lightly that she shivered. "This has all been too hard on you, hasn't it, sweetheart?"

"Loving you is never hard, Gabriel." The concern in his voice made her feel cherished and protected, and she liked it. She smiled at him, stretching languidly beneath his hand.

"That's not what I mean, love. You've grown thinner since the days on the *Revenge*. Too thin. And yet still...."

He frowned, puzzled, as he cradled the warm fullness of one of her breasts, then slid his hand lower, his fingers spread to span her pelvis. "I'll wager I'm gaining more than a wife with this marriage," he said slowly. "So which will you give me first, Mariah, a son or a daughter?"

Mariah flushed, startled that he'd guessed the truth.

He saw the question in her face. "My sister Sarah and her husband have six children, and Sarah's not the kind of woman to keep the details of their birthing to herself."

She swallowed hard, her confession tumbling out. "I wanted so much to tell you that night at Westgate, but I didn't want you to think I'd forced you to marry me."

"You should have trusted me, love." It saddened him to think of her so fearing his displeasure that she'd prefer to weather something like this alone. "By now you must know that no woman's ever been able to force me to do anything against my will."

"So you're not angry?" she asked uncertainly. "You'll welcome a child?"

"How can I be angry when the babe is mine? Ah, Mariah, I love you so much." He kissed her fondly, his lips lingering on hers. "I've always been so certain I'd never marry that I've never given much thought to children, that's all. But a little girl like you, plump and merry, that I could spoil to my heart's content—I'd like that just fine. Nearly as much as I'll like spoiling her mother."

"And if it's a boy?"

"Then I'll take the lad to sea with me, same as my father did with my brothers and me." He smiled crookedly. "You realize we'll have my mother on our doorstep begging for a place in the nursery. There's nothing she likes more than grand-babies, and I'm sure by now she thought she'd seen the last of hers. She'll be a trial to your own mother."

Briefly Mariah's joy faltered. Her mother had wanted her daughters married, but to have them out from her household into more fashionable ones of their own, not for grandchildren. If she'd thought herself too young for widowhood, she'd never relish being a grandmother, and Mariah couldn't imagine her mother offering any help at all when her child was born.

"I'll welcome your mother, Gabriel," she said softly. "You tell her that."

"We'll tell her together," he declared proudly. The longer he considered the idea of a family, the more precious it seemed. All he'd done, all he'd accomplished, even Crescent Hill itself—now he'd have someone to share it with. Someone to laugh with and work beside and cherish, someone he loved more than life itself. Before Mariah, he'd never realized how much that could mean. "We'll tell them all."

She had a sudden image in her mind of Gabriel standing on the highest crosstree of the *Revenge*'s mainmast, shouting his news to every ship in the Bridgetown harbor. The image was so at odds with her first world-weary impression of him that she couldn't help giggling, slipping lower on the pillow against his arm.

"Laugh all you please, sweetheart, I'll never tire of the sound." He laughed, too, her gleefulness contagious, and bent to kiss her again, tenderly. She seemed so young to him, scarcely more than a child herself, that he could hardly believe she carried his baby. Yet all her passion and devotion, all she'd done for him, came from a woman's heart, and again he marveled that such a woman was his. "I mean to make you so happy you'll forget everything that's happened on this godforsaken island.''

"It's nothing compared to what you suffered, Gabriel." As quickly as she could, she told him how she and Figaroa had rescued him. By the time she was done, his laughter had long since vanished, and with it, too, she realized unhappily, had gone the magic they'd created between them this morning.

"My father should never have let you go back," he said sharply. For a few precious hours he'd been able to forget Deveaux. But now all he could think of was how near he'd come to losing both Mariah and their child because of his father's carelessness, and what he'd have to do now to insure their safety. "To put you at that risk, after you'd escaped once, is unforgivable."

"He let me go because he believed I could help you," she answered with equal sharpness. To be cherished was one thing, to have her actions dismissed as the mere inattention of his father was quite another. "He loves you, Gabriel, if you'd ever let yourself see it. He would have tried anything to bring you back."

"It doesn't sound that way, not if he let you go traipsing off on your own!"

"I wasn't alone, Gabriel. Mr. Figaroa was with me, and he gave his life to keep me safe!"

"A sacrifice he needn't have made if my father had used better judgment." He ran his fingers through his hair, trying to decide his next move. "A good sailor, Figaroa. I chased him once, and he's one of the few—the *very* few—who can boast he outran me. I cannot thank him now, but I'll see to my end of the bargain. I owe it to him, and I owe it to you, for what you and your sister endured for my sake. Before I'm done, Deveaux will be dead."

Mariah stared at him, appalled by all his vow suggested. "But surely after the fire, he can't still live!"

Gabriel shrugged his shoulders with a carelessness that didn't fool her for an instant. "If he was within the house, no. But I've no guarantee he was, and if he wasn't—I'm sure he and I shall find each other."

"So you can risk your life all over again?" demanded Mariah bitterly. "That's what all this has been about, hasn't it? All the way back to the beginning, when you decided to sail my father's ship when the war began. You only agreed so you could come after Deveaux, didn't you? Maybe you even knew he was the one who owed my father five thousand guineas. I'm certain you sent Jenny and Elisha on the *Felicity,* and because of you Deveaux murdered every other person on board. If my sister had died in the middle of your selfish feud, Gabriel, I never would have forgiven you. Do you understand that? Never!"

Without looking at him she rolled swiftly off the bed and dressed as quickly as she could, her fingers shaking. He could make every promise he wanted to about their future together. She refused to be widowed before she was married, left behind with a child who'd never know its father.

"Mariah, listen to me," he began, taking her arm. She jerked free and he swore. "Damnation, Mariah, will you listen—"

She whirled around to face him. "No, Gabriel, you listen to me! Can't you understand that I love you too much to see you do this to yourself? This has nothing to do with kings or wars between France and England and Spain. This is a war between you and Christian Deveaux. I know now those men you killed in Newport were Deveaux's men, just like the men in the *Lady Anne*, and the man who kidnapped me, and every other wretched man I've seemed to meet since I met you! When will it end, Gabriel? When you're both dead?"

His expression was severe, unreadable. "Aye," he said slowly, "if that's what comes of it."

She couldn't bear to stand there and let him watch her heart break. She seized the empty water bucket from the floor and ran from the house. She ran until her lungs hurt, up the hill to the place where Figaroa had watched for the *Revenge*. Each morning while Gabriel had been ill she had come here herself, taking comfort in the sight of the sloop tacking back and forth off the coast, waiting for them to appear on the beach. But today there was no *Revenge,* no cloud of white canvas on the turquoise sea. After a week Jonathan must have finally abandoned hope and them with it, and returned to Bridgetown. God in heaven, why today of all days? Again she searched the whole sweep of the horizon, praying she was wrong, but there was nothing. Nothing.

With a tattered sob of frustration and pain she slammed the wooden bucket as hard as she could against the trunk of a gommier tree, the staves of the bucket shattering free of their hoops into the bushes. She threw the worthless handle after them, and sank to her knees on the ground, letting her head drop forward and her hair fall free to cover her grief.

"Mariah, love, look at me," Gabriel said softly beside her.

She had no strength left to face him, no will left to rise.

"Come along, poppet." As he lifted her to her feet she twisted away from him, facing out to the open sea but accepting the support of his arm around her waist. He held her lightly, not restraining her, and she closed her eyes and let her head slip back against the curling hair of his bare chest. Still soft and open from his lovemaking, her body melted treacherously into his as if nothing had changed between them.

"I—I was looking for the *Revenge*," she explained clumsily, her voice catching and breaking. "We could have sailed with your f-father today, but he didn't w-wait for us. Every other day I've seen him here, but today he's g-gone."

"The old man couldn't have stayed today even if he wanted to," said Gabriel. "Look at that sky. Wind's changed and we're in for foul weather, no mistake. Listen to me, Mariah, let me—"

"Gabriel, I don't want you to die," she whispered. She clutched his arm, wishing she shared his strength. "What else can I say to you? Please, love, please, for my sake, can't you end this with Deveaux now, with no more death?"

"Don't ask me that, sweetheart, because I can't." He sighed deeply and turned her in his arms. Gently he tipped her face up toward his, and Mariah saw the sadness that burdened his eyes. "God knows I've tried. When I came back to Newport and built Crescent Hill, I thought I could leave him behind. But he won't let me. As long as he lives, you and everyone else I care for will always be in danger. After what he tried to do to you and your sister, you must know that. And now with the child—Jesus, when he learns of that!"

She rested her cheek against his chest, his arm protectively tightening around her waist. "But why, Gabriel?" she asked sorrowfully. "Why does he hate you that much?"

"A long story, poppet." With another sigh he sat on the grass, pulling her into his lap. He'd come after her knowing it was time to tell her, but that knowledge wasn't going to make it any easier. "Long ago, when I was not much older than you are now, I was betrothed to a girl from Barbados."

She twined her fingers into his. "Catherine Langley. The one I resemble."

"So my mother's spoken to you, has she?" He smiled bleakly. "But she couldn't have told you everything because she doesn't know it. No one does, not the truth."

So why should he tell Mariah? Why tell her how careless he had been with his first love, why give her the reason he'd been afraid to love again? Until her, until Mariah. . . . Oh, sweet Jesus, let her understand!

"I was master of one of my father's ships," he began slowly, "a sugar sloop, and I was taking Catherine to visit her sister in St. John's. Deveaux was sailing for the Spanish then, a *guardacosta,* and he followed us. I'd warning enough, but because I was so hell-bent on impressing Catherine I let Deveaux come far too close, meaning to show her how fast I could make the sloop run. But the wind turned, and they captured us. They slaughtered nearly all of my crew, my friends, just like on the *Felicity,* for even then he didn't wish to be bothered with prisoners."

His fingers tightened around Mariah's, his voice strangely distant. "But Deveaux didn't let me die with them. By then he'd found the women, Catherine and her maid. He forced me to watch what he and his men did to them, there on the deck in the hot sun."

With the wind nearly gone, the heat of the noontime sun was blistering, the planking of the deck hot underfoot and the tar melted and dripping black from the rigging overhead. The air was rank with the smell of the blood of the dead men, the deck and the scuppers and the rail all stained red. Drawn by the smell, gray-bellied sharks followed the ship, turning and twisting sleekly through the clear water. Bound tight to the mainmast, he felt his own life's blood slipping away through the deep gash in his shoulder from Deveaux's sword and another in his thigh. Without the ropes around his arms and the strength of his own fury, he would have collapsed long ago.

Catherine's eyes were round with terror as they hauled her to the deck. Seeing Deveaux, his clothing and manner a gentleman's, she had begged him to save her, to show her mercy. He had smiled, and paid her pretty compliments until she, too, had smiled with relief. Then, still smiling, still teasing, he had slowly used his sword to cut the clothing from her body while his men held her, the blade slicing into her white skin until it ran with her blood. All the time he ignored her sobs of pain

*and terror, and when he was done, he had given
her to his men to use as they pleased.*

*And all Gabriel could do was watch in agony,
watch the woman he loved being torn apart by
men who were worse than animals. . . .*

He was shaking beneath the weight of the
memory, hugging Mariah tightly to his chest.
"When they were dead, he had their bodies
thrown overboard. I loved Catherine, mind? I
loved her, and she deserved so much more from
me than a death like that."

He closed his eyes, afraid to see the revulsion
that he knew would be in her eyes. *Now she'll
leave me. How could it be otherwise? Damnation, now that she knows the worst, I'll lose Mariah, too.*

"Oh, Gabriel, love, look at me." Mariah cradled his face with her hands, stroking, soothing,
seeking to comfort him any way she could. How
much this must have cost him to share with her!
Her cheeks were wet with tears for his pain, for his
lost love. She understood so much now. "It's done
now, Gabriel. It's done."

But he shook his head, not really hearing her,
and with a deep breath, he continued, unable to
stop until she'd heard it all. "I was still bound to
the mast when a British frigate recaptured the
sloop that night. The captain said I was a lucky
man to survive the attack. He was wrong. I knew
that attack was my own fault, and the only way I

could make it right for Catherine and the rest of them was to kill Deveaux. I left my father's service and turned to privateering, learning all I could so I'd be ready when I met Deveaux the next time. And I'm good, Mariah. The best.''

"I wouldn't have asked for you to captain the *Revenge* if you weren't," she said gently. "But you did find Deveaux again. You must have to have given him that scar."

"Oh, aye, the famous devil's mark." He took her hand from his face and turned it briefly against his lips, marveling that she hadn't shrunk from the truth or blamed him as he'd blamed himself all these years, and he found he loved her even more because of it.

And despite everything, she still loved him.

"We were both on 'Statia at the same time." His voice was stronger now, reassured by her love. "Not even at sea. Swords, in the courtyard before the customs house, with half a town's worth of Dutchmen there to watch. It was—" he smiled grimly "—quite a spectacle. When his men carried him away, I was certain he was dead. Doubtless he thought the same of me. But for what I'd done to his face, I became as much his enemy as he was mine, for as long as he lives. And I won't throw away your life the way I did poor Catherine's."

"But Deveaux is a madman!" cried Mariah. "There must be some other way to stop him besides fighting him all by yourself!"

"Oh, Mariah." He pulled her close, stroking the silk of her hair. Other women he'd known had always loved the dashing figure he'd made with a sword in his hand or the gold and gems he'd bring back from his prizes. But Mariah loved him as he was, not as some broadside hero. "Tell me, poppet, why did you come back to this island to rescue me?"

"Because I feared for you," she answered promptly. "Because I love you."

"And those, sweetheart, are my reasons, as well." He kissed her again before she could argue any more, wishing there was some way to take the worry from her heart.

"I know I can't ask you to accept what I must do," he said quietly. "All I hope is that you don't stop loving me, whatever happens."

"I'll never do that. I can't," she admitted, her voice husky with emotion. "And damn you, Gabriel, you know it."

"Ah, my brave Mariah, we do deserve each other, don't we?" He chuckled, lifting her to her feet as he stood. He pointed out to the sea beyond her shoulder, out to the white tips of sails just beginning to clear the horizon. "And it's just as well, for there lies the *Revenge*."

Chapter Seventeen

Gabriel's uneasiness grew as the *Revenge* loomed before them. The welcome from the men who'd rowed to shore to collect Mariah and him had been warm enough, with Ethan splashing through the surf with a coverlet flapping in his hands to wrap around Mariah, as if on so hot a day she needed it. But the subdued silence of the men as they pushed the boat back into the water wasn't natural, and as their captain, Gabriel didn't like it. He knew them too well to feel otherwise. Some sort of ill news awaited him on board the sloop, news they were reluctant to tell him, or else they'd be chattering like magpies among themselves.

Deveaux. It had to be Deveaux. Though every man who'd gone with Gabriel on the raid had returned—he'd asked that first off—and they'd burned the place to the ground as he'd ordered, it still had to be Deveaux that had them all on edge like this. So why the hell weren't they talking?

At the side of the *Revenge* he could see his father, hatless, his white hair unmistakable as it tossed in the breeze. At least he could count on his father to tell him the truth. That is, after the old man railed at him long and hard about how the woman he'd gone to rescue had rescued him instead. Gabriel's shoulders tightened just imagining it. Lord, he was tired, and a sight weaker than he wanted to be, not knowing what lay ahead.

Mariah rested her hand on the thigh of his torn, stained breeches, the same ones he'd worn when he'd been captured. "We're almost there, love," she said, leaning her head on his shoulder. "Almost home."

"Our home, poppet, leastways while we're in these waters. How many other ladies can boast of a dozen long guns in their parlor?" He tried to tease, but in return she only smiled wearily, and that worried him, too. Protectively he slipped his arm around her. Once aboard, he'd see her put to bed straightaway and not disturbed until the shadows beneath her eyes were gone.

He looked past the ship, to the horizon beyond. He hadn't been jesting with Mariah about the weather. To a landsman, the day would seem fine enough, the sky clear except for a few high, wispy clouds torn across the brilliant blue. But to Gabriel the air was too still, the shorebirds they'd left on the island as quiet as his men, the surface of the water glassy smooth. What little wind there was came from the south, hot and dry, a Spanish wind if ever he felt one, the kind of wind that this late in the summer never brought any English sailor any good. He sighed restlessly, his arm tightening around Mariah's shoulders. Maybe it was that wind alone, and not Deveaux, that made his men so uneasy.

The boat bumped against the side of the sloop, and Gabriel saw Mariah helped up the steep slanting side before he began up the rope ladder himself. He was painfully aware of how the men in the boat hovered around him, furtively eyeing the welts and bruises on his body and waiting to see if he, too, needed their assistance. With a growled oath he forced himself to make the climb alone. To lift his hands and arms upward to each rung was agony, and at the top, pale and sweating, he nearly fell over the side onto the deck. Like a great, clumsy flounder, he thought contemptuously, wishing he could square his shoulders before he must meet his father's scorn.

But it was his father's hand that steadied him and kept him from toppling over. "Good day to you, Gabriel, and welcome," said Jonathan evenly, his grip firm on his son's arm. "Mind you wear a shirt to cover those stripes when you greet your mother next, else she'll faint dead away."

"Father." Stupidly Gabriel could think of little else to say. He remembered how Mariah had insisted his father loved him, would do anything to have him back. "I didn't find Mariah, Father. She found me instead."

"No matter, boy, no matter." Jonathan cleared his throat self-consciously, frowning at the deck. "You're here and so's your lass, and let that be an end to it. We've other trials before us now."

"He wasn't in the house, was he?" There wasn't any need to say the Frenchman's name; they both knew. "He wasn't in the house, and he's still alive."

"You couldn't have known that, so don't go blaming yourself," said Jonathan sharply. "Burning out the bastard's nest was a good thing, a fine thing. Should have been done long ago, if anyone had had the courage to do it."

With the boat hauled aboard, the sloop immediately sprung back on course. For the first time Gabriel noticed that his father wore a sword at his waist and that the deck was already cleared for action. "Do you know where he's gone now? St. Pierre or—"

"I'll warrant about four points off the lee bar, where he's been all this week." Jonathan squinted off toward the horizon, shading his eyes first with his hand before pulling out his spyglass. "This little sloop of yours is a pretty sailer, Gabriel. She's led Deveaux's brig on a dance that's likely left him damning you for eternity. 'Course we didn't let him know you weren't at the helm.

Didn't want him guessing you were still on the island. Walker there did the honors."

Nearly as tall as Gabriel, Walker stepped forward, looking uncomfortable in Gabriel's hat and coat. "I didn't mean no disrespect, Cap'n," he said sheepishly, "but since ye told us yer father was cap'n whilst ye was gone, an' he ordered me—"

"You've done well, Walker, thank you." But beyond the man Gabriel could just make out a speck of white, the topsails of the *Chasseur,* exactly where his father had said Deveaux would be.

Jonathan followed his gaze, handing Gabriel his spyglass. "We've outrun him so far, but with this wind and all the press of sail he can set, I don't know whether we'll make it back to Carlisle Bay or not."

As Gabriel studied the ship that followed them with the glass, he understood the tension that was so palpable among the men who even now were straining to eavesdrop as unobtrusively as they could, hungry for a clue to their fate. For years he'd wanted the chance to fight Deveaux at sea, and now at last he had it. Exhausted though he was, Gabriel felt the exhilaration sweep through him. It was nearly done, their rivalry, nearly over, and he meant to be the winner.

He lowered the glass, meeting the expectant faces turned toward him. Now that he was back among them, on his own quarterdeck again, he felt the tension in their ranks vanish, replaced by eager enthusiasm. They knew their captain's reputation. Gabriel Sparhawk was the best privateering captain in the Caribbean, and the luckiest. To a man, they'd follow him anywhere.

And he wouldn't disappoint them. Bolstered by their faith, he began to plan rapidly, considering every way to even the odds or tip them in favor of the *Revenge*. With her twenty-four guns and Deveaux's crack crew, the *Chasseur* could outfight most frigates. Though the *Revenge* was swift and agile, with guns enough to intimidate merchant ships, she depended on speed to outrun or outmaneuver any larger, more heavily armed privateers or navy ships, ships like the *Chasseur*. The wind as it was now didn't favor the smaller sloop, and if the storm came as Gabriel expected, then they'd be doubly disadvantaged, without the weight and breadth to ride out a really heavy blow. But somehow he'd make it work, even if he had to keep running until the weather turned for them. He hadn't lasted this long without taking his share of chances. He would fight Deveaux, and he would win.

Jonathan rested his hand on Gabriel's shoulder. "Aye, son, I knew you'd be up to the task," he said with gruff pride that stunned Gabriel. "I've heard you're the best there is in a fight, and God willing, I mean to be there to see it."

Never before had his father been proud of what he'd done. Never had his father called him anything but a thieving pirate, a shameful wastrel, a sorrow to his mother. Never before had he spoken as if he loved him.

But as Gabriel turned to answer his father, he saw Mariah. She was standing in the shadow of the mainmast, beyond the pressing crowd of men, her arms around a slighter, younger blond woman as blandly fair to him as a porcelain shepherdess. Jenny West, he decided, the sister their parents had preferred, and at once he dismissed her. How could Jenny ever compare to his Mariah?

The sloop's deck canted, and the sunlight fell full on Mariah's face. She knew what was happening as well as any of the men, maybe more so. Holding her hair back with one hand, she glanced over her shoulder to the French ship, then turned toward Gabriel, her blue eyes in the bright sun clouded with a sorrow so deep it cut straight to his heart. How could he convince her that with the gift of her love to protect him he wouldn't die?

"Carry on then, Gabriel," his father was saying, "you're master here again."

"Nay, Father," he said slowly, his eyes not leaving Mariah. "I ask that you stay captain a little longer in my stead."

"You're in pain then, lad?" asked Jonathan with concern. "You seem well enough, but let's have Macauly look you over—"

Gabriel shook his head, raising his voice so he was certain she'd overhear. "I want you to stay captain long enough to marry Mariah and me."

"Sweet Jesus, Gabriel, can't you wait until Bridgetown for your mother's sake?" Jonathan frowned, thumping the deck with his stick. "Marry you! I wouldn't know how to do such a thing."

"Just read the words from Common Prayer, same as Reverend Thatcher would have." Over the heads of the others, across the decks, he watched her and waited. Her expression hadn't changed, and he wasn't sure she'd accept again. If she'd take him, he'd give her and their child his name now, and afterward, he'd give her Deveaux's flag as a wedding present. But, why didn't she say something, do something, beyond staring at him with those blue eyes? "Please, Father."

Helplessly Jonathan looked from Gabriel to Mariah to the French ship on the horizon and back again. "Oh, aye, very well, but let's be sharp about it. There's little time to lose. Come along, lass. Deveaux won't wait, and neither will I."

Slowly Gabriel stretched his hand out to Mariah, offering her his heart, his love, everything he was.

Mariah found she couldn't move, staring in silence at his outstretched hand. Long ago, at Crescent Hill, he'd offered her his hand like this, and though she'd hesitated then as she did now, she'd

finally accepted, and felt for the first time the thrill
that only his touch could bring her. How could either of them have guessed how far that touch
would lead? Since she'd first taken his hand, she'd
known joy and happiness, sorrow and pain, beyond any she'd ever dreamed possible. No matter
what she did now, he'd forever be an inextricable
part of her. Even if she turned away from him, he
would already have made her life infinitely richer
with his love. But was the joy worth the sorrow,
did the happiness surpass the pain? Was loving
Gabriel worth the risk of losing him?

"Lud, 'Riah, go to him," said Jenny, giving her
an impatient little shove of encouragement. "Go
on! If you don't marry Gabriel, you know Mama
will never, *ever* let me wed Elisha."

Slowly Mariah raised her gaze from Gabriel's
hand to his face, and found her answer in his eyes.
For his love she'd risk anything, and give him her
heart in the bargain. At last she smiled, and when
Gabriel came and kissed her, every man on the
deck cheered.

In the captain's cabin, they solemnly stood side
by side as Jonathan read the marriage service over
them. Jenny and Elisha and Tom Farr stood by as
witnesses, while Ethan hovered in the companionway, lamenting that he hadn't time to make a
proper wedding feast. But with the *Chasseur*'s
topsails now clear of the horizon, there was little
time for anything. No silk gowns or pearl brace-

lets, no velvet suits. Gabriel had barely pulled a shirt over his head and was still stuffing the tails into his breeches when his father began to read, and Mariah's wedding finery consisted of the tattered calico she'd worn to the island. Yet this time she knew he loved her, and nothing was worth more than that.

The *Revenge* swung over to another tack, and Mariah lurched to one side, thrown off-balance by the shift that the men compensated for without thought. Automatically Gabriel steadied her with both hands on her shoulders and left them there, his hands warm and sure on her skin. She listened to the old-fashioned words Jonathan was reading, hearing all the promises for the future the service contained, and she tried not to think of how her future with Gabriel might not last beyond this day. She let herself lean against him. He wouldn't leave her, not Gabriel, not her only love. And yet, happy as she was in her love, she couldn't quite forget the depth and power of Deveaux's hatred.

"I'm sorry, poppet, I've no ring for you on board," Gabriel was saying. "But once we're at Bridgetown—"

"Nay, son, your bride needs a ring." Jonathan tucked the prayer book beneath his arm and tugged the heavy gold signet from his little finger. "Likely this isn't the bauble she'd prefer, but she's a Sparhawk now, and it won't hurt for her to be reminded of it. Ethan can rig a rag about the band for now to make it fit.''

A wondering look crossed Gabriel's face as his father placed it into his palm. At once Mariah realized the ring's significance and she began to wonder herself. Had the two men really discovered the love that bound them together?

"On with it, Gabriel," said Jonathan gruffly. "The wind's freshening, and we can't be at this all day. With this ring . . ."

"With this ring, I thee wed." Gabriel slipped the heavy ring with the hawk intaglio on to her finger and closed her hand upon it so the oversize ring wouldn't slide off. "Ah, Mariah, how much I love you!"

Swiftly he caught her by the waist and pulled her close to kiss her, striving to swear again with his body the words he'd just spoken. With a sigh of contentment, Mariah melted against him, savoring the rightness of being in his arms.

Self-consciously Jonathan cleared his throat and snapped the prayer book shut. "Well, then, I say you're man and wife, and that's that. Come along now, Gabriel," he said as he edged past them to the door, "your wife can wait, but the wind and that French bastard cannot."

Reluctantly Gabriel lifted his mouth from Mariah's and sighed. "For once, Mrs. Sparhawk, the old man's right," he said, smiling sadly as he cradled her jaw in his hands, stroking little circles on her cheek with one thumb. "And as he said, you're family now, and must learn that he's accustomed to being obeyed."

Mariah blushed and smiled shyly, liking the sound of that Mrs. Sparhawk. "Doesn't he know," she asked, her voice low and husky for him alone, "how very bad we are at waiting?"

"Don't tempt me, love." He tapped his finger across her lips with mock disapproval. "But I must go, and I want you to stay here, where I know you'll be safe, and rest."

"I should rest? Gabriel, you're the one who—"

"Nay, don't argue with me, Mariah. I want you to stop fussing over everyone else and begin taking more care with yourself, mind? If it looks like they're going to fire on us, I'll have Ethan take you down to the hold."

He quickly kissed her again and then eased himself free of her embrace to rummage in the bulkhead cabinet for his pistols. Already the carpenter and his mate had squeezed into the cabin at Jonathan's beckoning, and with their mallets were thumping the deadlights into place over the stern windows in preparation for both a battle and the storm, whichever struck first. Ethan was busily directing two other seamen who'd come to carry the carved armchairs and the sea chests below into the hold for safekeeping, and overhead Mariah could hear shouts and feet rushing to obey Jonathan's orders.

She remembered it all from the time they'd nearly lost the *Marie-Claire*, just as she remembered the horror of being alone in the hold, huddled in the semidarkness as she'd heard the sounds of the fighting overhead and imagined every shot, every blow, striking Gabriel.

And now, when there was so much more at stake, she wouldn't do it again.

"I'm coming with you, Gabriel," she said, her hands fists at her side. "I'm not going to be stuffed away again like some wretched piece of furniture."

He turned and frowned at her, buckling the belt with his pistols and a knife around his waist. "Mariah, I can't have you risking both your life and our child's."

"What if I hadn't been willing to take that risk when Deveaux had captured you on the island? Where would you be now?" She rested her hands lightly on his chest, her left hand curled to keep the heavy ring from sliding off her finger. She swallowed hard, knowing that if she let her voice quaver with the fear she felt or shed one tear, he'd never agree. "Gabriel, I love you too much to leave you now, when I should be at your side. I always thought that's where a wife belonged."

"I remember promising to love and cherish, but I must have missed the part about the long guns," he said dryly. He sighed and shook his head. "Come along then, wife, for I know I won't be able to stop you. You've earned your place. But if they so much as open their gunports, down you go, mind?''

"Mind." She looked at him through her eyelashes and tried to smile. "And if you get yourself killed, Gabriel Sparhawk, I'll never forgive you."

But once on deck, perched on a coiled line near Gabriel at the helm, Mariah quickly realized that no one at all was going to die soon, except perhaps from the strain of peering at the French ship. By nightfall Gabriel had managed to stop the *Chasseur*'s advance and keep the distance between the two ships even, but from Jonathan down to the powder boys, they all knew it wouldn't be enough. Their only chance was to keep running until the wind lightened in the sloop's favor. Mariah thought back to how gleeful they'd been when the *Revenge* had pursued the *Marie-Claire*. How much better it was to be the cat rather than the mouse!

They ate their supper on the deck, biscuits and coffee and soup served cold because the galley fires were out for safety. Sometime during the second watch Mariah fell asleep on the deck, and when she awoke she found that Ethan had covered her with a quilt and placed a pillow beneath her head. It was the wind that woke her, whipping at her hair and cracking through the sails overhead, the standing rigging singing shrilly and the warm rain peppering her cheeks.

Stiff and sore, she clutched the quilt and pillow to keep them from blowing overboard. Beyond the patchy, tropical shower that soaked them she could see the *Chasseur* in the same place they'd left her, two points on their lee but closer now, both her topsails and mainsails clear of the horizon.

There was no teasing this morning from Gabriel, and only a brief, subdued kiss of greeting. He had braided his long hair into a tight sailors' queue, and his face was set and haggard, his green eyes red rimmed from lack of sleep. Without asking she knew they were in trouble.

"I thought we'd lose 'em in the dark," he said at the rail beside her, his voice raised over the wind and rain, "and now we'll never make Bridgetown. Look at that sky."

Through the clouds the sun hung low on the horizon, red as fire, and around it strange clouds eddied and swirled like flames. Rain streamed down from the clouds to the ocean in diagonal sheets, and the usually translucent Caribbean was dark and restless.

"Hurricane sky if ever there was one," he continued grimly. "We'll run for the cove at Bequia and pray the reefs will be shelter enough."

Though she'd never heard of Bequia, Mariah knew all too well what destruction a hurricane could bring. Her father had told her tales of the damage he'd seen in the Caribbean, houses and churches blown to pieces, trees plucked up by their roots like weeds, ships torn apart and the shattered pieces swept miles inland. Touching her new wedding ring like a talisman, she stared at the sun, now only a glowing smudge behind the clouds, and knew with the others that nothing Deveaux might do to them could rival the danger from the storm that swathed the bloodred sun.

"Bequia will be a hell of a place for a fight," shouted Jonathan in return. "He'll have us trapped tight as a fly in a jug."

Gabiel grimaced as he squinted into the rising wind. "If we don't reach Bequia, there won't be anything left of us for him to fight."

The wind and rain lashed at Mariah like living creatures, growing stronger by the minute as they tore at her sodden clothes and hair. She clung to the rail with both hands, fearing she'd be swept away otherwise, until she felt the solid band of Gabriel's arm around her waist to steady her.

They were racing as fast as they could for a low, green island before them. With the bay in sight, Gabriel had set every scrap of canvas the *Revenge* could muster, and two men fought to hold the wheel steady as they steered into the crests of the wind-driven waves. As they finally rounded their way into the harbor, the topsail shredded and the torn canvas whipped back like streamers, and the sloop lurched, unbalanced beneath the strain. At once Gabriel bawled out for the men to take in what remained of the sail, and as the topmen struggled to furl the heavy, wet canvas, other men dropped the sloop's anchor in the bay. The full force of the hurricane shrieked around them, the sky black as night. There was nothing left to be done now except to pray that they could ride it out.

But Jonathan was pointing toward the mouth of the bay, his curses audible over the wind. Ignoring the weather, Deveaux had swung the *Chasseur*'s head around so she fell broadside against the running sea. Every one of her gunports swung open, the black squares barely visible through the rain.

"That's madness even from a madman!" cried Jonathan above Mariah's ear. "She'll broach to for certain. God help the poor devils aboard!"

With their blasts muffled by the wind, the guns fired raggedly, twelve bright flashes in the gloom. Mariah gasped and clung more tightly to Gabriel, but in the storm the balls fell wildly astray from the *Revenge*.

The *Chasseur* wallowed in the trough of a wave, the water rushing into the open gunports before another wave plucked the ship up and swept her forward on her side toward the mouth of the bay and the coral reefs that guarded it. The smaller *Revenge* had cleared the reefs effortlessly, but the

Chasseur's hull ripped open and split on the sharp coral, her thick oak sides splintering like twigs. Men screamed and scrambled to cling to the slanting deck, but the waves relentlessly plucked them free and sucked them under. Mariah watched in horror, imagining too easily what might have become of the *Revenge*.

Amid the tangle of canvas and lines and splintered planking, the dark figures of the wreck's survivors swirled through the churning water toward the *Revenge*. Rivalries forgotten, the only enemy that mattered now was the sea, and already the sloop's crew was tossing lines out to them, pulling aboard the few able to catch the ropes. Too late a single boat pushed away from the wreck, so many striving frantically to cling to its sides that it nearly capsized, and Mariah looked away, unable to watch. That the Frenchmen had spent their last minutes trying to destroy the *Revenge* didn't seem important now. Of the one hundred and ninety men in the *Chasseur*'s crew, only a handful managed to reach the sloop.

With his arm still fast around Mariah's waist, Gabriel guided her down the companionway to the cabin. She was pale and shaking from exposure and all she'd seen, and she felt frozen to the center of the cabin's deck as the water streamed from her skirts, unable to move after being so battered by the wind. Without a word Gabriel came and held her, his hands sliding up and down the length of her spine, comforting her with his touch.

"It's done now, love," he murmured, his voice cracking with disbelief. "No more Deveaux, no more war. Only you and me, poppet. Only us. Dear God, Mariah, but I love you!"

Mariah's smile was tight, and with her cheek pressed against his chest she was perilously close to tears. Gabriel was finally free. The years of war and revenge were done. They could be in Newport long before their child was born. Their *first* child. She wanted more, just as she wanted years and years together with Gabriel. And now she'd have them.

They ignored the first knock at the cabin door, then the second. Reluctantly Gabriel acknowledged the third. Welsh's broad shoulders filled the doorway, his face grim beneath his curly sheep's-wool hair, while another man waited in the dark companionway behind him. "I wouldn't've bothered ye, Cap'n, but the bugger insisted."

At first Mariah didn't recognize the bedraggled man Welsh dragged into the cabin, not with his wrists bound with tarred cords and his wig and lace ruffles and the shoes with the cut-steel buckles all washed away by the storm. But then Welsh shoved the man full into the light of the swinging lantern, where there was no way for him to hide the scars on his face, and with a little cry Mariah shrank back against Gabriel.

"Bonjour, mon ancien ami," said Deveaux, his voice reduced to a croaking rasp. "I've come to grant you the field, Sparhawk. You are the victor. You have won. You've destroyed everything I ever held dear, *anglais,* and left me nothing but an empty, damned life. I congratulate you."

He glanced over his shoulder expectantly at Welsh, who, grumbled and wedged a scabbard with Deveaux's sword in it between his bound hands. "You surrendered your sword once to me. Allow me the folly, the indulgence of doing the same to you."

Clumsily he held the sword out to Gabriel, and for a long moment Gabriel only stared at it, the bright red-and-blue enamel on the hilt glittering like jewels in the lantern's light. Gently he set Mariah aside. Then he lashed out furiously at Deveaux, knocking the sword from the Frenchman's hands before driving his fist hard into the man's jaw. The sword clattered across the planks as Deveaux staggered and lost his balance, collapsing on the floor close to Mariah's feet.

"You ask me to treat you honorably after everything you have done?" demanded Gabriel, his breathing harsh. "After all the women and men you've made suffer, the lives you've destroyed for your own amusement, you dare ask for mercy? I won't do that for you, Deveaux. I won't do anything except take you to Bridgetown for trial, and see you hung as you've deserved to be since the day you were born."

Mariah pressed against the bulkhead, away from the man on the deck before her. With his close-cropped head bowed, he gasped for breath as he struggled clumsily to his knees and then to his feet, swaying unsteadily beneath the motion of the ship. If she didn't know him and all the wickedness he represented, she would have pitied him.

Welsh stepped forward. "I'll take th' bastard away from yer sight, Cap'n," he said. "There's plenty o' us below that want a chance t'pay our respects."

With his back to them still, Deveaux managed to draw himself upright, his head held high with his old arrogance. Then with a swiftness none of them expected, he turned and lunged forward, trapping Mariah against the bulkhead with his body. Clasped in his hands was a small pistol, and roughly he thrust the barrel against Mariah's cheek.

"Damn yer soul, ye lyin' little devil, where'd ye get the gun?" demanded Welsh. "We searched ye soon as ye dragged yer filthy hide over th' side!"

"Ah, but you searched only until you found the sword you expected." Deveaux smiled triumphantly. "*Très* careless for one of your men, Sparhawk. I'd recommend twenty lashes to improve his memory."

"Let her go, Deveaux," said Gabriel as quietly as he could, fighting every instinct to attack Deveaux, to throttle the last worthless breath from his body with his own hands. But he couldn't risk it with Mariah in his grasp. Fleetingly he thought of Catherine. Dear God, how had he let it happen again? His Mariah, his poppet, his *wife*, with her fate in Deveaux's hands! "You know odds are that your powder's too wet to fire."

"*Mais oui*, the odds are against the flint sparking and the powder taking," agreed Deveaux. "But there is still the chance, the tiny chance, that the gun might fire and your *bonne femme* would die. Is it a chance you wish to take, *mon ami?*"

With the sound of her heart pounding in her ears, Mariah didn't dare move, not with the pistol's muzzle cold against her skin, pushing relentlessly against her cheek and reminding her of how close to dying she was. God deliver her, she didn't want to die, not here, not like this. All she wanted was to live with the man she loved.

"When this storm is done, Sparhawk, you will put me ashore with all of my men, and any of yours that might wish to join me. I can be generous, eh?"

"Then take me as your hostage instead, and let her go," urged Gabriel. "I'm the one you want anyway, don't you?"

Mariah started, momentarily forgetting the pistol. "You can't go, Gabriel!" she cried. "If you do, you know he'll kill you."

"*Mademoiselle* is right. I doubt I could leave you alive, after you have left me nothing. Your life in exchange would be almost fair." He smiled, savoring their turmoil. "You leave her behind, and when you have kept clear of the harbor for three days, the girl will be waiting for you in Port Elizabeth. But if you try to be *galant* and return sooner, she will die. My terms, *anglais*. Or you gamble that the powder is wet. It is, you see, your choice as captain to make."

Outside the wind and sea still buffeted the *Revenge,* her timbers groaning and the rigging howling, but inside the cabin it seemed there was only silence. Helplessly Gabriel looked at Mariah, her blue eyes round with terror. The same way Catherine's eyes had been when she realized he couldn't help her.

Not again, dear God, not again! This time let him do the right thing to save the woman he loved.

"Don't do it, Gabriel," said Mariah, her voice quavering. Frightened though she was, she understood what he, too, was suffering. "If you let him go, you know he'll just kill me instead, the same way he would kill you, and I couldn't bear to live alone in a world without you! You know the gunpowder must be wet. Don't let him force you to do this for my sake, love. Gabriel, look at me. *Look at me! I'm not Catherine.*"

"*Petite folle,*" scoffed Deveaux. "*Certainement,* when he looks at you he sees only her.*"

"No," cried Mariah miserably, "that isn't true. I love him, and he loves me!"

Deveaux shoved her against the bulkhead, nearly spitting his words out in his vehemence. "Do not lecture me on the marvels of love, *mademoiselle!* For ten years Sparhawk has hounded me for the sake of his Catherine's memory, and he has ruined me in the name of his love. Love, fah! Will love bring me another ship and crew, or build for me another house? Can't you see that you're nothing to him beyond your resemblance to her?"

"Damn you, Deveaux, let her go!" thundered Gabriel, unable to contain himself any longer. "Mariah is my *wife,* you blackhearted bastard!"

Still trapping Mariah beneath his shoulder, Deveaux abruptly swung the pistol around to aim it at Gabriel. "Then tell me, Sparhawk," he asked mockingly, "do you love your little wife enough to die for her?"

Gabriel didn't flinch. "I love her much more than that," he said, looking steadily at Mariah's small, pale face. If Deveaux used the pistol's single ball to kill him, then Welsh would attack the Frenchman instantly, and Mariah would be safe. Gabriel would die for her if he must, but he didn't want to leave her, not now, not when their life together had only begun. "I love her more than you will ever know, Deveaux, you with your empty, loveless soul!"

But Deveaux wasn't listening any longer. Instead he stared past Gabriel to the small oval looking glass fastened to the bulkhead, staring with horrified fascination at his own reflection.

He hadn't seen his mutilated face in years, not since the surgeon had first taken the bandages away. It was so much worse than he wanted to remember. He was hideous, a monster with a face to frighten children and women. No wonder they gasped and looked away. Once he had been handsome, the kind of man that beautiful women desired.

Loveless, mon Dieu...

Gabriel saw Deveaux's attention waver, how the Frenchman let his grip on Mariah ease. Here at last was the second chance he'd wanted for so many years. For Catherine, for Mariah, and at last for himself.

In an instant Gabriel's knife was in his hand, in the air, then buried deep in Deveaux's belly. With a ragged gasp Deveaux dropped to his knees, the pistol still clutched in his hands, still aimed at Gabriel.

Heedless of the gun, Mariah ran to Gabriel's arms, shielding him as she defiantly met the eyes of the dying man before her.

"You too, *ma cher?*" asked Deveaux, each word painfully drawn out. "You, too, would die for love?"

From the deck he no longer saw the looking glass, but the memory of his reflection haunted him, mocked him. All he could see was Sparhawk and his woman, a woman who would give her life for his enemy's love.

Loveless . . .

His hands shaking from the effort, Deveaux lifted the pistol to his unscarred cheek and pulled back the hammer.

And against all the odds, the gunpowder was still dry.

Epilogue

Crescent Hill
July 1745

Mariah sat on the swinging bench that Gabriel had rigged for her from the elm tree nearest the house. The wind in the branches overhead did all the work. She could loll quite indolently with her feet tucked up on the cushions and still swing gently back and forth while the leaves above her rustled softly. This was her favorite spot on Crescent Hill, and now, with the summer's heat, the coolest, as well. She sighed with contentment, gazing out at at the bay before her, the fishing boats bound for Newport for the night like toys in the distance. From this same place this morning Gabriel had spotted the incoming sloop with his spyglass, and though he'd given up the sea and sailing, he still hadn't been able to resist riding into town for the news the ship brought. With any luck he'd be back soon before their guests arrived for supper, and Mariah smiled, considering all the ways they might pass that time together.

Beside her on the swing little Jon yawned and stretched his tiny fists up toward the leaves, trying to decide whether or not he was hungry enough to make waking the rest of the way worth his while. Mariah tucked the quilt more firmly about his legs, and that was enough to make up his mind. As soon as his eyes were open his mouth was, as well, with the full-throated howl that Mariah had heard so frequently in the three months since he'd been born. The sound of a man who already knew his own mind, declared Gabriel proudly, and Mariah agreed. The moment she lifted him to her breast he promptly stopped howling and began suckling, his infant contentment a mirror of her own.

Mariah touched her finger to the baby's cheek and at the little hands lying so peacefully—if also possessively—on her breast. She marveled at how much he resembled Gabriel already, the shape of his face and his size already marking him as a Sparhawk. It had been Gabriel's suggestion to name his son for his own father, and Mariah had immediately agreed, knowing the baby would be one more tie to draw them closer together. At Jon's baptism, she would have been sorely pressed to say which man had been the prouder, the new father or the grandfather. And then there was Damaris, who'd pluck her marvel of a grandson from his cradle as soon as she entered the house and declare him to be the most handsome, perfect child ever born.

"I knew I'd find you here, love," said Gabriel, pulling off his hat as he bent to kiss her, his lips lingering fondly on hers. "I'll have you know I missed you royally. It's quite sinful what marriage has done to me."

He shrugged out of his coat and kicked off his boots, settling with a sigh on the bench beside her. As the swing rocked back gently beneath his weight, Gabriel pulled Mariah and Jon against his chest and into his arms. With one foot he gave the swing another shove that sent them sailing through the air. Mariah giggled, and Jon stared up at his father with delighted surprise.

"So you've finally finished, you greedy little piglet," said Gabriel as he took the baby from Mariah so she could lace her bodice. "At this rate you'll be taller than your poor old man before your twelfth birthday. Soon we'll have to turn you over to Ethan for chops and biscuit."

"You'll steer clear of Ethan and his kitchen tonight if you've any sense," said Mariah. "He's beside himself with cooking and baking and polishing pewter that didn't need it. Do you know we'll be sixteen at dinner, not including the babies?"

Gabriel grimaced. "Sixteen?"

"Sixteen," repeated Mariah firmly, counting them off on her fingers as far as she could, "and every one of them's family. There's your sister Sarah and her John and their six, then your parents, and Elisha and Jenny, and my mother and Mr. Gosnold, and us. Sixteen."

Gabriel sighed dramatically. "If I promise to listen to Gosnold's story of his miserable crossing from London one more time, do you think he'll finally marry your mother?"

"Oh, hush, Gabriel, he's not so very bad." Mariah swatted Gabriel's arm, and he grunted in mock pain. "Besides, you can bear with him for my mother's sake. She's never been happier than she is now, with her plump old wool merchant to pamper and fuss over her."

"I'd rather fuss over you, poppet," he growled, nibbling at the nape of her neck. "Family or not, swear to me that you'll send the whole sixteen of 'em away as soon as the cloth is drawn so I can have you to myself. Swear it, and I'll tell you again how fortunate a woman you are."

"I'll swear, but I don't need you to tell me how lucky I am." She twisted in his arms and kissed him, slipping her hands into the front of his shirt to touch his chest and thinking how much her life had changed in the past year. "Very, very lucky."

Unhappy at being ignored, Jon squawked indignantly, and Gabriel nestled him into the crook of his arm where he could look up at both his parents.

"Ah, love, but you don't know the news of the harbor," said Gabriel as he gave the baby his knuckle to gnaw. "That brig we spied this morning was another capture by the *Revenge,* worth seven thousand guineas if she's worth a penny. Rawlin brought her in, and all he could say to any who'd listen was, 'Another prize for Miss Mariah!' "

"Mariah's prize," she repeated softly, smiling at the husband and son she loved so dearly. "Don't tell Mr. Rawlin, but the prize I have here is all I could ever want."

* * * * *

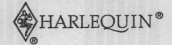

WEDDING SONG
Vicki Lewis Thompson

Kerry Muldoon has encountered more than her share of happy brides and grooms. She and her band—the Honeymooners—play at all the wedding receptions held in romantic Eternity, Massachusetts!

Kerry longs to walk down the aisle one day— with sexy recording executive Judd Roarke. But Kerry's dreams of singing stardom threaten to tear apart the fragile fabric of their union....

WEDDING SONG, available in August from Temptation, is the third book in Harlequin's new cross-line series, **WEDDINGS, INC.** Be sure to look for the fourth book, **THE WEDDING GAMBLE,** by Muriel Jensen (Harlequin American Romance #549), coming in September.

Take 4 bestselling love stories FREE

Plus get a FREE surprise gift!

Special Limited-time Offer

Mail to Harlequin Reader Service®

3010 Walden Avenue
P.O. Box 1867
Buffalo, N.Y. 14269-1867

YES! Please send me 4 free Harlequin Historical™ novels and my free surprise gift. Then send me 4 brand-new novels every month, which I will receive before they appear in bookstores. Bill me at the low price of $3.19 each plus 25¢ delivery and applicable sales tax, if any.* That's the complete price and—compared to the cover prices of $3.99 each—quite a bargain! I understand that accepting the books and gift places me under no obligation ever to buy any books. I can always return a shipment and cancel at any time. Even if I never buy another book from Harlequin, the 4 free books and the surprise gift are mine to keep forever.

247 BPA ANRM

Name _____ (PLEASE PRINT)

Address _____ Apt. No. _____

City _____ State _____ Zip _____

This offer is limited to one order per household and not valid to present Harlequin Historical™ subscribers. *Terms and prices are subject to change without notice. Sales tax applicable in N.Y.

UHIS-94R   ©1990 Harlequin Enterprises Limited

DESTINY'S WOMEN

Sexy, adventurous historical romance at its best!

May 1994
ALENA #220. A veteran Roman commander battles to
subdue the proud, defiant queen he takes to wife.

July 1994
SWEET SONG OF LOVE #230. Medieval is the tale of an
arranged marriage that flourishes despite all odds.

September 1994
SIREN'S CALL #236. The story of a dashing Greek sea captain
and the stubborn Spartan woman he carries off.

Three exciting stories from Merline Lovelace, a fresh new
voice in Historical Romance.

HARLEQUIN®

Don't miss these Harlequin favorites by some of our most distinguished authors!
And now you can receive a discount by ordering two or more titles!

HT #25525	THE PERFECT HUSBAND by Kristine Rolofson	$2.99	☐
HT #25554	LOVERS' SECRETS by Glenda Sanders	$2.99	☐
HP #11577	THE STONE PRINCESS by Robyn Donald	$2.99	☐
HP #11554	SECRET ADMIRER by Susan Napier	$2.99	☐
HR #03277	THE LADY AND THE TOMCAT by Bethany Campbell	$2.99	☐
HR #03283	FOREIGN AFFAIR by Eva Rutland	$2.99	☐
HS #70529	KEEPING CHRISTMAS by Marisa Carroll	$3.39	☐
HS #70578	THE LAST BUCCANEER by Lynn Erickson	$3.50	☐
HI #22256	THRICE FAMILIAR by Caroline Burnes	$2.99	☐
HI #22238	PRESUMED GUILTY by Tess Gerritsen	$2.99	☐
HAR #16496	OH, YOU BEAUTIFUL DOLL by Judith Arnold	$3.50	☐
HAR #16510	WED AGAIN by Elda Minger	$3.50	☐
HH #28719	RACHEL by Lynda Trent	$3.99	☐
HH #28795	PIECES OF SKY by Marianne Willman	$3.99	☐

Harlequin Promotional Titles

#97122	LINGERING SHADOWS by Penny Jordan	$5.99	☐
	(limited quantities available on certain titles)		

	AMOUNT	$
DEDUCT:	10% DISCOUNT FOR 2+ BOOKS	$
	POSTAGE & HANDLING	$
	($1.00 for one book, 50¢ for each additional)	
	APPLICABLE TAXES*	$_____
	TOTAL PAYABLE	$_____
	(check or money order—please do not send cash)	

To order, complete this form and send it, along with a check or money order for the total above, payable to Harlequin Books, to: **In the U.S.:** 3010 Walden Avenue, P.O. Box 9047, Buffalo, NY 14269-9047; **In Canada:** P.O. Box 613, Fort Erie, Ontario, L2A 5X3.

Name: _____

Address:_____City: _____

State/Prov.: _____ Zip/Postal Code: _____

*New York residents remit applicable sales taxes.
 Canadian residents remit applicable GST and provincial taxes..

HBACK-JS